VALIANT MINSTREL

The Story of Harry Lauder

VALIANT MINSTREL

The Story of Sir Harry Lauder

GLADYS MALVERN

Illustrated by Corinne Malvern

First Edition published 1943 by Julian Messner, Inc.

Copyright © 1943, 2013 by Gladys Malvern estate

ISBN: 978-1-5040-3023-6

Distributed in 2016 by Open Road Distribution
180 Maiden Lane
New York, NY 10038
www.openroadmedia.com

For Corinne
—ma wee bonny lassie—
wi' love.

CONTENTS

ACKNOWLEDGMENTS

The author wishes to express sincere gratitude for the gracious co-operation given her by Mrs. Franklin Delano Roosevelt, Mr. William Morris, Jr., and Miss Greta Lauder of Lauder Ha'.

VALIANT MINSTREL

The Story of Harry Lauder

CHAPTER ONE

Where," demanded Isabella Urquhart McLeod MacLennan
Lauder, "is wee Harry? Where can th' laddie be keepin' himsel'—an' it a *Setterday?*"

Six small round faces gazed up at her earnestly as she moved back
and forth from the table to the great open fireplace where a huge pot
of soup was bubbling invitingly, and the black iron kettle was making a
little gurgling sound and thick oatcakes were slowly turning a luscious
golden brown. The Lauder kitchen, with its low, smoke-blackened raf-
ters and its flagstone floor, was an immaculate and crowded place. The
floor was still damp from its recent scrubbing, and off in the far corner
was a wooden double bed, a homemade cradle beside it. Already set
for nine places, the table occupied the center space. A few straight-
backed, badly scuffed chairs were lined up on either side of it, and off
to the left was a large "dresser" with a glass front where Isabella kept
her dishes. From pegs on the door hung a dark woolen shawl, a man's

pair of pants, and several small, much-worn jackets of varying sizes. The walls, once whitewashed, were a dingy, dispirited gray.

Six children, the oldest, Matt, not yet seven, were playing in a group on the floor. Isabella, her ground-length dress faded with many washings, her wide apron tied about her buxom waist, put some tea in a large, earthenware pot and glanced concernedly at the battered old clock on the mantel. She was a competent, cheerful soul, was Isabella, but now she heaved a deep sigh of exasperation, for what with the ten of them, there was always so much to do in that shabby, incredibly little house.

Patching—why, it seemed to Isabella that she was forever putting patches upon small garments until there was scarcely so much as an inch of the original fabric left; and the washing! Eight children, the oldest only eight, meant almost interminable hours over the washtub. But Isabella was strong and energetic. It was not the toil she minded, it was the constant nagging anxiety about money. Scarcely enough to buy food for the lot of them from one week's end to the other. No matter how she schemed and scrimped there was rarely a penny left over to put in the kist on the mantel for that constantly anticipated "rainy day." And what would they do if John or one of the bairns got sick? John was a good, conscientious workman, but suppose he were laid off? How would they live? How would they buy medicines? Charity— oh, God save them from the horror of ever having to take so much as a tuppence of charity!

"Pigs," declared Matthew out of a long deep silence.

Isabella stopped and gazed down at him sharply. "Eh?"

"Pigs," he repeated solemnly, and then, as if by way of explanation, "Harry."

"Huh!" she frowned. "Pigs! An' it a Setterday!"

Saturday was the busiest day of all for Isabella, for on Saturday clothes must be prepared for church, and two days' cooking must be accomplished. The Lauders kept the Sabbath in the strict Scotch custom. No work was done and the children were allowed no games. All day Sunday the blinds in that tiny whitewashed cottage were drawn. No matter how inclement the weather, she and John went to the kirk in the morning and the children, shiny-clean, went to Sunday School.

Then when the gloaming hung softly and wistfully over the quiet land, Isabella would gather her weans about her and read them stories from the Old Testament.

Sunday meant the nearest thing to ease that she and John had ever known. They had no knowledge of what the world calls the good things of life. They had never traveled, had never enjoyed the luxuries that make for gracious living. They had known toil and sacrifice; they had known poverty—harsh, unremitting—but one clear, enduring, shiny thing they had, and that was a simple, unshakable faith in the goodness of God.

Sometimes Isabella mused that it would be nice to have a house a bit larger than two rooms, it would be nice to see what sort of place the rest of Scotland was. Of course, she and John had not always lived here in Musselburgh. John came from Edinburgh, and she came from the Black Isle in Ross-shire. Then there was Portobello a few miles away, where her oldest son, Harry, had been born on August 4th, 1870. She scowled. Where *was* the laddie, anyhow?

A fine help around the house, was Harry. Even now, even at eight, he could bathe the weans as well as she could; and when, some months ago she had been bringing the last one into the world, Harry had actually done not only the cooking for the family, but the washing as well.

"Pigs," said Matt again, with extreme seriousness.

"Aye. That's where he is, ye ken. Doon lookin' at Wattie Sandiland's pigs. He'll stand lookin' at th' pigs for hours, as if they were white angels oot o' Heaven. Your faither says it's because Harry's gaen tae be a farmer when he grows up. Aweel, it's a guid business. I mind ma ain faither was a carpenter, but Harry'll be a farmer, richt enough, th' way he's that fond o' th' soo craes. He—"

She broke off, put both reddened hands on her hips, and stood grimly waiting. He was coming home at last, and despite herself a fond maternal smile twitched at the corners of her mouth. Singing! Aye a one for singin'! Hymns that he had learned at Sabbath School mostly, and *Annie Laurie* and *The Campbells are Comin'*, and now and then one of the popular songs of the day that he had picked up—she never knew how.

He had a strong, sure voice for a lad of eight. Whenever Harry sang, he put such zest into it that it was all she could do to keep from singing with him. But this was no time for singing. *Now*, she reminded herself firmly, she was going to be very stern and teach the young rascal a lesson.

His song ceased as he entered the kitchen and he stood grinning up at her despite the severity of her frown. Small for his age, but strong and sturdily built, he was not—even Isabella had to admit it—what would be called a handsome child. His hair was auburn, straight and unruly. His nose was too big and his ears were too big, but he had a grin that was wide and contagious, and his small blue eyes had a perpetual twinkle in them, as if he found the world a delightfully amusing place.

So they stood, looking at each other. It was a ludicrous picture he made, his feet bare, his clothes patched and soiled, his auburn hair tousled from the wind. His straight little body, so small itself, was wrapped in a heavy plaid among the folds of which, cradled like a papoose on his back, was the latest Lauder infant.

He was not abashed at her frown. He understood her too well and loved her too much to fear her.

"A graund time it is for ye tae be singin'," she fumed. "That voice o' yours—I mind th' day ye were born. A gey row ye kickit up. Th' neighbors doon th' street heard ye roarin' an' cam' ower tae ask if ye was twins. Come here tae me."

He came, and turned his back to her without being told to do so. She unwound the heavy plaid and took the wean in her arms.

"D'ye mind it's a Setterday?" she scowled. "An' where hae ye been?"

The grin widened, the eyes were bright with excitement. "Mither," he ordered, his legs apart and his head up-flung, "hold oot your hand!"

Wonderingly, she did so, and he dropped a sixpence into it. She gasped. He had expected her to gasp like that. This was the proudest day of his life, the day he brought home to his mother the first money he had earned. His had been no carefree childhood. He knew the scheming which preceded the spending of every penny. And now he was able to help.

It was wonderful. He felt grown up and proud of himself.

Her eyes still on the sixpence, Isabella sank into a convenient chair as if the sudden shock of unexpected wealth had drained the strength from her legs. Then she looked up at her son.

"Where—did ye—get—this?"

"I earned it. I've been workin' a week for Wattie. There'll be mair *next* week, Mither! A whole sixpence! Wattie said if I'd help him feed th' pigs every day he'd gie me a sixpence every Setterday."

He expected her to laugh, but she did not. Her eyes were grave. She knew Wattie Sandiland. Every day he went around town collecting swill for his pigs. He was old, cranky, and he had a quick temper.

"I'm tae help him mix th' stuff for th' pigs," went on Harry, "and I'm tae help him dump it in th' soo craes every evenin'."

Her eyes filled with tears. "It's—no that I'm no gratefu' for th' siller, wee Harry," she told him softly, "but Wattie's an ould mon an' he's quick wi' his blows."

Harry laughed. He did not mind Wattle's irritability. The sixpence was the important thing.

She sighed. "Aweel, I'll speak tae your faither when he comes hame th' nicht."

He could not understand why she was not happy about the money. All the way home he had thought how she would laugh when she saw it, and how gay she would be as this week she would be able to drop a penny or two in the kist.

"Are ye fash wi' me, Mither?" he asked.

She smiled and patted his shoulder. "No, Harry, no. You're a guid lad."

"Then—tell us a story!"

Even the younger children knew that word, and now they all began to echo it, crowding about her eagerly, faces upturned and expectant.

"A story, Mither! A story!"

Isabella gave a deep, martyrlike sigh. There was work to do and little time in which to do it before John would be coming home from the pottery works; but often before this she had stopped in the midst of her labors to acquiesce in the demands for a story. She had, it seemed, an unending fund of stories, and she delighted in telling them as much as her brood enjoyed hearing them. And what hair-raising tales they were! Stories of the Scots clans; stories of bogles, ghosts; stories of witches and water-kelpies and fairies.

The infant still in her arms, the seven older children squatting in a semicircle about her, Isabella's eyes widened ominously, and her voice sank to a deep, impressively sepulchral tone.

"Once—upon—a time—"

Harry, Matt, George, Jock, Alec, Bella, Mary, Jean—there they were, all silent as little statues. Now and then as she stressed dark, dread happenings in the Scottish glens, one of them shivered and gave a quick, apprehensive glance over his shoulder.

As the story was ending, John Lauder came in, swinging his lunch pail. The children scrambled to their feet and ran toward him, clutching at his knees, pulling at his coat.

"Faither!" cried Matt, "Harry's made some siller!"

Isabella, the baby balanced on one arm, walked briskly over to the fireplace and began stirring the soup with a long-handled ladle.

"Aye, John, it's true. Harry's made a sixpence helpin' Wattie Sandiland wi' his pigs."

John smiled. He was a short man in his late twenties, slender and hardy. "It'll be guid experience for him," he declared cheerily, "it wull so. Th' lad'll be a farmer when he grows up. Let th' flea stick tae th' wa'."

Like the proverbial flea sticking to the wall, Harry showed up at Wattie Sandiland's soo craes promptly every evening for two weeks. He was ambitious, was Harry, and eager to please. Engrossed in his work, he mixed the swill and stirred it energetically with a long stick. Then, straining his mucles until his young face was blood-red and puffy, he lifted the heavy tins and dumped them into the trough.

But at the end of two weeks Isabella's fears were realized. Her son came home one evening, his face swollen from a blow of Wattkie's hand, his backside raw, his bare legs bruised. It did not matter that he had been unmercifully beaten. What mattered was that he had lost his job.

"It wasna' ma fault," he explained lugubriously to his mother, "one o' th' pigs deed. She choked on a biscuit that was i' th' swill an' deed. An' Wattie said I shouldna' hae let her eat th' biscuit."

He sobbed a little after he went to bed that night, not only because of the pain in his body but because his pig-feeding career had ended. Yet he had tasted the joy of earning money, and he meant to be out looking for other employment as soon as school was over on the morrow.

"Hae ye said your prayers?" asked Isabella from the doorway.

In his sorrow, he had forgotten to pray. Now, stiffly, he climbed out of bed and knelt.

> "As I lay me doon this night tae sleep,
> I pray th' Lord ma soul tae keep,
> If I should dee before I wake,
> I pray th' Lord ma soul tae tak."

When he had climbed back into bed, Isabella with her candle walked away from the door and the tiny house was still. Harry lay there wondering what it would be like to fall asleep now and not to wake up in the morning. And what was a soul, anyway? And what would the Lord be doing in Musselburgh prowling around in the dark for the soul of wee Harry Lauder?

Years later the millions of people who saw him, applauded him, knew him, flattered and catered to him never suspected that before he went to sleep he never failed to repeat that ageless prayer which had so puzzled him as a boy.

It was some days before Harry succeeded in finding other employment, but he heard at last of a man who needed boys to pick strawberries. The road was dusty and the sun was hot. The man who gazed down at him was tall and stem, with a long face and small, suspicious eyes.

"Weel, whit do ye want?" he barked.

"Hoots, I came tae pick your berries!"

"Hmm. Hoo ould are ye?"

"I'm eight, sir."

"Hmm. Can ye whustle?"

"Huh?"

"Can ye whustle?"

Even at that early age Harry was at a loss to understand exactly how being able to whistle was going to mean success as a berry picker, but he was eager to oblige, and promptly began a lusty whistling of *Annie Laurie*. The big man listened and nodded.

"Weel, take this can an' get in there an' start pickin'. Mind ye *keep* pickin' an' keep *whustlin'*!"

The gardener had discovered that boys who whistled could not eat his berries at the same time. There were many boys in the wide field, all of them whistling a different tune. Up and down the numerous long rows the gardener walked, listening. If a boy stopped whistling, it meant that he had started eating. So the boys whistled, and at the end of the day each received fourpence.

Harry's berry-picking experience lasted only two days. At the end of that time he limped home to his mother, his backside again smarting. There were no tears this time. He was learning to take these things philosophically.

The berries had been tempting—luscious-sweet, dusty, hot and juicy. Whistling like that for hours at a time, one's throat got dry. Surely, a fistful of berries popped lightning-swift into one's mouth would be as refreshing as nectar. He withstood the temptation manfully the first day, but the second day he succumbed. Just as he stuffed the fruit into his mouth, the boss popped up, it seemed, from nowhere, caught hold of his collar and yanked him to his feet. The gardener reasoned that the punishment he was about to inflict was justified, for it would serve as an example to the others. So Harry was beaten again while his fellow-workers went on whistling.

Years later, when Harry Lauder was famous, when people were inviting him to luncheons and banquets, they wondered why it was that their guest of honor would never eat strawberries. Why, they said, it seemed *as if the very sight of them brought him pain!*

Paying jobs for an eight-year-old boy are not the easiest things in the world to find, and to Harry it had become of tremendous importance that he make money. To him, a sixpence seemed a fortune. Poverty was all about him, not only in his own home, but in the "wee but and bens" of his neighbors, something omnipresent, inescapable. This was the ugly kind of poverty which had to scheme for weeks before it could take a pair of boots to be mended at the cobbler's; yet through it all, theirs was a cheerful house, for Isabella had learned to bear poverty with patience and even a certain gallantry, since she never expected to know anything else. She had a family to raise, and she considered it was her duty to raise them to be, not great men and women, not scholarly or rich or famous, but straight and clean and dependable. Imbued in Harry Lauder from babyhood was the creed that a promise must be scrupulously kept, that one must always pay one's debts, and think thrice before one made them; that one must save rigidly; that one must expect to work for what one got—and work hard.

Ingrained in him, too, even at that early age, was an intense love of country, of his own Scotland with its sharply, strongly molded hills, its deep green woods, its swift-running rivers, its wide, brooding valleys and its broadly sweeping moors, melancholy, tranquil. No festive, feminine land is Scotland. It is a masculine and virile land, rugged, moody, sometimes kindly, sometimes cruel, but always beautiful and proud. This ardent love of country had been instilled into him from his schoolmaster, a gruff, bearded man named Fraser. It was not enough for Fraser to teach his students how to read and write and do sums. Scottish history was Fraser's favorite theme. He expounded upon it eloquently. He drilled it into them day after day—stirring, glowing, inspiring were the tales he told of Bruce, Wallace, Robert Livingstone, Burns, Scott. It would be pretty tragic, Harry often thought, to be born an Englishman or a Norwegian or a German instead of a Scot. Young Lauder was proud that he had had the great good fortune to be bom in Scotland. He thought his country must be more lovely, greater, than any country on the face of the earth. Later, years later, he was to make people all over the globe feel that they, too, knew and loved Harry Lauder's Scotland—the Scotland of the plain man, the wee hooses, the glens, the heather, the lassies, the gloaming, and the "braw, bricht, moonlicht nichts."

"Scotland," he announced one day in the schoolyard, "is th' bonniest country i' th' whole *wor-r-rld!*"

An English boy, twice Harry's size, who had lately joined the school, disputed this.

"It's not 'alf as good as England," he declared, scornfully.

Harry gasped. Why, this was nothing short of sacrilege! For a moment he stood, his short, thickly set body tense, his bright blue eyes flashing and incredulous, his face red with anger. Then of a sudden he pounced upon England, lashing out with his small fists. England was stronger and bigger, but Harry hung on. They rolled in the dirt, they kicked and punched and yelled.

An hour later Isabella saw her son limping down the narrow, dusty road. His face was bruised and battered. One eye was already discolored; his clothes were torn, but his head was up—and he was singing "Draw the Sword, Scotland," singing it lustily, with unmistakable bravado. He had been beaten, but he had fought for his country.

He was nine now, and he had been unemployed for almost a year. No one wanted a pig feeder, no one wanted a strawberry picker. There was nothing to do but help his mother around the house, play nursemaid to his younger brothers, and take the wean out for an airing strapped among the heavy folds of the warm plaid on his back.

Musselburgh was a neat little town, fronting on the sea, a place of small, one and two-story stone houses with sloping slate roofs. There was a wide beach with sands of rich golden hue. Up and down this beach went the fishwives wearing bright, full skirts and 'kerchiefs, selling mussel broth and "buckies," which was the local name for the periwinkle, a small shellfish. Here on the beach with the other children, young Harry played, and here he sat alone, his eyes staring somberly out to the horizon, asking himself how he could make a few pennies to help his mother.

His third opportunity came one early spring day when he wandered down to the Musselburgh station. There were crowds of boys lounging about, all of whom sprang to attention when the train from Edinburgh pulled in and men carrying golf bags stepped out of it. Instantly the golfers were surrounded by an army of ragged, screeching boys. "Carry your clubs, sir? Carry your clubs?"

Harry Lauder observed it all thoughtfully, speculatively. Obviously, one could not carry a bagful of clubs on one's back and a wean at the same time.

He raced home, dashed breathlessly up to his mother, and turned his back to her while she unstrapped the infant. Hurriedly, he told her all that he had seen.

"It's a braw business," he maintained.

"Aye. I've heard many rich men came tae Musselburgh tae play their golf on th' Musselburgh links. An' how muckle wull ye get for carryin' their bags?"

"I dinna ken, Mither."

He was off, tearing down the street again. Presently he had joined the crowd of urchins who were waiting for the next train.

"How muckle wull ye be gettin' for tae carry th' clubs?" he asked eagerly.

"Twopence a round. Why?"

"I can carry clubs," he told them.

They laughed goodnaturedly. "Hoots, look whit wants tae carry clubs! Why, he's nae bigger than th' bags themsel's!"

"He's naught but a wean!"

He was still small for his age, and younger than any of the rest, but when the train pulled in, and they tried to shove him out of the way, he found that he could dart under their arms and reach the very front of the line. Young though he was, his voice was amazingly strong and clear. It rang out, topping the others in a quick, sing-song chant: "Carry your clubs, Mister? Carry your clubs, sir?"

The bag grew heavy at the end of a long day, but sometimes a man would give the boy an extra penny. This was pleasant work, better than feeding pigs, better than picking berries. There were days now when Harry Lauder earned the unheard-of sum of sixpence (about twelve cents), and sometimes even ninepence. His short legs were tired when the game ended, but he ran home to his mother, his blue eyes glowing, and tossed his earnings into her lap with a lordly gesture. It was worth everything, just to see that broad smile creeping over her face and up into her eyes.

He had been caddying only a short time when he discovered a means of augmenting his income. Golfers in those days used what were called "gutta" balls. A club striking these balls sometimes split them in two. To the caddies that was a happy moment, for they were permitted to salvage the pieces. In the evenings Harry boiled these pieces in an old stew pot until they were almost the texture of clay. Then he sat at the kitchen table, carefully, patiently rolling the pulp while it hardened, shaping it into a long tapering cylinder, and finally after several hours, a gutta ball was transformed into a hard, tough whip which could be sold to the pony drivers in the mines.

Coming home from the links late one evening when he was eleven-and-a-half, he found that his father had already returned from the pottery works and was seated at the kitchen table. Isabella stood, her work-worn hands on her hips, her young face anxious.

"I'm no likin' it, John," she said firmly. "I'm no likin' it at a'."

John smiled coaxingly. "You'll like it when ye get used tae it."

"England!" she muttered. "Tae leave Scotland for England. I've a feelin' nae guid wull come o' it, John. We'd best be stayin' here, mind I'm tellin' ye. Ye ken I hae th' feelin' we should stay where we are."

Harry stood, the money in his fist forgotten. Leave Musselburgh? Go to England? Why, this was incredible! Neither of his parents paid the slightest attention to him. Isabella's face with its firmly chiseled features had a strained, almost frightened expression. Her husband smiled and assured her that Whittington Moor in Derbyshire was a very fine place to live, and besides, Pearson's Pottery Works there had offered him more money.

"You'll no be scoffin' at a bit o' extra siller," he told her.

She shook her head gravely. "It's—a—feelin' I hae," she answered, her voice dull with foreboding. "Nae guid wull come o' oor leavin' oor ain folk, John. Ma heart's nae i' this move. Ye ken I've nae mind tae be leaving Scotland. I'll gae, but I dinna like it."

He laughed again, rose, patted her shoulder affectionately.

"It's a—feelin' o'—*danger*" she insisted.

Again he laughed. Danger! What danger could there be in Whittington Moor? What danger could there be in a man of thirty-two earning more money? Was it not a man's duty to improve his position when he got the chance?

She sighed. "Aye. Aye. We'll gae, but I'm telling ye, mon, ma heart's no i' it."

Yet she set to work energetically enough packing her skillets, and in a short time the Lauders were on their way to Whittington Moor.

To John and the children the trip was gloriously exciting. It was the first time the children had been on a train, and they stared with wonder-bright eyes out of the windows, while Isabella, very prim, tight-lipped and dignified, kept telling herself that there was nothing to fear, that this feeling she had of impending danger was very, very silly. Why should she feel like this? Why must every turn of the train wheels increase her apprehension? What could possibly happen to them in Whittington Moor? John was only thirty-two, hale and full of life. She was a few years younger, strong and healthy. The bairns—oh, dear God be good to them!—were strapping, vigorous youngsters. And it *would* be pleasant having a bit of extra siller each week. No, there was nothing to worry about, nothing at all; only—oh, if they could only turn right around and go back to Musselburgh!

Arriving at Whittington Moor, the Lauders rented a cottage no larger and even more ramshackle than the one they had left in Musselburgh. When they had been there only a few days John came home from the works one evening, and Isabella knew at the first glance that he was sick. The Lauders were a strapping, healthy brood, and to Harry it was strange and a little terrifying to have illness in the house and to have to be telling the younger children to keep quiet all the time. The doctor came and went, talking in low, solemn tones to Isabella. She listened, her hands clasped tensely, her tortured eyes riveted upon his face. She was looking pale, these days, and Harry knew that she was sitting up every night by his father's bed. Pneumonia. The very word had a funereal sound.

Two weeks after their arrival in Whittington Moor, Isabella came out of the sickroom closing the door softly behind her. She was sobbing wildly. It was the first time she had cried during these seemingly endless days, and her sobs tore at Harry's heart, hurting him like knife-thrusts. He felt uneasy and helpless as he stood watching her for some minutes. She sat there in the old chair by the window, and now and then she lifted her tear-swollen face ceilingward, crying out in agony, "Oh, God! Oh, God!"

Fearful, he came close to her and spoke in a hushed voice. "Mither, is he—is Faither—worse?"

"Harry! Harry!"

She caught him to her, pressing him hard against her body. He felt her tears on his cheek.

"Mither, dinna greet," he pleaded.

"Harry, your—your faither's—deed."

"Deed!"

"Aye. Aye. God help us. God help us a'! Hoo'll we live th' noo? Hoo'll we live, th' nine o' us? Ah, ma puir laddie!"

The hideous thought of charity which had haunted her all the days of her life now loomed like a specter. There would, she knew, be only enough insurance to bury John and bring herself and her bairns back to Scotland. And then what? What then? Charity! She shuddered.

"Ah, God hae mercy on us," she moaned.

Harry blinked back the tears and straightened his shoulders. In that moment he knew a deep sense of his own responsibility. No longer did he feel like a child.

"Mither," he pleaded softly, stroking back a wisp of her fine hair, "dinna greet. I love ye, Mither. I love ye. I'll never be leavin' ye. I'll work, Mither."

"YOU! You're no twelve yet, wee Harry. What can *you* do?" she queried distractedly.

His young voice rang out solemnly. It was not a boast, it was a vow, a vow that he was making, not to her, but to himself. "I'll *work* for ye, that's what I'll do. I wull so. I'll work for ye. I'll tak' care o' ye, Mither. *I'll tak' care of all of us!*"

CHAPTER TWO

Even though there was death in it, and tears, nonetheless, thought young Lauder as the train carried them back to Scotland, it was a bonny, bonny world. All the days of his life he remained very sure of that. It was a bonny world to him when later he left the sunlight behind and went down into the blackness of the earth. It was a bonny world to him when he saw it torn and bloody with war. It was, he maintained, a bonny world and well worth saving.

Now, despite the weeping of his mother, despite her pain and her fears, he knew within himself a quiet confidence that the world was going to let him make a living for himself and his family. He had not the faintest idea how he was to accomplish this. He knew nothing beyond the fact that they had only enough money to take them to Arbroath where his mother had decided to go because she had relatives there.

Ah, but it was good to be back in Scotland, he mused, when they had crossed the border. The air of Scotland was different from the air of England. It had been, surely, a grand adventure, this riding in a train, but evidently it was soon to end, for his mother had stopped weeping and become very busy wiping Alec's nose, setting Jean's bonnet to rights, helping Matt on with his jacket, and pushing back George's hair.

Arbroath. Arbroath. Harry repeated it to himself several times, liking the sound of it. Would Arbroath, he wondered, be like Musselburgh?

It was vastly different from Musselburgh, he knew that the minute they stepped from the train. He could see chimneys, tall chimneys, factory chimneys. Arbroath was a small, busy, industriously prosperous town of about twenty thousand inhabitants. Here were engineering works, shoe factories, huge flax mills. The harbor was a bustling, noisy place where great boats from Russia and the Baltics brought in enormous quantities of flax which was speedily transported in large horse-drawn carts to the mills.

The Lauders trooped along the main street, Isabella leading the way, the baby in one arm, the other hand holding a battered and bulging valise. Matt and George were holding on to the sides of her shawl, their free hands clasping the strings of large, inexpertly wrapped bundles. A few yards behind came Harry, also laden with bundles, while Bella and Jean clung obediently to his short, tight little coat. Alec trotted along sturdily in the rear. Their few sticks of furniture were coming along by a later train. The valise and the bundles held the family wardrobe.

It was a somber, narrow street, devoid of any such pleasantry as a tree or a garden.

They were passing one of the mills now—Gordon's Flax Mill, read the sign over the wooden gates. It was evening, and great streams of workers were pouring into the already crowded street. Harry watched them, his blue eyes alight with interest. Presently he saw a group of children, boys and girls of about his own age, leaving the mill. Did they work there? And if they did, why couldn't he? A boy of his own age was walking tiredly beside him.

"Do ye work i' th' mill?" asked Harry.

"Aye. I'm a towie."

Harry had no idea what a towie was, but he asked the boy if he thought *he* could be one, too.

"Aye. If you're under fourteen ye can be a part-timer like me. If you're fourteen, ye can work fu' time."

"Hoo muckle would ye be gettin' fer tae be a part-timer?"

"Twa' shillin's a week."

"Whit does it mean tae be a part-timer?"

"Ye go tae school one day an' ye work th' next. Th' school's run by th' mon that owns th' mill. Stumpy Bell's th' teacher."

"Could I *say* I was fourteen, maybe, an' work fu' time?"

"No. They hae inspectors. Weel, I turn here th' noo. G'bye."

"G'bye. I'll be seein' ye at th' mill!" he promised cheerily.

When the Lauders had settled down in Arbroath, they managed to exist without charity. Occasionally Isabella made a few pennies doing washing, baking, sometimes minding a neighbor's brood as well as her own. This, with the two shillings (fifty cents) which was Harry's weekly wage at the mill, was enough to pay for a shelter and barely sufficient to keep them from starving.

Though he was not yet twelve, Harry lost no time in securing a job at Gordon's. It became, presently, a matter of dull routine, working twelve hours one day and going to school the next.

Being even a part-time towie was hard and monotonous. It meant moving at top speed like a rabbit in a cage, over the same stretch of floor a hundred times a day. When the tow had passed through the heckling machines, the towies collected it, brought it to large receptacles, dumped it in, and then stamped on it to press it down. Then back to the machines for more tow. There was never an end to the tow, never an end to the receptacles. The place was badly ventilated, and the air was heavy, especially in summer.

There was no use complaining. Tiresome though the work was, one must thank God for it, and pray that it would continue. The two shillings a week he earned was scarcely enough to feed a family of nine, and time after time Harry would go to a new mill claiming stoutly that he was fourteen. For a day or two he might work, his eyes and ears as alert as those of an animal, painfully on alert lest the inspector catch him. There were times when he would hear the inspector's voice or catch sight of him before the man saw him. This meant a feverish scampering to hide behind some of the machinery until the inspector should be gone; but the man was not always considerate enough to announce his coming beforehand, and inevitably Harry was sent back to part-timing again. Finally he resigned himself to this, only counting the months until he would be fourteen.

But months are long. Back and forth, legs aching, muscles strained, the towies ran from machine to receptacle. If for a minute during that twelve-hour day they stopped stamping and paused to ease the stinging pain in their legs, the overseer roared at them, threatening them with the loss of their jobs. All day long one looked forward to the next day, which was school; and at school even while dodging the blows of Stumpy Bell, one dreaded the *next* day, which was the mill.

School was held in an old kirk. The schoolmaster was a stem, irascible man called "Stumpy" because of one leg which was considerably shorter than the other and encased in an iron brace. The slightest mistake was to Stumpy an infuriating thing. He never, however, caned the students. He had a more efficient method. There was always that iron boot with which to kick them. But despite his short temper and his sudden, often unexpected kicks, the boys held no grudge against Stumpy. At least, he was impartial in his kickings, and if the iron foot did not happen to strike a bone, it did not hurt *too* much.

Saturday was always schoolday, and Harry soon found a way to increase the family income on Saturdays. By rising at five o'clock he could deliver one hundred and fifty copies of the *Arbroath Guide* and still be on time when the school bell rang. Scotch winters are harsh, Scotch rains are torrents, Scotch winds are high and biting. Delivering the *Arbroath Guide* meant trudging miles along the roads when everyone else was asleep. It meant battling against the winds and the rain and the mud, but it meant, too, an extra ninepence every week, it meant extra milk for the younger children.

It was not Stumpy, it was not the mill, it was not the paper route that Harry hated. These dwindled almost to nothingness in comparison with the nightly tussle with the tow. This was the most nerve-shattering task of all. You loathed it, rebelled at it, but you kept on doing it—because you had to, because doing it meant an extra shilling and sixpence at the end of every week.

Mrs. Lauder and her boy Harry were not the only ones in Arbroath who "teased" tow night after night. Many of the poorer families supplemented their incomes in this manner. By applying for the work at the factories, the factory would dump at your house a hundred pounds at a time of old string, old ropes, old ship's rigging. This must be "teased" into tow so that it could be woven into coarse cloth, perhaps for the sails of a ship.

When the frugal supper was over, dishes washed and the younger children in bed, then came "towing time." The rope, the string, was piled in a high, unlovely mound on the kitchen table. The candle was lit. Isabella and her son Harry sat side by side in the candlelight teasing the tow. They never worked less than two hours, and often they labored until midnight. After working for an hour, the muscles of their hands and wrists grew stiff and cramped. The rough tow tore into the flesh of their fingers, so that all ten fingers were bleeding, and there were little pools of blood on the wooden table which Isabella wiped off with a wet rag and went on "teasing" again. Fingertips grew so sensitive after a time that every move, every slight pull at a piece of string tore its hot way up their arms and into their elbows.

Harry made no sound, but night after night his eyes filled with tears that presently came streaming down his cheeks, tears of pain and tiredness. But Isabella was determinedly cheerful. Her face gray-pale in the flickering light of the candle, she would force herself to smile at him.

"Laddie, laddie, we mustna' greet. It—" she winced in spite of herself as her skinless fingers tore at a rope of exceptional stiffness, "it willna be long before we can stop an' gae tae bed an' rest. Did I ever tell ye th' story aboot th' time ould Angus MacDonald met a bogle i' th' glen?"

And the story would be told. She managed to stretch it out until the work was over for the night, and only then the story broke off, and she reached out her bleeding fingers, caught her boy to her, and they would cry together—not for pain any longer, but for gladness that the night's work was over.

But in the mornings when the autumnal mists lay like softly illumined silver over the moors, and in the evenings when the long twilight was languid and pungent with the smell of the peat, then it was easy to forget the unraveling of the ropes, then it was good to sing as he strode to and from the mill or played among the ruins of the ancient abbey. There was always *Annie Laurie* and *The Campbells are Comin'* and the hymns, but lately there was a particular song which kept running through his head and would not let go of him. It came humming its presumptuous way into his brain after he had said his prayers at night, as he ate his porridge in the morning, as he entered into the rough and tumble sports of the schoolyard.

> "Though poverty daily looks in at my door,
> Though I'm hungry and footsore and ill,
> Thank God I can look the whole world in the face,
> For I—am—a—gentleman still."

Much as Isabella loved to hear her boy singing, there were times when she wished he might choose some other melody. "Can ye no sing saethin' else, wee Harry?" she asked at length. "Sing one o' th' toons ye heard at th' Band o' Hope meetin'."

It was Isabella who insisted that Harry join the Band of Hope. He had been reluctant to do so at first, but now he was glad, for these meetings were his only diversion. If it meant several hours longer with the tow to make up for it, Harry decided, the meetings were well worth the price.

For they *sang* at the Band of Hope meetings.

Boys and girls who joined the Band of Hope pledged themselves to abstain from strong drink. At these meetings there would be speeches on the evils of liquor, but afterward they would all sing hymns or some of the old Scotch songs, and sometimes during the evening the superintendent would call upon a few of the children to come to the platform and sing or give recitations.

For Harry the attraction of these meetings was the singing. There was nothing on earth he enjoyed more. He sang with gusto.

"Shall we gather at the river,
The bee-tee-fu', the bee-tee-fu' riv- ver?"

And the other hymns—Throw out the Lifeline, Do Thou with Hyssop Sprinkle Me, Oh, Love that Will not Let Me Go.

Singing, you could forget old Stumpy and his rages and his iron boot, you could forget the noise of the machines at the mill, you could forget the piles of rope on the kitchen table.

"Now," beamed the superintendent on a particular evening in mid-spring, "which of you children will favor us with a song tonight?"

There was an interval of silence. Bob Hannah, the boy who sat next to Harry, gave him a sudden nudge. "Why don't *you* sing?" he whispered.

Harry looked startled. What? Him? Sing? Stand up there before a crowd of people and sing all *alone*? It was one thing to sing with others, it was one thing to sing when you thought no one was listening, but it was another thing just to stand alone and sing with people looking straight at you. Not that the idea was entirely new to him. He had often wondered how it would feel to do a thing so daring as that, and secretly he had even practiced *Annie Laurie* and several of the old Scotch hymns, but always when the invitation came he remained quiet, too shy to come forward.

"Oh, now," coaxed the superintendent, "surely *somebody* has a hymn for us tonight? Or a recitation? Johnnie? Johnnie Yeamans?"

Again that nudge, more compelling now. "Go on, Harry! Go on! Get up an' sing!"

Before Harry realized what he was doing, he found himself on his feet.

"Ah! Here's little Harry Lauder! Come right up here, Harry."

All eyes were upon him. There was a deep, abysmal hush. It was too late to back out now. Harry walked to the platform. Then he was standing there, facing everybody. It was a bleak and terrifying moment. He gulped, blushed, suddenly realized he had hands, and sought desperately to put them somewhere. A little girl tittered, and the superintendent said, "*Ssh!*" Then silence again.

"Go on, Harry," smiled the superintendent encouragingly.

But Harry could not go on. Not a word of *Annie Laurie* could he recall, not so much as a line of a single hymn. His mind groped feverishly in the midst of what seemed a black and interminable void. How did *Draw the Sword, Scotland* go? But though he had sung it a thousand times, the very tune now completely evaded him. He experienced a dreadful moment of sheer panic. There was only one song that remained stubbornly with him in that never-to-be-forgotten moment, and presently he heard himself singing it.

> "Though poverty daily looks in at my door.
> Though I'm hungry and footsore and ill . . ."

There had never been anything quite like this at the Band of Hope meetings. His short, sturdy legs apart, his bare feet planted firmly upon the wooden boards of the platform, Harry Lauder proclaimed to the world in his first public appearance that he was a gentleman still.

And his world believed him.

When he finished, he had his first taste of applause—and applause is a heady, dazzling thing. He loved it, welcomed it, wanted to hear it again. Why, it had not been difficult at all, standing up there and singing before a crowd! It was just as easy—just as easy as *anything!* Would he sing again? Just let them ask him!

He felt proud of himself as he walked home through the darkness, proud and glad with the applause still ringing in his ears. It had been a glorious and stimulating experience. Livingstone must have felt just like this when he discovered Victoria Falls. Rabbie Bums must have felt like this when, in 1787, he saw the first Edinburgh edition of his poems.

Only a few weeks afterward, while the sound of applause was still vibrating in his ears, a traveling theatrical company announced their appearance in Arbroath. Strewn everywhere were posters, gaudy and impressive. They showed a picture of a watch—an Abyssinian gold watch. In addition to the regular performance, the management proposed to hold an amateur contest, and this rich, handsome watch of pure—genuine—real—bonafide—guaranteed Abyssinian gold would be presented to the winner.

Imagine, thought Harry, as he read the glowing description, just imagine actually owning a genuine Abyssinian gold watch! He stared at the picture of it longingly. For two nights following he could scarcely close his eyes for thinking of the fine gold watch which somebody was going to win just for singing. In the mornings he left the house earlier than usual so he could go and read the poster and look at the picture of the watch again.

As he stood there on the third morning he was joined by two small friends, Bob Hannah and Johnnie Yeamans. Fascinated, the three children stared in utter silence for a long time.

"It's at th' Oddfellows' Ha'," announced Johnnie.

"An Abyssinian gold watch!" gasped Bob at last in a small, awed voice.

"It'll be worth muckle siller," declared Johnnie, who seemed to know all there was to know about watches. There was a longish pause. "It's no as if it was just a plain ould *gold* watch," he went on, "but it's an *Abyssinian* gold watch!"

"Aye," murmured Harry a bit breathlessly.

"Why do ye no try for it, Harry?" asked Johnnie.

"Me?" queried Harry, as if the idea had never until this moment invaded his mind. "*Me?*"

"Aye. You'd win it. Ye sang graund at th' Band o' Hope meetin'. It's no everyday a person has a chance tae win an Abyssinian gold watch, ye ken."

"True," nodded Harry gravely.

"And," put in Bob, "we could sell it later an' get muckle siller for it."

"We?" questioned Harry, with a sudden hint of coldness in his voice.

"Aye. We could divide th' siller."

"Weel," said Harry thoughtfully, "I might try for th' watch, but I'll no promise tae divide th' siller wi' ye."

The question was settled, then. He was going to sing in the Oddfellows' Hall. Never had he worked more zestfully than he did that day at the mill. It was wonderful to sing in a theatre. It was wonderful just to *sing*. It was wonderful to be alive. It would be wonderful having a watch. Wonderful. Wonderful. Even the heckling machines were wonderful when one came to think of it. All the world was suddenly wonderful.

As the night of the contest approached, however, both Isabella and her son were nervous. She had not the money to go to the theatre to see him, but she had washed and mended his clothes, she stood over him to make sure that he scrubbed behind his ears, she smoothed his straight, unruly hair before he started out.

She smiled at him encouragingly. "Mind ye sing *loud*, laddie."

Harry's blue eyes had a strained, rather wild look.

"Dinna fash yoursel' if ye dinna win th' watch," she called, as he walked out into the gloaming.

Again Harry Lauder stood waiting for his turn to sing. Oddfellows' Hall was crowded. His legs seemed suddenly to be made of jelly. He heard the catcalls from the gallery as they laughed and jeered at the singers preceding him. He smelled the ancient eggs. He had not known it would be like that. He had anticipated a polite, quiet, friendly audience such as he had faced at the Band of Hope; but here, why, if a singer did not please them, they booed, stomped, they threw rotten eggs and soft tomatoes and cabbages so old they were slimy. It was terrifying. It was ghastly.

"All right," said a man in shirt sleeves who seemed to be in charge, "it's your turn now, laddie."

Into the glare of the footlights walked a very little boy. Once he was facing the audience all nervousness left him as if it had never been. He felt confident and glad. He looked straight at them, walked directly down to the footlights—and grinned. At once the strange Lauder magnetism, the sureness of him, made itself felt. The crowded theatre lapsed into silence.

"Though poverty daily looks in at ma door," sang the strong, boyish voice, "Though I'm hungry and footsore and ill—" instinct, something wise yet untaught, made him pause dramatically; then his head went up with a sudden, heroic, challenging movement, and the young voice rang out in a note of triumph, "Thank *God* I can look th' whole wor-r-rld i' th' face—for *I—am—a gentleman* still!"

Again that burst of applause, louder, more insistent than it had been at the Band of Hope. Who had taught him the dramatic value of that pause? Who had schooled him in the technique of "getting a line over"?

He just knew these things, and even then he sensed how necessary they were. For the moment he had forgotten all about the watch, forgotten himself and his world, and remembered, *felt*, that he was a gentleman still. And because he felt it, his audience felt it. Suddenly, now that his interval of triumph was over, the watch did not matter. It had been enough just to sing, just to experience that strange consciousness of mastery, just to hear the applause.

He walked home that night with the Abyssinian gold watch ticking joyously in his pocket. Its ticking stopped after a few days, and before the month was over all the fine, shiny Abyssinian gold had worn off, but if you were to visit him today at his home in Strathaven, sixty years later, he would show you that very watch.

Many traveling companies gave amateur contests in Arbroath, for these were becoming the rage in 1882 and 1883. Never a chance came to sing that Harry Lauder did not eagerly clutch at it. He spent his spare time learning other popular songs and even thinking out certain gestures to go with them. Isabella's front room, which heretofore had included only the barest necessities, now became gay with clocks and vases, mustache cups and andirons which Harry was forever winning. Every moment she could spare she spent polishing these trophies.

"Come an' see th' ground fire-iron that oor Harry won!" she would say proudly to the neighbors.

Everywhere he went, these days, wee Harry was pressed to sing. He had no "voice." The only thing that could be said for it was that it was strong and flexible. It was never his voice which people came to hear. It was not the appearance of the singer himself, for his was definitely a homely face and a short, though hardy body.

Yet more and more, people were clamoring to hear him sing. People enjoyed his singing as much as he enjoyed singing to them, and through his singing, life became to Harry Lauder a perpetual adventure, eternally interesting, marvelously worthwhile. He asked little of life except to keep working and keep singing. Nothing else mattered much.

He was fourteen when, returning from the mill one evening, his mother handed him a letter.

"Read it," she said. "It's frae your Uncle Sandy i' th' Black Country."

Harry put aside his lunch pail, hung up his jacket on the back of the kitchen door, and reached for the letter. "What does he say?" he asked.

"He says that th' bairns wull be growin' up. He says that i' Hamilton there'll be mair opportunities for a' o' us. He says we maun gae tae Hamilton."

To Isabella, Harry had now become "the man of the house," and she frankly sought his opinion upon every occasion. She watched him now as he read the letter. His uncle Sandy MacLennan was a miner in the Black Country, which was what the Scots called the mining district near Glasgow.

"Whit d'ye think, laddie?" asked Isabella.

"Hoo far is Hamilton frae Glasga', Mither?"

"I dinna ken. Maybe aboot—ten—twelve miles. Weel, what d'ye think, Harry?"

"I think if there are opportunities i' Hamilton, Hamilton's th' place where we maun be," answered Harry readily. "I might get work i' th' mines."

"Th' mines? You? You're no fourteen yet. Ah, it's that conceited you're gettin', Harry, whit wi' your singin' an' a'." She smiled fondly at him. "Weel, laddie, if ye think it best, we'll gae tae Hamilton. We couldna' be worse off than we are here. We'll gae, then, God helpin' us. I'll write your uncle th' nicht an' tell him—"

"Tell him th' Lauders are comin'!" declared Harry.

CHAPTER THREE

Situated in the lowlands, Hamilton, a town of around forty thousand, was distinguished by the fact that it was the center of the Black Country, the coal and iron mines; besides these, it boasted of the proud Hamilton Castle, a Georgian palace with great Corinthian columns, set in the midst of magnificent grounds. The Prince of Wales, later to be crowned King Edward the Seventh, had visited the palace only six years previously. When, however, the Lauders arrived in 1884, Hamilton failed to be impressed. It was a busy, smoky place, almost twice the size of Arbroath, with steel mills, blast furnaces and iron foundries.

Uncle Sandy was a "bottomer" in the coal mines. He had responsibilities of his own, and he could offer the Lauders no financial aid even had they asked it. He could, however, take Harry around and introduce him to the "gaffers" and see if any of them needed a "boy."

Returning home the first night after Uncle Sandy had taken him to the mines, Harry's eyes were so bright that at first Isabella suspected that the lad must have a fever.

"Mither!" he cried jubilantly, "I'm tae get ten shillin's a week an' I gae tae work tomorrow!"

She stared at him incredulously. "Ten shillin's?"

They both thought it was much too good to be true. Ten shillings— (two dollars and fifty cents)—in one week? Uncle Sandy had been right, this was indeed the place of opportunity.

As each day of the first week passed, the boy grew more and more impatient for the big moment when he would receive his wages. Ten shillings all at once! He would take it home and dump it in his mother's lap. They would kiss each other and laugh and feel rich.

But with the arrival of Saturday night, Harry discovered that the gaffer had collected both his own wages and those of his "boy"—and left Hamilton.

It was a blow too severe to be borne stoically. A week of anticipation for the moment when he would bring his mother ten shillings, and now there was nothing.

He could not tell his mother what a frightful experience it had been. He could not explain to anyone how it felt to leave the clean, warm sunlight and descend into the slimy darkness of the mine. There had been something terrifying about the sensation of the air pressure in his lungs. He had felt all the time as if he were choking to death. The men told him one grew accustomed to it after a while. The smell down there, the darkness, the dampness, the black walls on every side—no, he had never told his mother how awful it was. Every muscle of his body ached from the work he had been called upon to do, but he had stood everything, always dreaming of that moment when the gaffer would hand him his ten shillings.

He was frankly crying when he reached the "but and ben" where they had found shelter. When he told her what had happened, his mother cried, too. The uncertainty of finding another job occurred to them and they wished now they had stayed in Arbroath.

But there were no tears on Monday morning when Harry went back to the mine and waited for the arrival of Gibbie Pitcairn, the general manager. Pitcairn was a big, brawny man with a deep and bellowing voice. Harry walked directly up to him and before Pitcairn could speak, blurted out all in one breath what had happened on Saturday night.

"Hoo ould are ye, lad?" asked Gibbie.

"I'm fourteen i' August."

Gibbie gave the boy a great thump on the back. "Weel, you'll be a guid collier yet. Keep a stout heart i' ye th' while. I'll put ye tae shiftin' wagons at th' pit head."

"Ye wull?"

"I wull so. An' you'll get your nine shillin's when th' week's up. Whit d'ye say, lad?"

"Done!" declared Harry.

When the second week had ended, it was no longer a woebegone little figure that burst into that tiny ramshackle cottage. This time he had his wages—not in his pocket but tightly clasped in his fist. Isabella was seated at the kitchen table and he opened his hand, dropping the coins into her lap. She gave a glad little cry, kissed him, and then the two who had weathered many storms together, sat side by side at the table counting over the money. It would have been difficult to tell whether her eyes or his were the brighter. They counted the money once, twice, three times, while the younger children, sensing that something unprecedented was happening, grouped closely about the table staring in wonderment.

"It's—Harry's *pay*," whispered Matt, and there was awe in his voice.

"It's—Harry's—*pay*," repeated Bella, deeply impressed.

"An' whit'll we *do* wi' it a'?" asked George, his eyes saucer-round and grave.

"Mither!" cried Alec, "can we hae mince pies?"

"Mither!" echoed Jock, "can we hae mince pies wi' Harry's pay?"

Isabella, after careful consideration of the matter, decided that, as a celebration, they could have mince pies.

Though he had been employed there only two weeks, Harry had already become a favorite with the men at the mine. Hardy, rough, good-natured, they were eager to be entertained. Their lives were drab enough, spent day after day in the darkness, and during lunch hour someone was always sure to call out, "Where's wee Harry th' noo? Gie

31

us a bit song, Harry!" Harry was a friendly, obliging little soul, and he sang the same songs to them over and over.

He had been working only a few weeks when Pitcaim told him there was a better job open and he could have it if he wanted it.

"I want it," Harry answered, and then by way of second thought, "whit is it?"

"A trapper. D'ye ken whit a trapper is, lad?"

"Aye. A trapper opens an' closes th' wooden gates that controls the air currents tae th' mines. Whit pay wull I be gettin'?"

"Fifteen shillin's."

"A *week?*"

"A week."

"Done!"

Each mine had gates. It was the trapper's business to open and close the heavy wooden gates for the pony drivers when they approached with their loads of coal. The pony drivers were big, stalwart men, and if a trapper did not open the gates quickly enough he was apt to receive a lash of the pony driver's whip—those hard rubber whips which Harry himself had so often made from gutta balls. A trapper must be constantly at his post, for the opening and closing of the traps meant air currents far below. Yes, opportunity was here, for here Harry knew that by keeping his eyes open he could learn to be a pony driver. Drivers earned the enormous sum of a pound a week.

A few months later he was glad that he had made it his business to watch and learn how to be a pony driver, for Gibbie told him he could have such a job if he wanted it.

Want it? Of course he wanted it. Not alone for the extra money it would bring, but because he had come to love the patient, hardworking, intelligent ponies.

"You're only a wee bit laddie fer a job like that," said Gibbie, "but I've noticed you're a guid hand wi' th' ponies."

"Wull I get ma pound a week like th' ither men?"

"Ye wull."

"Done!"

Isabella no longer looked worried. They paid only three shillings (seventy-five cents) a week for rent, and there was never a Saturday night that she could not drop something into the kist.

Sometimes Harry assured himself that nobody on earth would want anything better than this. True, it was hard work and he had to walk a mile every day to and from the colliery, but he loved the ponies and the ponies came to know and to love him.

Harry's deepest affection was centered upon Captain. Day after day Harry and Captain worked together, and Harry was positive that Captain understood every word that was said to him. The carts Captain pulled hour after hour along the narrow winding levels of the mine were called "hutches." A train of these hutches was called a "rake." One day Harry and Captain were on their way down. The hutches were empty and the rake was a long one. Somewhere below them in the darkness was the coal "face" which was their objective. Only the tiny lamp fastened to Harry's cap illumined their way. The way led through a long silent tunnel, immediately beyond which was what the men called a "drift."

A drift meant that some years before, this particular part of the mine had collapsed. Now it had been cleared again and a narrow path had been cut through leading to the lower levels. As if by mutual agreement, Harry and Captain always hurried when they had to go through the drift. Day after day as they left the tunnel and approached it, Captain's pace would increase. Man and horse both seemed to feel that there was something uncanny and unsafe about that long, somber stretch that was the drift. Today, as usual, as he neared the end of the tunnel, Captain's hoofs moved quicker. The tunnel was behind them now, and they were approaching the drift. Then suddenly, just as he reached it, Captain stopped.

"Go on, Captain," urged Harry gently.

But the little horse did not move.

"Go on, Captain," begged Harry, his voice impatient now. "It's th' drift. D'ye no ken it's th' *drift?* Gee-up, Captain!"

Captain remained immovable.

"Whit's th' matter wi' ye, Captain? Gee-up, I say! Wull ye hae us stand here a' nicht?"

Harry had never taken the whip to Captain, but now when further

33

distracted pleas and commands proved unavailing, he brought his whip down sharply on the horse's flank. Captain winced, turned his head, looked around at his young master reproachfully, but he made no move.

"Gee-up!" shouted Harry desperately. "*Gee-up!*"

Scarcely had he spoken than there was a strange sound, like a deep groan. It is a sound that every miner knows and dreads. It is a sound that means destruction and terror and death. It is a sound that is heard only a second or two before a cave-in. Quickly now, the boy and the horse rushed backward into the haven of the tunnel. Then it came— the deafening, sickening roar, as tons of stone filled the great cavern below. Quivering, suddenly limp, Harry flung his arms about Captain's shaggy neck.

"Ye kent it, Captain! Ye kent it was comin'! Ye saved ma life th' day—ye ken that, too, don't ye? Don't ye, Captain?"

No one on earth prized his friends more than did Harry Lauder, and it was a sad parting which took place between him and Captain some months later; but he had heard of a chance for a job as a water-drawer over at the Allentown Colliery. It meant a slight increase in his income. He was familiar with all branches of work in the mines now, and he knew full well what it meant to be a waterdrawer. His body no longer ached from the labor. His muscles had grown strong as those of a man. At fifteen he *was* a man, with a man's responsibilities, doing a man's work, getting a man's wages. It seemed to him sometimes that he had left his childhood back in Whittington Moor.

Things have changed in the Allentown Colliery since 1885, but at that time it was known as a "wet pit." Water constantly seeped into it. The "drawer" labored during the night when the men had gone. He bailed the water with great pails, pouring it into wagons. There were no pumps for this purpose. Alone night after night, the fifteen-year-old boy labored. There was no time for idling. He must work for ten hours. If at the end of that time he had failed to bail from forty to fifty tons of water, he knew that he would lose his job. It was lonely, desolate work.

He sang now, not because he felt like singing, but because he knew that he had to. Singing was a kind of defiance against the cold water, against the aloneness and the blackness, against that awful, vaultlike silence. He was allowed fifteen minutes a night to eat the bread and cheese he brought from home. Though he needed this brief respite and the food, he always dreaded "piece-time," for then the pit rats came, thousands of them, racing out from every cranny, from behind every rock. Pit rats are huge and hungry. In the darkness their small eyes glowed like phosphorus. They waited for "piece-time," the time the drawer sat down and took from his pocket the food he had brought. Then in great, eager hordes, from all directions the glow of their eyes moved closer, and at last they swarmed about him, fighting one another for the crumbs that he dropped.

No human soul labored in the mine during the night except Harry Lauder and Jamie McCulloch. McCulloch was a roadman. His station was a vast distance away from the deep pit where Harry worked. Jamie was middle-aged and kindly.

One night, after he had been a few weeks at the Allentown pit, a curious thought came to Harry as he watched those thousands of huge, ravenous rats moving toward him. He tried to tell himself it was silly. He kept saying that he must not be afraid. But the idea grew, the horror of it increased, mounting, ever mounting, until it reached a very crescendo of terror.

Those rats, he decided, were possessed of diabolical intelligence. Behind one of those rocks they had held a meeting and had decided to attack him. They would all surround him like this, coming closer, ever closer. Then at some fiendishly prearranged signal—at any moment now—they would leap for him, all of them at once. Their sharp claws would dig into his eyes, into his body. They would crawl up his legs. They would sink their little knifelike teeth into his neck. They would suck out his blood. . . .

He shrieked in agony, but there was no one to hear. Then wildly, still shrieking, he started running—up—up—up—into the fresh, clean air, up out of the darkness, up away from the rats with their sharp claws and their gleaming, watchful, bloodthirsty eyes.

"Jamie! Jamie!" he screamed.

"Here. Here I am."

"Jamie! Jamie!"

"Whit's th' matter wi' ye, lad?"

"Th'rats! Th'rats!"

Jamie's voice was quiet, firm, reassuring. "Aye, there are muckle o' them, but they're harmless, Harry. Do ye no ken they're harmless, lad? Och, a braw laddie like you tae be afraid o' a few rats! They've never hurt anyone yet. It's just that they *like* humans, tha's all. They're— *friendly*. Here, sit doon. They *like* th' sassiety o' humans. Do ye think I'd tell a lee tae ye, lad?"

White-faced, his eyes bright with horror, the boy stared up at Jamie. Jamie was calm and smiling.

"Sit doon, lad. Sit doon th' noo. We'll both sit doon a bit taegither. We'll bide a wee here taegither—an' we'll sing. We wull so. We'll sing. Ah, 'tis a graund thing, a bit song, when you're lonely an' afraid."

The two of them sank upon the ground, close together, and Jamie began to sing.

> "Maxwellton's braes are bonny,
> Where early fa's th' dew . . ."

Harry sat, listening for a time to Jamie's singing. His breath was coming easier, his heart had ceased its fearful thumping against his ribs. He had been foolish, of course. It would not, could not happen again. He would make friends with the rats. As Jamie said, they had never hurt anyone yet.

He was singing with Jamie now, happily, lustily. He felt strong, and his body felt comfortable again. He would have to work doubly hard to make up for this time he had lost, but they sang several more songs together, their voices echoing weirdly through the empty caverns. At last the boy rose.

"Weel, thanks, Jamie."

"You're gaen back th' noo?"

"Aye. Guid nicht, Jamie."

"Guid nicht, laddie."

Harry descended into the mine again, singing. The rats were there, peering at him furtively. He could hear them, see the gleam of their eyes, but now he did not mind them any more. He sang as his big pail rang out against the stones, as the black, icy water sloshed up over his knees, a song he had not thought of for a long, long time.

> "Though poverty daily looks in at my door,
> Though I'm hungry and footsore and ill,
> Thank God I can look the whole world i' th' face,
> For I," he told the rats, "am a gentleman still."

Many were the songs he had learned and many the songs he had sung since the day when he had flung forth *The Gentleman* at the Band of Hope. Here in Hamilton he had become better known for his singing than he had been in Arbroath. It was his hobby now, and one that brought him never-ceasing delight. He would take a popular song and change it to suit himself, always trying out new little characteristic touches upon every audience. He was still singing for prizes at charity bazaars, church affairs, amateur contests, anywhere and everywhere.

His work continued steadily at the mines and at sixteen he was a full-fledged miner, but during his times of idleness he could now and then afford a cheap seat to see other singers, to watch them, study them. He never ceased experimenting on his own audiences. He found that there were little tricks which brought sure-fire laughs, while other tricks, which he himself might think funny, fell flat. These he discarded at once. It was not alone himself that he had to please, and he was swiftly coming to realize that. He was learning a great deal. He was learning how to foster a laugh when once it had started, barely a ripple from some far comer of the house. Real vaudevillians called it "humoring the laugh." Harry knew no theatrical vernacular as yet, but already he was well versed in the art of "humoring the laugh."

Too, by the time he was seventeen he realized the value of watching people—people he met, people he passed in the streets, learning to take mental and even penciled notes of how this one walked, how another used his hands, how another held his head; odd touches of costume, a wry smile, a certain kind of walking stick, the tilt of a hat— all these were becoming increasingly important.

He was dressing for his songs now, and sometimes he would see a shawl, or a coat, which exactly fitted a character in his mind. He saved his money, and when he had enough he bought the article. Always he was adding to his knowledge of stagecraft, always he was improving, always his characterizations were growing a little more convincing—sometimes humorous, sometimes wistful.

It had seemed so easy at first just to stand up there and sing a song; but now he was realizing that there was infinitely more to a song than the singing of it. It had to have a character in it; a real, living, lovable character; someone people would understand and remember. It was the plain people of whom he sang. It was the plain people with whom he associated. It was the plain people of Scotland that he brought forth finally into the glare of the footlights—an old man with his pipe, a young boy with his slate, a lover off to meet his lassie. He was getting no money for his performances, but he was getting a keen sense of satisfaction, and that was payment enough.

By the time he was eighteen the financial situation at home had eased considerably. His brothers were growing up now, and they, too, found work in the pits. These days he could look back and smile at the time he had been a pony driver, the time he had been a drawer. He worked hard, for the more coal he cut, the more money he made, and Harry Lauder was never known to consider money unimportant.

At eighteen he was still short and stocky. His face was strong, slender, with a high forehead, a prominent nose, and a firm, well-shaped mouth. He wore his hair neatly parted on the side, and his grin was as wide, as quick as ever. Swinging his pick into the soft coal, he knew a certain joy in the fact that he was a good miner, and that he was always assured of a job at any of the collieries. He had a reputation for reliability, for steadiness and industry, and for never breaking his word.

Yes, there was a certain joy in knowing himself to be, at eighteen, as good a miner as any in the pits, but his delight was his singing. Nothing, he thought, could be more important than that.

"Why d'ye never gae walkin' oot wi' a lassie, Harry?" asked Matt one day.

"I've no time," answered his brother, "for such foolishness."

"D'ye like th' lassies?"

"Aye. Aye. I like th' lassies, but they tak' up a mon's time seathin' awfu'."

What with the work in the mines, what with singing at contests, and practicing his songs in the evenings at home, he had little time to think about love and lassies. But when love came, one mid-summer evening shortly after he had passed his eighteenth birthday, it came with the suddenness of lightning, and Harry Lauder knew that he had been all wrong.

For there was only one thing that mattered in this bonny world— and that was love.

CHAPTER FOUR

Had anyone told Harry Lauder when he awakened that braw Sunday morning that before nightfall he was going to be "tap-salteerie" over a lass, he would have laughed and said they were having a "dwam." In the first place, nothing ever happened on a Sunday. Sundays never varied. The shades were drawn, excluding the willful brightness of the sun, which was going right ahead with its business because nobody had told the gaudy thing that this was the Sabbath. Every shop was tightly closed. The voices of children were hushed. In her best black dress and shawl, Isabella marshaled her brood sedately to the white kirk around which the gravestones huddled. In the afternoon she read the Bible to the younger children.

"And it shall come to pass, if thou shalt hearken diligently unto the voice of the Lord thy God, to observe and do all his commandments which I command thee this day. . . ." She looked from the page to see her oldest son picking up his cap and moving toward the street door.

"Where are ye gaen th' noo, Harry?" she asked.

"Just for a wee bit stroll, Mither."

"You'll no be late for your tea?"

"No, Mither."

"There's bannock and gingerbread an' apple jelly."

"I'm only gaen for a bit stroll," he repeated, and closed the door behind him.

She sighed. "He'll be thinkin' aboot those songs o' his an' come i' late for his tea. Aweel, I suppose a lad might do worse than be thinkin' aboot a *song* on the Sabbath."

Isabella was right. Harry, thinking about a new song he was learning, strolled idly through the town, puffing nonchalantly at his pipe, forgetting the passage of time. Now and then he passed someone he knew, and they bowed with grave circumspection, remembering that it was the Sabbath. There were few people on the streets. The world seemed restful and quiet, and there was little to divert his attention from his new song. Realizing presently that it was late and he had promised his mother to be back for tea, his pace quickened as he moved toward home. He had gone only a little way when he heard the sound of music and turned toward it as naturally, as involuntarily, as a flower turns to the light. Even before he reached it, he knew what the music was. It was a group of Salvation Army people holding one of their curbstone meetings in the Black's Well. Already a small crowd had gathered in a circle about them.

Joining this circle, Harry shoved his pipe into his pocket and stood for a time listening to the thumping of the big drum and the tinkle of the tambourine. He watched the stout, bearded, middle-aged man who labored over the huge drum, for he was a "character" which someday Harry might want to reproduce, and then suddenly everything was blotted out—the drum, the drummer, the tambourine, the fact that his mother was waiting at home, the song he had been studying. Harry Lauder's heart began some queer and alarming antics. It was not the man with the drum who had created this havoc. It was the girl to the right of him, one of the small group of townspeople.

There was an appealing freshness about her, as if she had just that moment been created and had not yet been contacted by the fog and the soot of this common, workaday world. She was a little thing, small-boned, daintily fashioned. Her full skirts were ground length—a simple, homemade cotton dress with a narrow ruffle about the hem, a tiny woolen shawl which just covered her narrow shoulders, and a small, prim bonnet tied with ribbons under her chin. Beneath the bonnet was a sweetly sensitive face, with a delicately chiseled nose, a mouth that was red and tender, a mass of soft, glistening dark curls in which lurked surprisingly more than a glint of copper, and eyes of the clearest, cleanest blue Harry had ever seen.

He could not stop looking at her. Surely, surely, only something that had stepped spang out of heaven could be as lovely as that. They were singing a hymn now, and she was smiling a little as she joined in. Presently she felt the intensity of his gaze. Their eyes met, and for a long, pulsing, dynamic moment held. She stopped singing. As the boy opposite continued to stare, she blushed and finally turned her eyes away. There was nothing of rudeness in his staring.

It had the raptness, the gladness of a young priest gazing at an angel.

He had never seen this girl before, and now he told himself that all the world contained nothing sweeter, nothing more desirable. This, he knew, was love, and love was a wild jumble of beauty and tumult; love was electric and glorious and terrible. Vaguely he had assumed that someday he would fall in love, but he had never dreamed love could be so awful and so wonderful as this.

A man whom he knew slightly came up and stood near him. "Why d'ye no sing, Harry?" he whispered.

"Eh?"

"Why d'ye no sing?"

"Jock, that lassie—that lassie—d'ye ken who she is?"

"Whit lassie?"

"Whit?"

"Aye. Whit lassie?"

What lassie, indeed! Were there others?

"Yon. That one. Th' wee lassie wi' th' blue een. By th' drum, mon, by th' drum!"

"Oh. That's Annie Vallance. Lives oot at th' Bent."

"Annie Vallance!" The very name was lovely and musical. "Annie Vallance. Ye ken her, Jock?"

"No tae speak tae."

"Would she be any relation tae Tom Vallance?"

"Aye. She's his sister."

"Tom's sister!"

He did not know how long after that it was that the meeting ended, the crowd dispersed, little Annie Vallance moved away, and little Harry Lauder stood looking after her as she went. Only when she was out of sight did he start walking. He walked and walked, paying no attention to time, no attention to the direction in which he went. Annie Vallance was his and he knew it; he knew it as surely as he knew that he existed.

It was late when he returned home and his mother scolded him for missing his tea. He scarcely heard her. Eat. How could a person think about food and be in love at the same time? That night he found that he could not sleep. Annie Vallance. Annie Vallance. Annie Lauder. He felt weak and strong at the same time. Mind and body were now in a state of delicious ferment.

His usual energy was lacking next morning at the mine. He seemed to move in a kind of haze.

He knew that the more coal he mined the more money he got, but now he would drive his pick into the black rock before him—and leave it there for minutes at a time, standing motionless, staring at nothing, his brain repeating two words: Annie Vallance, Annie—Annie Vallance.

The man working beside him gazed at him worriedly. "Whit's th' matter wi' ye, Harry? Are ye sick, mon?"

"No. Aye. No. I dinna ken." He sighed, yanked his pick from the coal.

At noon he went hunting for Tom Vallance. Tom was slightly younger than he, but for a long time, in a rather casual way, they had been friends. There was, he noticed, a strong family resemblance between Tom and Tom's lovely sister; they were both slender; both had that finely modeled nose.

Harry lost no time in coming to the point. "Tom," he asked, "wull ye introduce me tae your sister?"

His mouth full of cheese, Tom looked at him in amazement. "What sister?"

"Annie."

"Oh. Nance?" Tom laughed. "Many's th' one that comes around askin' me for an introduction tae Nance. Aye, Harry, aye."

"When? When?" queried Harry tensely. "Th' nicht?"

"Aye. Come around tae th' hoose th' nicht." Tom laughed again. "Mon, ye look as if you've got it bad."

"I hae, Tom," answered Harry, miserably. "I'm i' love wi' her an' it's seathin' awfu'."

He had a sudden fondness for Tom, too, because Tom was her brother, and someday Tom would be his own brother-in-law.

"I'm gaen tae marry Nance, Tom," he announced.

"Weel," admitted Tom, "she might do worse, but I'm thinkin' ye won't be marryin' yet awhile. Nance is only fourteen."

Though shabby, overcrowded and small, the Vallance home could boast of a plush parlor set, on the backs and arms of which were handmade lace doilies. The family was a large one, and Nance was the oldest daughter. Already she knew as much about housekeeping and taking care of children as her own mother did. Jamie Vallance, her father, was a big, stern-faced man, the underground manager of Pit Number Seven. He was a man who was known to stand no nonsense from those who worked under him. He was fair and honest, but no one dared take advantage of Jamie, for his fists were huge and tough and he could out-fight any man in the mine. Harry knew Jamie by sight, but Jamie did not yet know that Harry Lauder existed. Harry was glad that Jamie was not at home when he called at the Vallance home that night.

Nance. She was lovelier, even, than he had thought her. Her hair had more copper in it than had been noticeable under the bonnet. Her eyes were shy and her voice was gentle.

"D'ye ken you're mine, Nance?" Harry was saying five minutes after he had met her.

She laughed softly.

"I mean it. I love ye, Nance Vallance. I'll love ye as long as I live. I'm nearly daft wi' th' thinkin' o' ye. Just let anyone *dare* tae tak' ye from me!"

"Hoots, but you're sure o' yoursel'," she said.

"Aye," he answered feelingly, "I'm sure—I'm verra, verra *sure*."

And now Harry Lauder had a lassie of his own to roam with in the gloaming. But he realized that it was not only a question of winning Nance, he must win Jamie as well. Pit Number Seven was located in a small village on the outskirts of Hamilton, and because Jamie was its underground manager, here Harry promptly applied for work.

He was meeting Nance regularly in the evenings away from the house now, for the tiny place where she lived was always too crowded for Harry to tell her how beautiful she was. Though her mother knew that she and Harry were sweethearts, Jamie remained in ignorance of the fact that his eldest daughter was being courted by one of his own men. But Harry saw to it that Jamie liked him. As Jamie walked along the workings, the voice of young Lauder was sure to ring out with a genial good day and a friendly question as to the state of Jamie's health. Never had he worked harder than he did now, for not only must he make enough money to equip his own home, but he must prove to Jamie that he was industrious and dependable.

A year passed, and Harry and Nance were planning their wedding.

"Ma faither willna' like ma marryin', Harry," she told him. "Ma mither knows aboot us, but she hasna' said anything tae ma faither. He'll think I shouldna' leave them—ye ken there's sae muckle tae do around th' hoose, whit wi' th' bairns tae raise an' a'."

"I'm no afraid o' your faither," declared Harry, but his voice was a trifle shaky. He thought of Jamie's fists, his quick temper. "An' why should he no let me hae ye, Nance? I've proven tae him I'm steady an' trustworthy."

"Aye, Harry, aye. But—we'd best say naethin' th' noo. We—we'll bide a wee."

"Aye. When I've twenty pounds i' th' bank, Nance, that'll be enough tae buy th' furniture an' rent a hoose. An' then I—" he took a deep breath, "then I'll speak tae your faither."

His mother was glad that her boy had fallen in love with such a fine girl as Nance Vallance. Isabella believed in love and early marriages.

She was in her forties now, and growing stout. Life was easier than it had ever been. Her children were growing up and the boys were working steadily in the mines. One by one they would all be marrying and settling in homes of their own, which was right and natural.

At the end of another year, when Harry was twenty and Nance was sixteen, he had managed by dint of rigid economy to accumulate twenty pounds.

It was a Saturday night in late April and he and Nance were strolling through the city, looking in the shop windows, planning their home. Every lower-class Scotch home had a "dresser." Scotch housewives considered this the most important piece of furniture of all. Here would be the dishes, the best ones braced neatly against the back, the less important ones stacked in shiny piles, the cups displayed to advantage. The dresser would have the place of honor in Nance's kitchen. On the shelves would be immaculate doilies which she herself had made, and on the top would be one of the clocks Harry had won with his singing.

"Do ye think we could afford *that* dresser, mon Harry?" asked Nance, pointing to one in the shop window.

"If that's th' one ye want, Nance, we can afford it," he answered promptly.

"It's verra dear—" speculated Nance, "three pounds ten—but it's lovely, Harry. Och, th' way it shines! Weel, we'll think aboot it—" they started walking again. "Oh!" gasped Nance suddenly. "Oh!"

"Whit is it, Nance?"

"Faither! Here he comes. He hasna' seen us yet."

"I'll speak tae him th' noo!" exclaimed Harry impulsively.

"Th' *noo?*"

"Aye."

"Weel, I—er—I'll be waitin' for ye around th' comer."

"*Pray!*" begged Harry.

"*Aye!*" she answered feelingly—and left him.

CHAPTER FIVE

Suppose Jamie got angry and wanted to fight him? Harry's distress increased as he walked along the street toward his prospective father-in-law. Suppose Jamie said no, then what? Jamie looked bigger, huskier than ever.

"It's a braw nicht, Jamie," he began brightly.

"It is so, lad. It is so."

There was a pause. The younger man glanced about wildly in search of a conversational topic.

"I—er—I see by th' papers there've been labor riots i' London."

"Aye. Workin' men holdin' mass meetin's i' Hyde Park."

Another pause. Harry realized, with an unmistakable sense of relief, that they were standing directly in front of the Royal Hotel.

"Wull ye—hae a drink wi' me, Jamie?"

"Aye. I don't mind if I do, lad."

They turned and walked into the bar.

"An' whit'll ye hae, Jamie?"

"A wee hauf."

"One wee hauf," ordered Harry, "an' one—lemonade."

"Weel, I'm glad tae see ye don't drink, Harry."

"No sir." Harry was plainly nervous now, and wishing he had prepared his speech beforehand. There was another pause.

The boy's jaw set firmly and his eyes took on a defiant look. "Jamie," he announced suddenly, "I'm i' love wi' Nance."

"You're—*whit*?"

"I'm i' love with Nance an' she's i' love wi' me. I want tae marry her—richt awa', Jamie."

Jamie stared. For some minutes he was utterly speechless.

"*Oor* Nance?" he asked incredulously.

"Aye."

The barmaid set down the drinks and Jamie swallowed his beer in one great gulp. "Th' same," he ordered.

There was a long, uncomfortable silence. He looked at Harry, and Harry met his eyes fully and squarely.

"I love her, Jamie. I'll aye love her. I love her wi' ma whole heart an' soul."

"Lad, it's a problem. Little did I ken I'd hae a problem like this put tae me th' nicht."

The boy's eyes filled with tears. "I'll mak' her happy, Jamie. I'll do ma best tae mak' Nance happy."

"Swear!" demanded Jamie.

Harry lifted his right hand solemnly. "I do. I do, Jamie."

"You—an' oor Nance," muttered Jamie, as if he were finding it difficult to grow used to the idea.

There was another long pause. The barmaid set the second glass of beer before him, but he drank it slowly.

"Weel," declared Jamie at last, "if ye love her an' she loves you, then—then tak' her, lad, an' may joy be wi' th' twa o' ye."

Harry began to laugh. He grabbed Jamie by the hand, and a moment later he had slapped the money for the drinks down on the bar and was racing out the door.

"Here! Hae ye seen a ghaist?" called Jamie. "Where're ye gaen?"

"Tae Nance. Tae tell her th' news. She's waiting for me around th' corner!"

He never stopped running until he found her.

It was nearly eleven when he left her that night. In all the world there were no two people happier than they. For hours they strolled up and down Lanark Road, blissfully planning their future, their house, their wedding, their furniture. So far he had had no ambition beyond that of being a miner, but now for the first time he wanted to be rich, really rich, to have servants to wait upon his lady, to buy her jewels and carriages and castles.

"Th' best i' th' world ye should hae, Nance. Th' best i' th' world belongs tae ye. It does so. I'll work harder than ever. An' one o' these days, darlin', I'll be buyin' ye a silk dress an' a coach tae ride in!"

She laughed and pressed his hand. "A carriage! What would I be wantin' wi' a carriage?"

"Oh, if I could only mak' masel' a great mon for ye, Nance! If I could only gie ye a graund hoose wi' hot water i' it. An' someday I wull. Trust me, Nance. Hae faith i' me. I'll make ye a lady!"

Again she laughed, softly, caressingly. "Och, you're daft, mon Harry. Whit else i' th' world matters tae me but just *you?*"

It was spring and it was moonlight—a full, healthy moon sailing briskly and serenely in a great silvery nest of clouds. Harry stopped, turned Nance about until she faced him. There was an ethereal quality about her in the moonlight, her eyes had taken on a new depth and mystery. A little choked cry escaped him, and he caught her to him passionately.

"You're so bonny," he whispered; "you're so sweet. You're as sweet as—as th' heather i' th' dell!"

They were really engaged now. Everyone knew that Nance Vallance and Harry Lauder were "walking oot." There were no long engagements in the Black Country. When a lad and lassie were definitely engaged, then there was nothing to do but find the house, buy the furniture, publish the banns, and have the wedding.

Finding the house was easy. There was a group of miners' cottages in Weavers Land. These small dwellings had been built by the owners of the mine where Harry worked. The rent was cheap, only three and sixpence a week, a sum which fitted nicely into their budget, for now Harry was earning three pounds a week.

Immediately after they rented it, the small house was painted and papered all fresh and gay for the new tenants, and now came the joy of buying the furniture. It would, of course, be bought for cash out of the twenty pounds Harry had so painstakingly saved. There would be no debts.

Nance's taste was as modest as his own. There must be the dresser they had seen in the window, the beautiful, shiny dresser; a bed, a kitchen table, a few chairs, a cheap bit of carpet for in front of the fireplace and a lamp—this was all the furniture needed. Dishes and cooking utensils would come as wedding gifts. They had carefully calculated the sum they could spend. It must not, Nance decided in her practical way, be more than fifteen pounds. When all purchases were completed, she had shopped so carefully that the total actually came to less than this, which left all of five pounds in the bank.

Harry, impatient to see the house complete, could not even wait for the shops to deliver; instead, after working hours, he carted everything to Weavers Land himself, piece by piece. People laughed at him when they saw him, hurrying through the streets of Hamilton, the kitchen table balanced on his head.

Mrs. Vallance and Mrs. Lauder were now gloriously busy. The older women, feeling almost as if they were brides themselves, scrubbed the new house until it shone. Harry washed the windows, polished the floor, put up curtains. At last it was ready, spic and span and gleaming. It was such a wee house, and it looked more cheerful than ever when Isabella brought over some of the vases and the fenders that Harry had won with his singing.

Next there were the wedding invitations. The Lauders and the Vallances worked on these for several nights, making out lists of likely "customers." The list completed, the Lauder boys and the Lauder girls, as well as those of Nance's brothers and sisters who were old enough, went about to friends and even slight acquaintances selling the invitations at eight-and-sixpence for double tickets. Like other poor people in the Black Country, Harry and Nance were to have a "pay-weddin'," and the celebration was to take place in Lesser Victoria Hall.

A wedding was considered a very great and hilarious occasion. A bride and groom naturally wanted all their friends and acquaintances to share their happiness. But this required an enormous amount of food, which the poor folk could not afford. Consequently, it had long been the custom to make the guests pay an entrance fee in order to partake of the wedding feast.

The parish church "cried" the banns for three weeks, and for three weeks the banns were posted for all the world to see in front of the registrar's window. It was, thought Nance and Harry, beautiful to read their names together like that. Every night they strolled past the registrar's window, ecstatically reading the notice.

Finally it came—the 18th of June, 1890, their wedding day.

Only the immediate families were gathered in the immaculate front room of the Vallance home. There were times when the groom felt that he would never be married standing up. Surely, his legs would not support him that long. His hands were trembling, his throat felt dry. He took out his pipe, fingered it nervously.

"Put your pipe i' your pooch!" his mother whispered sternly.

Meekly, he obeyed her.

"Hae ye got th' ring?" Matt asked in an undertone.

Unable to speak, Harry nodded, his eyes upon the plush-covered table which had been transformed into an altar. He looked, his mother thought, very elegant. She had pressed his Sunday suit, and he wore a new white shirt. It was the first white shirt he had ever owned. His collar was high, uncomfortably high, and now it seemed to Harry that the thing was slowly choking him to death. The tie he had chosen for the occasion was the gaudiest he could find—a vivid yellow background with bright green polka dots. His shoes were new. He stood there waiting, painfully conscious of his hands. He tugged at his collar and felt his tie. He took out his penknife, toyed with it nervously, returned it to his pocket.

The minister rose, gave a slight clearing of his throat, took his place gravely behind the table. Then the door opened, and there was Nance—Nance, radiant, composed, smiling. Her outfit had been Harry's wedding gift—it was a simple white dress that swept the floor in the current mode, and a small poke bonnet tied under her chin with wide crimson ribbons. They took their places side by side before the minister.

"Dearly beloved . . ."

It was the typical "pay-weddin." The ceremony over at last, the families hurried to Lesser Victoria Hall where the pay-guests were already assembled. The guests had spent eight-and-sixpence for their tickets, but it was, they all admitted later, a worthwhile investment. The tables were laden with steak pie, potatoes, carrots, cabbages, rice pudding with raisins, tea, pastries, Scotch whisky.

Jamie, dressed in his Sunday suit, silenced the chatter long enough to say grace. Grace over, he raised his head. "Weel," he called in his hearty voice, "fa' tae!" (which is Scotch for "Pitch in, folks").

Everyone obeyed with alacrity. At the main table, close together, sat the bride and groom. Harry had not been able to eat anything all day, but now he found himself surprisingly hungry. The serious business of eating over, there were toasts to the Queen, to the bride, the groom. There were speeches, songs, recitations. At eleven the tables were cleared and the dancing began. At five next morning the wedding celebration was over.

At eight, Mr. and Mrs. Harry Lauder left for their honeymoon. Nance always maintained that no bride ever had a lovelier honeymoon—a whole day in Glasgow! There were shops in Glasgow, all kinds of shops, tramcars, splendid restaurants and theatres. They strolled along George's Square admiring the municipal buildings. They saw the great shipyards. But most of their honeymoon they spent in McLeod's Wax Works. Later, they climbed a tramcar and rode all the way to Barlinnie Prison. Next, they wandered along the Clyde and watched the river steamers. Then it was time to return to Hamilton.

As she sank into the plush seat of the train, Nance sighed contentedly. "It's *guid* tae be gettin' hame," she murmured.

Years later, these two, sweethearts still, were to take many trips over the whole world together, but once homeward bound, Nance would always give that deeply contented sigh and declare that, "Oh, it was *guid* tae be gettin' hame!"

Home. Their own home. What, Harry wondered, was there left in all the universe to want? He would not have changed places with a king. His own home, the wife he worshiped; good, steady, honest work, friends—and the chance to sing.

On Monday morning he put on his old workclothes again and returned to the mine. Already it seemed natural and beautiful to be working for Nance, to be coming back to her when the work was done, everything safe, everything forever settled.

His newly found happiness as a benedict did not interfere with the amateur singing contests in which he continued to compete. Nance encouraged this. She was proud of his singing, she enjoyed it as much as his audience. At home, she was always on hand to watch him when he rehearsed his new songs in the kitchen. He learned to rely upon her judgment. Nance had as sure an instinct as Harry's as to what would and what would not appeal to an audience. Neither of them had any thought that Harry would ever make any money with his singing. Nowadays he was in demand, not only in Hamilton itself, but he was often invited to sing in the out-lying villages. People putting on a soirée, a bazaar, a local concert, were sure to seek out Harry Lauder. He never refused, not even when he had to pay his own train fare to some neighboring town.

But there came a night in Larkhall when, instead of winning a prize, he received five shillings (one dollar and a quarter). To be actually *paid* for singing! It was fantastic. It opened up an entirely new train of thought. Why, people were willing to *pay* to hear him sing!

"D'ye no see, Nance? If they paid once, they'll pay again! I might make quite a bit o' siller on th' side!"

"Aye, Harry, aye. They're no fools i' Larkhall."

"Imagine, Nance, actually gettin' paid for singin'! Weel, when they ask me again, I'll tell them I'm gettin' paid for singin' th' noo. I wull so"

Came the dreadful thought that, perhaps, if they had to pay, they would not ask him to sing any more; they would not want him to sing!

But to his surprise and delight, they did.

Even when they found they could no longer get him for nothing, they still wanted him. As months went on, he never received less than five shillings every time he sang, and sometimes even as

53

much as ten. He began to realize he was no longer an amateur, but a professional.

Yet to rest upon his laurels was unthinkable. He wanted better songs. He bought make-up, and night after night, a mirror propped before him on the kitchen table, he studied how to use it. He learned to blend in the grease paint, which came in little cylinders. He experimented with crepe hair and "stickum" for whiskers. He bought brown "liners" and found out how to make his face look middle-aged, old. It was all eternally interesting. His costumes, too, were becoming less crude, more authentic. Steadily, a great entertainer was emerging.

He discovered that there were song writers in Glasgow ready to sell their wares for little. Sometimes he bought these songs, changing them to suit himself and Nance. He was learning the art of facial expression and certain distinctive tricks with his voice, the "Lauder touches" that were different and clever.

There were times when he thought he would like to be a great tragic actor. He studied Hamlet, Romeo, Othello, Lear. But when he presented excerpts from these masterpieces on the stage, people laughed so uproariously that he realized tragedy was not his forte.

Nowadays original tunes took an odd way of popping into his head. Seemingly they sprang out of nowhere. He treasured them, hummed them, improved them, put words to them. They were lilting, simple, catchy tunes which people could whistle as they left the theatre.

Gradually the thought impressed itself upon him that he might even get on the real stage, somehow. Perhaps he might even travel all over Scotland.

He had been married a year when he received a letter postmarked Glasgow, from a man named McGill. Mr. McGill had heard, he wrote, of Mr. Lauder's success around the city of Hamilton. Would Mr. Lauder care to sing in Edinburgh? Mr. McGill was sorry but he could only afford to pay train fare plus one pound.

"One pound!" Harry gasped.

"Does it say—a *pound?*" asked Nance incredulously.

"Aye. It says it i' black an' white."

"A whole pound for one night's singin'! Dear! Dear!"

An hour before traintime, Harry was waiting at the station. When he returned, he talked so fast Nance could scarcely follow him. They had liked him in Edinburgh—a great city like Edinburgh—which was used to the best performers in the land! They had laughed and fairly rocked the theatre with applause. When he had finished, important song writers came backstage, offering him new songs.

"You have personality!" one of them had declared excitedly.

Personality. Harry Lauder had not thought of such a thing before. Personality—what was it, exactly?

"And I bought some graund new songs, Nance, frae a fellow named Tom Glen. One of them is called *Tooraladdie.*" Before she could answer, he began to sing it for her:

> "Twig auld Tooraladdie,
> Don't he look immense? . . ."

When he had finished, Nance was nodding appreciatively. "It's guid, Harry. It's *guid!*"

"Aye. And wait till I tell ye th' costume I've planned for it! It'll mak' a church deacon smile. It wull so."

"Ye say this fellow Glen sold ye th' words. Where did ye get th'music, mon?"

"Ah, that. I made that up masel'. Nance, ye ken, I believe I could write ma ain songs?"

"Of course ye can, Harry," she agreed knowingly.

"This Tom Glen, he supplies a lot of Scots comics wi' songs. Here's anither I bought frae him. I paid five shillin's for it. Listen. It's called, *Wha Deed an' Left ye th' Coat?*"

When he had sung it, Nance was laughing. "It's *guid!*" she declared.

"Aye, they're guid songs, but I've got tae find songs even better. I can earn *more* than five or ten shillin's a nicht, Nance. One o' these days I'm gaen tae hae a try at th' real stage!"

"*Harry!*" she gasped; and then, after a moment's consideration, "Weel, why shouldn't ye?"

But he went on, eager enough to earn those five or ten shillings which supplemented his wages at the mine. Always he was practicing, preparing himself for what might come—who knew when? The big chance. With every performance he gave, he was gaming something, especially the "feel" of an audience, learning how to hold them with a more reliable power, learning to sense the minute he stepped down to the footlights whether an audience would laugh easily or whether he must exert himself and *force* it to laugh. For it was completely under his dominion. It would respond to him. It would do what he wanted it to do. Only one must know how to handle it. It was never the same audience. In its very silence, it told him about itself. Sometimes it said, "I'm *ready* to laugh, Harry." Sometimes it said, "You're supposed tae be funny, are ye? Weel, I *dare* ye tae make me laugh!" Whatever its message to him in that first moment when he stepped out from the wings, he met it with a smile and a sense of assurance. He knew that a laugh was the most contagious thing in the world—let one person start it, and it spread, it grew, it swelled in volume momentarily, as he himself encouraged it, ordained it, sustained it.

Singing in Motherwell one Saturday night, a fellow performer approached him.

"What's your name?"

"Ma name? Lauder. Harry Lauder."

"Well, Lauder, you've got a good act."

"Ye think so?"

"I know it, and I've seen a lot of them in my time. Look here, why don't you send your name in for the competition in Glasgow? It's called 'The Great Comic Singing Contest,' and it's being put on by the Glasgow Harmonic Society."

"Whit's that?"

"Oh, it's one of those temperance organizations. They put on affairs Saturday nights and serve tea and cookies. The point is, they want to keep people out of the saloons. They put on long programs and good ones. Usually they even bring over a real star from the London Halls. The place is always packed."

"Weel, thanks, I'll send i' ma name."

"Good luck, old man."

When his name had been accepted, Harry found that he was to receive one pound for his performance. Not until the train sped toward Glasgow did he begin to realize what a momentous step this was. If the people liked him, the Harmonic Society would engage him to sing at future entertainments. But the thought of being pitted against a real star from London alarmed him. Almost, he wished he could back out. Suppose they booed him? Suppose he had to come back and tell Nance that they had booed?

But he came back to Nance that night with the news that he had been engaged for a series of entertainments in Glasgow.

His neighbors and fellow-workers were regarding him now with a new respect. He was a real actor. He was associating in Glasgow with other real actors. They were inclined to make fun of him, however, the Sunday he first wore the coat with the astrakhan collar.

The idea for such a coat had come to him from one of the actors appearing with him in Glasgow. In those days an astrakhan collar was the badge of the successful thespian. The minute Harry realized this, he knew that he, too, must have such a collar. His theatrical engagements in Glasgow enabled him at last to buy a small strip of the fur, and proudly he stood over Nance while she sewed it on his old coat. Wearing that coat now he felt like a being set apart from the rest of the humdrum world. The coat had become to him a symbol. He wore it everywhere. When the weather was too warm, he carried it over his arm.

The thought kept recurring these days that he might even give up mining. As he was becoming more and more in demand, it was increasingly difficult to keep working in the pits. Plainly, he must decide either to dispense with the mining or the stage. He could not do both.

For days, for weeks, he and Nance discussed the matter. It was not an easy decision to make. The stage or the mine? The stage, he knew, was a precarious livelihood, while the mine meant steady work and a definite amount of money coming in regularly at the end of every week. It was not, he kept telling himself, as if he were alone. There was Nance depending on him. No, no, it was foolhardy to give up the mine. But *could* he give up the stage—now? Could he forget about it forever and merely content himself with singing for his friends?

"Whit shall I do, Nance? Whit shall I do?"

"'Tis yoursel' ye maun please, Harry," Nance told him in her gentle way.

"I'm no denyin' there's a fascination aboot th' stage, but I mustna' let that sway me. I maun keep a level head on ma shoulders an' do whit wull be richt i' th' long run."

"Hoo can ye ken whit wull be richt i' th' long run?"

"True; but—do ye think I'm guid enough, Nance? D'ye think I'm guid enough tae mak' a livin' on th' stage for th' twa o' us?"

"You're better than many I've heard, mon Harry."

They talked about it all night. They considered it from every possible angle. They were very young and they were trying to be very wise.

"We canna look ahead tae whit's comin', Harry. 'Tis your ain life ye maun live."

"True, but it's a sair risk, Nance."

"Aweel, if ye fail, ye can aye gae back tae th' pits."

"True, but—no, I'll stay i' th' mine. I wull so."

"An' gie up your singin'?"

"Aye. Th' gaffers hae been fine tae me. They've given me hours off an' even days off when I've asked for it tae fill ma stage engagements, but I canna' expect them tae gae on doin' that. It's no fair tae them, Nance. Och, whit shall I *do*, lassie?"

"Ye maun please yoursel'," she said again.

A few nights later, tired after his day's work, he was in the kitchen lounging in front of the fire reading the *Evening Citizen*. Outside, great gusts of wind-swept rain beat noisily against the windows. Presently, above the sound of the wind and the rain, Nance heard him calling to her. She turned from her dish washing, drying her hands on her apron.

"Whit is it, Harry? Whit is it?"

"Look. There. An advertisement. They want a comedian for a six weeks' tour this summer."

"Tour? Six weeks? Where?"

"A Scottish tour, it says. You apply by letter tae this person named Kennedy i' Glasga'!"

"Six weeks!" she gasped. Six weeks away from home. Six weeks away from the mines.

"Nance, whit would ye think—if I—if I—just—had a try at it?"

She smiled. "Ye maun please yoursel', Harry."

"Weel, it—it—it wouldna' hurt just tae write th' letter an' mak' th' application?"

"No," she agreed.

"They may tak' no notice o' th' letter, but it could do no harm tae *write* it."

"No," she said again.

A week later a telegram arrived. Harry stared at it for a long time. Never before had anyone sent him a telegram.

"Would it be—frae Glasga'?" he asked boyishly.

"Open it, Harry!" Nance caught his arm excitedly.

And even as he did so, Harry Lauder had a curious feeling that that telegram was going to change the entire course of his life.

CHAPTER SIX

All day Nance had spent running back and forth from her house-work to the front door, her eyes anxiously scanning the street down which her husband must come. He had left for Glasgow early that morning to see some exalted personage named Kennedy. He had looked, Nance thought, very thriving and important, wearing his white shirt, his Sunday suit and the coat with the astrakhan collar. Although she had tried valiantly not to show it, she had been apprehensive these last few weeks. Her Harry was confronted with two roads—one that led into the glare of the footlights, the other that led into the blackness of the mine. Who knew which was the wiser choice? After all, wise or foolish, it was Harry's happiness that mattered. To Nance, it did not matter *where* he was happy, just so long as he was happy.

As for herself, she loved this wee house, she asked nothing bet-ter. She was managing very well on Harry's three pounds a week, although it never quite added up to that, because he was still contributing to the support of his mother. The stage held no glamour for Nance, but whatever the life Harry wanted, that was the life *she* wanted. Now, because all of a sudden it seemed doubly precious, she polished the dresser as tenderly as if it were a living, breathing thing. Stage people had no dressers like this. They lived a vagabond existence, always traveling, lodging in strange places, owning nothing more than a trunk or two.

The polishing finished, she began mixing a batch of scones. Always she took great pride in her scones and her pastries. Nance knew the same enjoyment in her cooking as Harry knew in his singing. It would be odd, she thought, living in restaurants, never having a stove of one's own, not having to plan meals and peel potatoes. She could almost pity women who had never experienced the fun of housekeeping. Her scones in the oven, she shoveled more coal in the iron stove, and hurried to the front door again. He was coming now. Walking fast, almost running in his eagerness to get to her. That meant that he brought good news. She waved to him gaily from the humble doorway.

Harry caught her in his arms and held her close to him. "It's a' richt, Nance," he said as he kissed her.

She laughed, helped him off with his coat, and stood holding it, her hands fondling the astrakhan collar.

"Sit doon an' tell me aboot it, Harry."

"Weel, th' Kennedys are a mon an' his wife. For years every summer they've been takin' oot tours i' th' sma' toons. This tour is no for six weeks, it's for fourteen weeks."

"Did ye get th' job, Harry?"

"I did so."

"Whit did they say?"

"They said their ain comic, th' one they had engaged, canceled the engagement wi' them at th' last minute. If they hadna' been in a fix, I suppose they'd never hae taken *me*."

"An' how muckle siller wull ye be gettin'?"

"Thirty-five shillin's a week. At every show I'm tae sing three songs, but it's no only ma songs I'll be singin' tae earn it. Durin' th' day I'm tae see that th' luggage gets tae th' station frae th' theatre, an' frae th' theatre tae th' station. After that, I'm tae gae around th' toons seein' that th' bills for th' show are up. Then I'm tae be th' stage carpenter, an' after that, I'm tae tak' th' tickets at th' door."

"Dear! Dear!" she murmured, deeply impressed. "I'm thinkin' you'll be as busy as ye are at th' mine." Her eyes filled with quick tears, tears of relief that he had the job, tears of sadness thinking of the fourteen weeks when her Harry would be away from her, actually on tour with a regular theatrical company. A new world, a new life lay ahead—a life that was strange and hazardous.

"Your heart's i' your singin', mon Harry," she murmured softly.

"Aye, Nance, ma heart's i' ma singin'. A collier's existence is hard an' drab, aye doon i' the earth an' never seein' th' sun, never knowin' th' clean feel o' it on ma face."

"Of course, if ye fail ye can gae back tae th' pits."

He straightened his shoulders and looked full at her, his eyes very grave, his large mouth set firmly. "Only I willna' fail, Nance. I willna' fail. I'll mak' guid, Nance. I *willna'* fail!"

"No," she answered steadily, and her faith in him gave him greater assurance. "No. I'm thinkin' that when a body's heart is i' a thing, a body willna' be failin' i' th' doin' o' it. Weel, mon Harry, when d'ye start?"

"We *open*" he announced impressively, "next Monday nicht i' Beith."

"Ye—whit?"

"We *open*. On th' stage, Nance, we never start or we never begin at such an' such a time—we *open!*"

"I see. I see. It's no only a new life, a new world, 'tis a new language we hae tae learn."

"I could hardly wait tae get back tae tell ye. Nance—are there—tears i' your een?"

"It—it's just that—that it's such an adventure, Harry. It's like—like we're leavin' a' that we knew behind us. It's such a great change. I'm just no used tae th' thought o' it."

"I ken hoo ye feel, Nance. I only pray I'm doin' th' richt thing."

Next morning he went back to the mines again, working the entire week until Saturday noon. Had he, he wondered when Saturday noon came, grasped a pick for the last time? All week he had known a keen anticipation for the moment when he would resign. He had even prepared a carefully worded speech which he considered dignified and impressive, and which he would recite to the mine manager. Now at last the time had come when that speech would be delivered.

"A word wi' ye, Mac," he began.

Faces blackened, bodies odorous with perspiration, the two men faced each other.

"Weel?" asked Mac.

"I've seathin' tae say tae ye th' noo."

"Weel, say it, mon. Say it."

"I'll no be resumin' ma work i' th' pit. I hae accepted an engagement—a theatrical engagement. I'll no be comin' back."

"Ye—whit?"

"I hae accepted a theatrical engagement. I'll no be resumin' ma work i' th' pit."

"Hoots!" said Mac, and stared at Harry's small, begrimed figure wonderingly. "You're gaen awa' wi' a real theatre troupe?"

"Aye. We—we—*open* i' Beith, that's i' Ayrshire, ye ken."

Mac smiled. "Weel, success tae ye, lad. An' I'm no sayin' I wouldna' be glad o' th' chance tae see th' fine country th' Lord hae made masel'. You're a guid miner, Harry, an' I'm no sayin' you're no a guid comic, but—you'll be comin' back tae th' pits, mon. Aye, you'll be comin' back!"

"No," answered Harry. "This is ma last day i' th' pits." He reached out his hand and Mac shook it heartily.

As Harry walked away he heard Mac calling after him. "You'll be *glad* tae be comin' back, mon Lauder!"

In the gloaming that Sunday evening, Nance and Harry strolled down Lanark Road hand in hand, both curiously silent. Fourteen weeks seemed an eternity. They kissed often and Nance cried a little, because it seemed inexpressibly sad to think of not to be waiting for him to come home in the evenings, not to be cooking scones and steak pies, broth, porridge, and haggis for him, not to be mending his clothes and listening to his songs. But she let him go with a smile next morning, waving to him as he turned the corner.

Once on tour, Harry was supremely happy. Being stage carpenter, ticket taker, bill poster, baggage man and comedian left little time for idleness, but no matter how hard the work, it was done in the fresh, clean air. For so many years, ever since he was fourteen, he had spent his days down in the ground like a mole. His palms were callous from the pick.

It was wonderful to be traveling about, to be seeing his beloved Scotland. The tour began in Ayrshire, continued into Dumfriesshire, wandered through the Border district, and ended at last in the Midlands. Harry pitied the men in the mines because none of them had had an opportunity to travel like this. None of them knew how beautiful was their own Scotland.

The Kennedy company played a new town every night. Harry learned that these were never "trips"; in the vernacular of the stage they were "jumps." A "long jump" meant getting up at six o'clock and even earlier in the mornings. A "short jump" meant the hitherto unexperienced luxury of remaining in bed as long as one wished. How monotonous and colorless a miner's life seemed in comparison with this! This was freedom.

Seeing Burns' tiny clay cottage just two-and-a-half miles out of Ayr was almost like going to a shrine. He had never imagined he would actually see this place, actually stand inside it. Here a great poet had been born, way back in 1759. And when Harry reached Dumfries, he went at once to the home where the poet had died, in 1796. Awed, silent, Harry looked about, only wishing that Nance were here to share this unforgettable experience with him. Here Burns wrote one hundred songs, the songs most beloved of all the songs of Scotland—and in payment received five pounds, a picture of "The Cotter's Saturday Night," and a shawl for Jean, his wife. Here, along this very road he had walked, a robust, hearty Scot with dark, glowing eyes. There was the very kettle where he had heated the water for his too-frequent toddies. Harry wanted to remember everything about this place so that he could make Nance see it all as he was seeing it. He bought a book of Bums' poetry and began to memorize it on the trains.

As the tour approached its end, young Lauder began to worry. How was he to get another engagement? And when? Had Mac been right? Would he have to go back to the pit? Now it seemed quixotic, even stupid, to have given up his work in the mine. Hadn't his mother always taught him to "ca' canny"? Yet, even though he had sent Nance a pound a week, he had managed to live so economically that he had saved twelve pounds in the fourteen weeks.

But when he returned home there was an offer already awaiting him. True, it was only an offer for a single night's work, but it was to pay the hitherto undreamed-of sum of one guinea. One guinea for one night's singing?

When he had read the letter containing the offer, he hugged Nance again, and dropped the twelve pounds he had saved into her lap with a magnificent gesture.

"Och, th' world's a graund an' beautiful place tae be livin' i', Nance," he affirmed.

"It is so, Harry. Losh, twelve pounds! An' I saved nearly ten frae th' pound a week you've been sendin' me!"

"Ten pounds ye saved, Nance? Hoo?"

She smiled. "That's ma ain business, but save it I did. Come, let's sit here by th' fire an' tell me a' that's happened tae ye."

"Weel, we made some long jumps an' some short ones. We—"

"Ye made—whit?"

"Jumps, dear. Jumps. It's a theatrical term for trips, ye ken."

"Oh," nodded Nance, and charged her mind to remember this, for now she, too, must learn the new language of the theatre-actors.

"Och, Nance, d'ye ken how a bird maun feel when it's set free o' th' cage? It's so I'm feelin' set free o' th' pits. It's *such* a bonny world wi' th' sun shinin' i' it! Ma mither used tae tell me when I was a lad, aboot th' guid fairies an' how they would be wavin' their magic wands an' changin' everything intae beauty. That's whit's happened tae me, Nance. A guid fairy came along an' waved her wand."

She laughed. "But, Harry, mon, how did ye manage tae save a' this siller? Ye didna' do *that* by th' wavin' o' a wand. Every week ye sent me a pound. How could ye live on sae little, mon? It maun cost a lot tae gae tae hotels an' a'."

"Hotels? Are ye thinkin' I lived i' hotels? Th' ithers did, but not me. I hardly ever paid mair than a shillin' for a night's lodgin'. In Stirling-shire I slept wi' a dog."

"A dog?"

"Aye, an' a guid dog he was, tae. Ye see, i' th' toon there was only one hoose where I could stay for th' price I had tae pay. Th' lady said she'd gie me blankets an' a pillow an' I could sleep on th' floor. So when I went intae th' room where I was tae sleep, there was a fine bed wi' a dog i' it, a lurcher he was. Th' dog was tae hae th' bed. I was tae hae th' floor. He was a prize dog, a racer, an' they were proud o' him. Weel, I mind it was rainin' ootside an' I hae no likin' for sleepin' under th' rain. So I agree tae sleep on th' floor i' th' dog's room. So that nicht I came hame frae th' theatre. I rolled up in ma blankets—but och, Nance, th' floor was hard, I'm tellin' ye!"

"Puir Harry!"

"Weel, just after I'd gone tae sleep, I felt saethin' wet against ma face. It was th' dog lickin' me. So as long as he was friendly, I slipped i' his bed, an' he beside me. I had a fine sleep. I did so." He chuckled retrospectively. "And then—then—I mind th' time o' th' ghaist."

"Ghaist?" Nance's blue eyes widened. "Ghaist? You're no tellin' me, mon Harry, that ye slept wi' a *ghaist?*"

He sighed dramatically and shook his head. "That was a terrible nicht. It was a wee hoose an' an ould widow woman lived alone i' it. As far as I could see, there was but one room, th' kitchen, but I didna' think much aboot it because it was late an' I had tae see tae th' baggage an' th' postin' o' th' bills. Weel, the ould widow woman said when I came back frae th' theatre I'd find th' door on latch an' th' kettle on th' hob so I could mak' masel' a cup o' tea. Weel, when I got tae th' theatre, one o' th' troupe said he didna' ken whit he was gaen tae do, because he hadna' been able tae find a place tae sleep." Harry paused, his eyes upon Nance, calculating the effect of his words.

Nance was the perfect audience. Her slender, girlish body was tense. Her eyes were as wide as the eyes of a child, and, indeed, she did look like a child tonight, with her dark curly hair parted neatly in the middle, and her red lips slightly apart.

"Aye? Aye?"

"Weel, so I saw a chance tae save siller an' I said he could share ma room if he'd pay his hauf. Distributin' th' bills, I'd given th' grocer a pass an' he'd given me a box o' crackers free. So we took th' box o' crackers an' we came hame tae make oorselves a bit tea. Ah, I mind it was a wild an' roarin' nicht. Th' wind moaned like a soul i' torment, an' th' trees swayed back an' forth like crayturs that were damned. But in the wee hoose, everything was verra, verra still. We made th' tea an' ate th' crackers an' we went tae bed. Weel—" he paused for emphasis, "aboot three o'clock i' th' mornin'—"

Nance gave a quick, apprehensive glance over her shoulder. Her voice was faint. "Aye?"

"We heard a noise."

"Whit kind of a noise?"

"Weird. Like someone chokin'. It was faint at first, so faint we couldna' tell where it came frae. Th' fire was oot an' th' room was pitch dark. Jamie an' I lay there whisperin' an' shiverin', askin' each ither what we'd better do. Th' sounds kept comin' louder an' louder an' at last we couldna' stand it. I got up an' ma hands were tremblin' so I could hardly light th' candle. There was a big wardrobe i' th' room, an' th' sounds seemed tae be comin' frae there. I could hear Jamie's teeth chatterin'. 'It's over there i' th' closet,' he whispers, 'gie me th' candle, Harry. You gae first. Dinna be afraid, mon, I'm richt behind ye!'"

"Oh!" gasped Nance, and her small hands were tight in her lap.

"Th' sounds kept gettin' worse. Jamie was tremblin' frae head tae foot, an' I'm no sayin' I was any too steady, masel'. Him behind me holdin' th' candle, we crept tae th' closet. I opened th' door—and a *body* rolled oot at oor feet!"

"Harry!"

"Jamie was that excited he let th' candle touch ma backside. I screamed bloody murder. Then *he* began tae scream. An' then—"

"Weel? Weel?"

"Th' *body* began tae scream. Jamie dropped th' candle an' th' room was pitch dark. I knocked against a chair, fell over it, went sprawlin' heid first. Th' noise we made brought th' neighbors. Whew! What a nicht!"

"But th' body, Harry! Th' body! Th' deed body!"

"I dinna recall sayin' it was deed," he answered with a sly smile.

"Whose body was it? How did it get i' th' closet?"

"It was the ould woman. Puir soul. She needed th' siller, so she thought she'd sleep i' th' closet, but she didna' ken that she wouldna' be able tae breathe i' there."

"Dear! Dear!"

"Oh, Nance—Nance, th' things I've seen wi' ma twa een! I've seen th' hoose where Rabbie Burns deed at Dumfries, an' I've seen th' place where he was born, an' I bought ye a book o' his poems. Ah, it's a wonderful book, Nance. I've learned every one o' his songs since I've been awa'. It's a bonny world we're livin' i'—a big, fine world wi' th' braes, an' th' lochs an' th' rivers an' a'."

His mother, his sisters and his brothers were all proud of him. Working in the mines during the day, and either rehearsing or playing on the stage in the evenings, he was seeing little of them. None of them except Alec had any desire for the stage. Watching his brother, Alec began to think that it would be rather a fine thing to be an actor. He started practicing songs of his own, and though later everyone admitted that he had considerable talent, he lacked that singular magnetism possessed by his older brother.

Already Harry had become a local celebrity.

Neighbors came in to hear of his adventures, gazing at him now with something like awe. Friends whom he met on the street treated him with a new deference. None of them had traveled beyond Glasgow. He was, and a bit cockily he admitted it, no longer an amateur, but a real professional. It was good to walk through the town wearing his coat with the astrakhan collar. It was good to wear a white shirt every day. It was pleasant to wave a friendly hand at his old pals as they hurried to work in their stained, grease-soaked clothes. It was pleasant to know that they were envying him and alluding to him now as an "artiste."

But weeks and months were passing. He scanned the newspapers, since in those days the smaller companies often advertised for actors through this medium. He answered every ad, but no replies came. As weeks passed, the money so conscientiously saved began to dwindle. Day after day he and Nance watched for the postman, but the postman never stopped at the little house in Weavers Land.

"It wull come tomorrow," Nance always told him cheerily.

But the letter did not come. Always there was the hope at night that it would, indeed, arrive in the morning mail. He knew that Nance was praying all the time that the Lord would *please* send Harry an engagement.

Both she and Harry had been confident that there would be no difficulty in getting further work on the stage. Nance knew what it would mean to him to have to go back to the mines. It would be admitting to his friends and neighbors that he had failed. They would sneer at him, laugh among themselves.

Christmas Eve. In cottages throughout Scotland old and young were gathered about fireplaces, the old ones in comfortable chairs, the young ones on the floor or on stools, and the old ones were telling ghost stories.

Always before, Harry and Nance had been part of these family groups, but tonight they knew they could contribute nothing to the holiday mood. At the kitchen table sat Harry, his head in his hands, his body leaden with despair. Oh, thought Nance, only let her say the right thing to comfort him, to give him courage!

"So, it's over, Nance. It was—just a dwam, anyhoo. It was tae guid tae last. I might hae known it couldna' last."

She put her arms about him, her small body deluged with a tenderness so exquisite that it was perilously close to pain. The words she spoke seemed to her inadequate. She realized the futility of words to express the love that she felt. If only her love could enfold him, shield him, wipe out this turmoil in his soul!

"No, Harry, no. Dinna say that, mon. How can it be over when they liked ye an' they clapped until their hands were raw, an' they shouted for more of ye? That wasna' a dwam, mon Harry, that was real an' true."

"But it's ower, Nance. I ken how I've heard th' artistes talkin'. They'll talk o' some great star, some person who had made a hit even i' *London*—an' they'll say, 'Ah, puir so an' so! *He's finished.*' Th' stage is like that, Nance. One day you're i' demand an' th' next day nobody wants ye. Weel, I maun face it. It's like that wi' Harry Lauder. There's no evadin' facts. He's finished—finished—finished!"

"No, Harry, no! You've your whole life ahead tae prove whether you're finished or not. You canna' say you're finished until you're finished wi' *livin'.* You're only twenty-two, Harry. Think o' th' graund life that's ahead!"

"Th' graund life," he scoffed. "Th' life o' th' blackness o' th' pit— that's a' that's ahead o' me, an' weel ye ken it."

"I ken naethin' o' th' kind!" she answered sturdily. "I ken if ye go back tae th' pits you'll no be stayin' there."

"No, I'm a failure, Nance. Th' world's had enough o' Harry Lauder. I tried. I failed. We maun admit it, dear. I was a fool, that's a'. Weel, frae today on, I'll renounce a' thought o' makin' a livin' on th' stage. I'll gie th' whole thing up—just—forget aboot it, like a mon awakenin' frae a pleasant dwam."

"No, Harry. Your chance is comin'. I'm *tellin'* ye, Harry!"

"How can ye ken?" he asked wearily.

"It's a feelin' I hae. I'm that sure. I'm as sure as I'm standin' here. This is—why, it's—" she *must* keep her voice steady, "—it's—naught but a wee bittey delay, tha's a'."

He moaned. "I *can* sing, Nance. I *can* mak' people happy. I can mak' folks laugh an' forget their worries. I ken I can."

"Of course ye can. Of course. Of course. It's a talent ye hae, a gey talent, a talent for makin' folks happy. D'ye think th' Lord would gie ye a talent like that an' then let ye bury it i' th' ground like th' mon i' th' Bible? Th' talent ye hae is th' talent th' good Lord gie ye. It's a talent ye maun *improve,* a talent ye maun *increase.*"

Her words were sweet and comforting. Miserably, he reached out for her and leaned his head against her while she smoothed back his hair with gentle hands.

"*You* believe i' me, Nance?"

"I do, Harry. I believe i' ye—an' I'm proud o' ye! I ken your chance wull come. I ken that this is—losh, 'tis just th' beginning. There're graund things ahead o' ye!"

He did not believe her, but it was comforting to listen to her, to look into her shiny blue eyes, to know her love and her faith. Aye, he had fought the battle with himself. He knew now he could give up his dream. He could go back to the mines, and he could go cheerily. He could withstand the jibes of his comrades, too, taking it with a smile— because there was Nance.

He walked away from her and she stood watching as he took down his old mining clothes, greasy, ugly, ill-fitting.

He had known it would not be easy, withstanding with equanimity the good-natured raillery that greeted him as he joined the throngs of miners returning to work after the holiday.

"Weel, Harry, so ye came doon i' th' world, eh?"

"Thought he was a bit better than th' rest o' us, didn't he? Him wi' his fur collar an' a.'"

"He *had* tae come back because he couldna' make guid on th' stage. Just a stuck-up comic!"

"Awed, Harry, ye tried, anyhow. Ye *tried*."

"Thought ye was resignin', Harry! Gaen tae get your hands dirty th' noo?"

It irked him, but Harry took it all and grinned. He swung his pick as lustily as he had ever done, for in those days a man could work as hard and as long as he pleased. Each night when he was on his way home, he fought the persistent expectancy for the letter that would bring another offer from the stage. But even if the offer came, he told himself stoutly, he would not accept it. No, that was over. That was a beautiful, glistening bubble that had burst. What was he, after all, but a miner? No, his mind was made up. He would be a miner the rest of his life. And it was not, he speculated, really bad, being a miner. It was good, honest work, and he must be grateful for it. But often he would find himself staring wistfully at the coat with the astrakhan collar. Well, if the world did not need his songs, at least it needed the coal that he cut.

He had been back at the mine only a few weeks when several offers arrived from managers of bazaars and concerts around Hamilton, but Lauder firmly refused them. His singing days were over. There must be no more fantastic dreams. A man, however, could not help glancing at the tubes of make-up from time to time, and fingering over the costumes. There was no harm in that.

"Harry!" called Nance as he entered the house one blustery Saturday night. "Harry, there's a letter!"

His heart gave a great leap, but he forced himself to assume an air of indifference. A letter? What of it? What did it matter now? He would fight this love of the footlights. What would result from another excursion into the world of the theatre? Only disappointments, only disillusionment.

He opened the letter and read it. Then he read it again.

"Weel?" asked Nance, whose eyes were fixed upon him steadily.

"It—" he looked at her in wonderment, "it's frae MacDonald. It's frae J. C. MacDonald himsel'. You've heard o' him, Nance? Ye ken who he is?"

"Aye. He's a famous Scots comic. He has his ain companies. They're called—"

"They're called 'MacDonald's Merrymakers.' They're bigger than th' Kennedys. Th' Kennedys played only th' sma' toons, but MacDonald's Merrymakers play only th' bigger cities!"

"Whit does he say?"

"He says—" Harry swallowed. Here, indeed, was temptation. "He says that he's never seen ma act, but he says that—that he's heard guid things aboot me."

"There!" Nance's voice had a glad note of triumph. "There! Ye thought they had forgotten wee Harry Lauder! An' here's a mon like J. C. MacDonald that's been hearin' guid things aboot ye! Is—is that a' he says, Harry?"

"No. He says he's not as weel as he should be an' he canna' fulfill an engagement for ten performances at Grenock Town Ha'. He says—he asks me tae—tae tak' his place!"

"You? Tak' th' place o' J. C. MacDonald?"

"Aye."

"For ten performances only?"

"Aye. He—he'll pay me three pounds."

"Three pounds for ten nights' work?" The sum was staggering.

"Aye. It says so i' black an' white. Three pounds. At first I couldna' believe ma een. Three pounds. Here, read it yoursel'."

Nance read the letter and re-read it.

"Whit shall I do?" he asked at last.

She knew how ardently he wanted to play those ten performances. She alone knew what it meant to him. He watched the slow smile creep over her face.

"Please yoursel', Harry."

"Weel, I—I think I'll tak' it."

"Guid!"

"These ten performances—they'll be like—weel, like havin' a last graund fling. A mon's got tae be sensible, Nance. A mon's got tae mak' a livin', a mon's got tae be *sure* o' makin' his livin'. An' I *am* sure i' th' mine. I've thought it a' oot clearly an' calmly. Th' stage is wonderful. But this wull be th' finish—just these last ten performances. Where's th' pen? Where's th' ink?"

Again the greasy trousers were put away and the coat with the astrakhan collar taken out. Again the make-up tubes were handled lovingly, and Harry was practicing his songs in the kitchen. It was only for ten days, he kept telling himself, and then he would go back to the pit again, this time for good. He was resolutely determined upon that.

Returning from Grenock, he hung the coat with the fur collar far back in the closet so that he would not even see it when the door was opened. Again he went back to the pit. There was no battle this time. He had fought it all out with himself that Christmas Eve, and now all inner conflict was over.

But a few days later another letter arrived. Again the call, the irresistible siren call.

The letter was from a firm named Moss and Thornton which owned a circuit of halls in the north of England. They had heard of Harry Lauder through J. C. MacDonald, who had spoken glowingly of him. On the strength of MacDonald's praise, they were in a position to offer Mr. Lauder a month's booking. The tour would end in Glasgow.

"I'll tak' it," announced Harry, "and this time, Nance, *this* time—"

"This time you'll stay on th' stage?"

"Weel, maybe I willna' stay on th' stage, but I canna' gae on as I hae been, workin' i' th' mine an' then leavin' it, an' then gaen back tae th' mine again."

"Aye, Harry. It ought tae be one thing or th' other."

"You're richt, Nance. This is ma last chance. If I dinna mak' guid th' noo, I never wull. Anyhow, th' mine managers willna' stand for me leavin' again an' again like this. It's no fair tae them. This time for guid or ill, I'll say guidbye tae th' mines. If I canna' mak' a success as a comedian, I'll get another kind o' job above ground. I wull so. I open i' Newcastle. I've a month's tour promised. Only a month. We canna' ken whit wull come after."

"It'll be th' first time you've played tae an English audience," said Nance.

"True. It wull be a test. I might fail, but whatever happens, I'm sayin' guidbye tae th' mines—forever."

CHAPTER SEVEN

Except for the two weeks in Whittington Moor, this was the first time Lauder had been out of Scotland, yet not even the smallest Scots towns had received him more graciously than did the English provinces. They yelled for encore after encore. Before the brief tour was finished, agents in London began to hear of a new Scots comic named Lauder. Upon his return to Hamilton he found fifty letters awaiting him, each containing offers for engagements.

"Hoots!" he exclaimed when he had read them all, "if I'm that guid, I'll not sing for less than a guinea-and-a-hauf!"

Even at this hitherto undreamed-of figure, he was promptly engaged for a second tour by Moss and Thornton. Lauder was more sure of himself now than he had ever been. He had studied the English audiences and toned down his Scottish accent, for his unfailing sense of showmanship told him that an audience must easily comprehend what the actor is saying. Not satisfied to be "just another

Scots comic," he was still seeking better songs, constantly perfecting his technique, always trying out different effects, retaining some, discarding others.

Ambition at this time became, not only a stimulus but a tyrant. Not alone for himself, nor even for Nance, did he want money and success now; it was for John, his son, who had been born November 19, 1891, and named for Harry's father. The Lauders had already moved from Hamilton and taken a small cheap flat in Glasgow. Money, and much of it, had become imperative. John was to have a real boyhood; John was to be a gentleman; John was to have a splendid education, the best the world could give him. John must never experience the hardship and poverty which his father had known. Harry Lauder told himself that henceforth he must never stop, never be satisfied with anything less than the very pinnacle. To accomplish this, he must never cease striving to improve.

He had absolute faith in himself and his ability. His job, as he saw it, was bigger than merely entertaining people—his job was to be so good that he could make people forget that they were being entertained. His job was to make people forget themselves, their fears, their troubles, even to make them forget for a time that they were in a theatre, and that he was an actor paid to amuse. He began to intersperse stories between songs. He told these stories in a confidential, intimate manner which vaudeville performers everywhere tried later to imitate.

Vaudeville! The color, the scope of it! It was a world of fantasy, endlessly kaleidoscopic.

Every vaudevillian made it his business to "catch" the other fellow's act, especially if that act was a success. It was inevitable that Lauder should be watched and copied by his own profession.

Vaudeville at this time was the rage. The greatest theatres in the world were built and dedicated to vaudeville. Vaudeville acts—called "turns" in England—were endless in variation and novelty. The bill, however, followed a general pattern. On the better circuits it usually consisted of seven acts, and lasted from an hour and a half to two hours. The headline act ran the longest of every act on the bill, but even this scarcely ever ran over twenty minutes. Twenty minutes was considered a long act.

These bills were planned with utmost care. Part of the science of laying them out was to eliminate all conflict. No two acts on the same bill must be alike. Also, acts had to be placed on the bill according to the amount of stage space they required, for the stage had to be set and re-set many times during a single performance, and there must be no delay between one act and another. When a vaudeville performer said he played his act "in one," he meant that he used only a few feet behind the footlights. An act which played "in two" used half the stage, while an act playing "in three" used the full stage. The star act, or headliner, was the act which received billing above all the others. This always preceded the closing act, and the utmost care was taken in regard to the act which preceded the headliner.

Almost invariably a vaudeville performance opened with what was known as a "silent" or "dumb" act—an act in which no words were spoken, no songs were sung—jugglers, wire walkers, tumblers, contortionists. This was generally followed by a song and dance team, which was either a man and a woman, two men, or what was termed a "sister" act, which played "in one."

The third act was usually a "sketch"—a short playlet either comedy or drama—using the full stage. The fourth act might be a musical, or a blackface, a tramp, a ventriloquist, a tap dancer. The fifth act might be a "girl" act. Then came the headliner, and following this came another silent act—a bicycle, an acrobatic or a trained animal act.

These acts each had separate agents and separate bookings. They rarely appeared on the same bill more than once, and except in isolated instances, they never returned to the same town twice in a season.

Vaudeville had among its ranks the finest talent in the world. If one were successful, it promised a long season with consecutive bookings, and the better circuits, such as the Orpheum circuit in America, paid enormous salaries. That the time would ever come when there was no vaudeville was unthinkable. Vaudeville, called "Variety" in England, was a part of the national life. Countless acts never got beyond the smaller circuits, being satisfied with what was called "split weeks" in suburban towns; but whatever the circuit, the life was intensely competitive. An act which made a hit was sure to be copied by hundreds of imitators.

Vaudeville was a world of its own. It employed vast armies of skilled workers which the public never saw—costume designers, "patter" writers, joke writers, sketch writers.

Lauder knew that he must have better songs, he must continue to improve, he must work unceasingly toward perfection if he were ever to earn more than his guinea-and-a-half, for now he realized that there was practically no limit to the money that was to be made in vaudeville. Only a year before he had considered himself fortunate to earn as much as fifteen shillings a week, and now he was actually refusing offers of one guinea.

Nance was proud of him, and a little breathless about all this. Sometimes she told herself that it simply could not last. But it did. Harry kept on working when other Variety artistes were idle and grumbling. No sooner was one engagement finished than another was waiting. He was known and loved all over Scotland now.

It was the autumn of 1896. Peace between Italy and Abyssinia had been declared, and Ethiopia was assured of her independence. The Queen of Madagascar had given the French resident control of the island. There had been trouble in the Philippines and a revolution in Cuba. In America President Cleveland had recognized Utah as a state, and in Scotland Harry Lauder was accepting a six weeks' engagement with Donald Munro's North Concert Company for five pounds a week.

Sometimes an impresario like Munro would assemble an entire vaudeville bill, maintaining the entertainment intact for several months. To a vaudevillian, "solid" booking was something to be dreamed of, prayed for, schemed for. To be "booked solid" for a definite length of time meant that there would be no intervening weeks of idleness, or what was naïvely termed "resting," between engagements. Even to be booked solid for six weeks meant that for six weeks one did not have to worry about meeting expenses.

This six weeks' solid booking brought Lauder infinitely more than his salary. It brought him the fine and enduring friendship of Mackenzie Murdoch, who was only a month younger than Harry, and already a well-known Scots violinist. Lauder always maintained that he would rather hear Mac play the old Scottish airs than listen to the greatest virtuoso in the world. To him, Mac never played so well as he did when he and Harry were alone—and Mac would get out his fiddle and play for an audience of one.

In the vernacular of the stage, the Munro tour was "packing 'um in." Munro was making money so fast that he was kept busy counting it. Next summer he intended to take out another company and had already approached both Murdoch and Lauder on the subject of re-engagements.

"Mac," began Harry one day as they were strolling idly about a small town, "I was thinking—if Munro can make a' this siller, why can't we do th' same?"

"True, Harry. What's to prevent us from taking oot a company of oor ain? We're th' chief drawing cards. We're th' topliners. Weel, why should we make a' this siller for Munro? What's to prevent us from taking oot a concert company of oor ain?"

"Say next August, Mac? We could both accept other bookin's i' th' meanwhile. We could engage some guid acts and we could arrange a route through other towns besides th' ones Munro plays. He's a graund fellow, is Munro. I wouldna' like to compete wi' him."

"We'll call it 'The Lauder-Murdoch Concert Company'! How much siller hae ye saved, Harry?"

So they began to plan.

Already their joint resources were sufficient to pay rail road fares, salaries, and advertising costs. Meanwhile, there were bookings ahead for each of them, bookings in which Harry's salary was as much as two guineas. Out of this, of course, must come transportation, costumes, hotel expenses, commissions to agents. Nance had been good at saving what was left over. She had economized everywhere possible, but when she learned that Harry was now determined to risk every penny, she only smiled and told him that he must please himself.

Every spare moment they could find, Lauder and his partner spent planning the tour which would begin the following summer. They fancied themselves as managers, and when at last they actually saw the bills printed with THE LAUDER-MURDOCH CONCERT COMPANY in bold type, they shook hands and laughed like two boys.

* * *

By spring the company had been engaged, the itinerary planned for a different town every night. Not only would Lauder and Murdoch each present his own act, but they would serve jointly as press agent and treasurer. Once the tour began they were constantly together, eating together because they enjoyed each other's society, and rooming together to save expenses. Arriving in a town, they would walk through it, arms laden with posters. In and out of shops they went, asking for window space in which to display the placards in exchange for a free pass to the show.

Before the first week had ended they were beginning to regret that they had not accepted Munro's offer instead of striking out for themselves. Why, they asked each other forlornly, didn't the people come to the theatre? Their troupe was a good one. In addition to themselves there was a tenor, a ventriloquist, a soprano. Harry had added several new songs to his repertoire, one of which was *Tobermory*, the other *The Lass of Killecrankie*. Yet they were playing almost to empty seats. He and Mac had invested one hundred and fifty pounds in this enterprise, all they had in the world. In Sterlingshire they played to exactly eleven people.

The tour over, they returned to Glasgow. "Weel," sighed Mac disconsolately as he sank beside his partner in the train, "I suppose you'll want to quit, Harry?"

"Quit? No. I want tae tak' out anither troupe next summer!"

"I'm glad to hear ye say that. That's the way I feel, too. We'll try again. We've each pretty solid bookings ahead o' us for the winter, and we'll save every cent we can."

"We'll tak' oot another company. We'll increase the advertisin'!"

"Aye. Aye. We'll go to different towns. We might get back all we lost."

And they did.

Harry's letters to Nance the following summer were full of encouragement. Things were going so well, in fact, that they could now afford to engage a man to act as secretary and to attend to the duties of bill poster.

"The mon we want is hard to find," declared Mac. "He maun be a mon we can trust. He maun be honest, sober and reliable—and an easy fellow to get along wi'."

"Findin' th' mon we want is the easiest thing i' th' world, Mac. He's ma ain brother-in-law, Tom Vallance! I'd depend on Tom as much as I'd depend on masel'."

So Harry sent for Tom Vallance and Tom laid aside his miner's pick and lamp forever, for never again throughout the long years of Harry Lauder's travels was Tom Vallance separated from him. Everyone who knew Lauder knew Vallance, for Tom became friend, dresser, confidant, manager, secretary, bodyguard.

As each year the tours continued to show a substantial profit, sometimes even reaching as much as a hundred pounds a night, this constituted undeniable success. Mac and Harry would return to their hotel night after night carrying a leather bag heavy with coins and sit up until the small hours counting them. They had both known extreme poverty and now the sight of so much money spread out before them seemed nothing short of a miracle.

After they had collected the money at the end of each performance, they were never quite at peace until it was placed safely in the bank the next morning. One Saturday night they were playing in a small town near Glasgow. There was a train which they could catch directly after the show which would bring them into Glasgow a little after midnight. This meant that they could spend all of Sunday at home with their families. To be at home with his wife and son was to Harry ever a precious opportunity. He decided to take advantage of it. The money was counted and placed as usual in the small leather bag.

"You'd better take a cab frae the station," advised Mac.

"Aye," agreed his partner feelingly. "I'll run no risks wi' a' that siller."

Arriving at the Buchanan Street Station in Glasgow, the bag clutched tightly in his hand, Harry jumped into a cab and gave the address of his apartment in Dundas Street. How surprised Nance would be to see him! He leaned back, visualizing the scene which awaited him. It was only a two-room flat and the kitchen served as a bedroom. Nance would be asleep in the big double bed, and John, almost eight now, would be asleep in his own bed—a fine, blond sturdy lad, tidy as a cherub. Harry would let himself very silently into the big kitchen. . . .

"Hey!" came the driver's voice. "Here ye are, mister!"

Harry awoke with a start. "Eh? Eh?"

"This is Dundas Street."

"I must have been asleep. Aye, this is th' place."

So eager was Harry to get to Nance that he fished the amount of his fare out of his pocket, and dashed into the house, the clap-clap of the horse's hoofs echoing behind him down the silent, empty street.

Moving on tiptoe, he hurried up the stairs, fitted his key noiselessly into the kitchen door, and began silently to undress. He was robed only in his underclothes when he remembered the bag with the money.

"Oh!" he cried aloud, and stood there for a moment immovable.

"Harry?" came Nance's voice. "Harry? Is it you?"

He did not answer. He lit the gas and stood staring wildly about, his eyes searching for the bag. No, he had left it in the cab.

"Harry!"

For once her husband was completely unmindful of her presence. He seized his trousers and made a wild rush for the kitchen door.

"Harry! What ails you?" she called. "Harry! You'll no be gaen oot o' this hoose wi'oot wearin' your troosers!"

But the door had slammed after him. He bolted down the long flight of stairs and not until he reached the lower hall way did he realize that he was still clutching his trousers. Stopping long enough to don them, he rushed frantically into the silent street. A policeman idly leaning against a lamppost saw a disheveled, barefooted man dash past him—a short man with a wild look in his eyes.

"Here, you!" called the policeman.

But the strange apparition did not halt. The policeman started in pursuit and was presently joined by another.

"It maun be an escaped lunatic," decided the first officer.

At last the barefooted man turned toward Buchanan Station.

"Ah!" cried the second policeman breathlessly, "he's tryin' to make a getaway!"

It was now well after one o'clock. Except for a single cab the station was deserted. The driver on the seat was dozing. Suddenly a strange apparition bounded beside him on the box, had him by the arm and shouted: "You're th' one I'm lookin' for!"

"Help!" screamed the cabbie. "Police!"

"Where's ma money? Gie me ma money!"

"Let me go. I don't know anything about your money. Police! Murder!"

"Ma money! Where is it? Where is it?"

"Police! Police!"

"Ma money! Where is it? Where is it?"

"Help! Help!"

In his efforts to release himself from his assailant, the cabbie rolled off the box and into the street, the barefooted man on top of him. Seemingly bored with the rumpus, the aged horse turned his head to see two men rolling on the ground. One of them kept saying something about "money" all the time. It was a curious spectacle, even to a horse.

Like genii emerging from the shadows, the two policemen each grabbed a man.

"Now! What *is* a' this?"

"Ma money!" shouted the barefooted man frantically. "He's got ma money!"

"That's a lie. He's been ravin' aboot money. I never seen no money. Here, whit're ye holdin' me for?"

"Ma money! It was i' a leather bag. I left it i' this cab. Where's ma money?"

One of the policemen flung open the cab door. "Is this th' bag?"

"Aye. Aye. That's it. That's it."

"Better count it and see if it's a' there," suggested the other officer.

Four weary men sank in a line along the curb. Harry counted his money. "It's a' here," he declared.

The next night in Mac's dressing room when Harry had related the incident, he added, "I had tae pay an extra cabfare back tae Dundas Street, I had tae gie th' cabby some siller for accusin' him, an' I had tae gie th' coppers seathin'. Noo, Mac, I was thinkin', shouldn't that extra expense be charged tae th' *company?*"

"It should not," answered Mac with promptitude. "It's your ain lesson and you'll pay for it. What kind of a Scotsman are ye, anyhoo, to be forgettin' a bag o' money?"

Life to Lauder was now gloriously, wondrously full. There was this fine friendship with Mac, there was the cozy little flat on Dundas Street, there was success, there was Nance, there was the boy. Hour after hour he and Nance would sit together planning the future of the bairn.

"Do ye think, mon Harry," Nance would ask, "do ye think we might someday be able tae send him tae *Cambridge?*"

That would take money—more money, even, than Harry was making at present, but he answered quickly. "Aye, Nance. He'll gae tae Cambridge. We'll see that oor John has every advantage th' world can gie him. Nance, Nance, I want ma boy tae be proud o' his faither!"

"I want—" Nance answered softly, "John's faither tae be proud o' his *son.*"

"I am, Nance, I'm proud o' him now; and when he grows up—"

That was their constant refrain—"when he grows up."

He was a handsome child, straight-limbed and cheery. He had Nance's nose, but he had Harry's mouth and chin. It seemed incomprehensible now that they had ever lived without him. He was a source of constant delight, constant conversation. Their lives were centered in this boy. Every new song Harry sang seemed now something which would help him to secure the future of his son.

New songs were constantly being added to his repertoire. Sometimes to Mac he would sing over an original tune which was running through his head and Mac would orchestrate it for him. It was not only tunes which Lauder was creating—a phrase would often keep repeating itself in his mind for days at a time, eventually it would develop into a chorus and a verse. The songs in themselves were trivial, but the music was catchy and easily remembered.

Between the summer tours of "The Lauder-Murdoch Concert Company" Lauder's winter bookings were now taking him more frequently across the border into England. Even Liverpool had received him enthusiastically. He began to consider the possibility that one day he might even play in London. Why not? Why not try—at least *try*. But he hesitated. Was he quite ready for London? Was he good enough?

No Variety artiste could ever claim to have really arrived until London had accepted him.

Occasionally, he mentioned the matter to his friends. There is not a performer in the history of the theatre who has made a success in some particular territory, but that his well-meaning friends advise him to remain where he is. Lauder was no exception. Why not, his friends asked, leave well enough alone? Wasn't he doing beautifully where he was? London audiences were hard, critical, cold.

"I'm as guid as some great London stars I've seen," answered Harry doggedly.

"True," they argued, "but maybe they have a pull, maybe they've just had luck."

"Luck!" he scoffed. "There's no such thing as luck an' there's no such thing as Fate. People who sit doon an' moon aboot luck an' Fate are just lazy, that's all."

Meanwhile, there was not a town or city in Scotland that did not receive him with open arms; there were the English provinces which were coming to know him and applaud when in the slot at each side of the proscenium the card was inserted announcing that the act to follow was "Harry Lauder, Scotland's Pride"; and, of course, there were the pleasant summer tours. With Tom taking care of the business details, Harry and Mac had time to practice their golf.

"If you gentlemen like to fish," said the proprietor of the hotel at Castle Douglas, "the fish in the lake are so plentiful that they practically jump in the boat. If you like, I'll lend you my own rowboat and my fishing tackle."

Harry looked at Mac, Mac looked at Harry. "Aye," nodded Mac, "we're verra fond o' fishing."

"They say fishin's a graund sport," remarked Harry, as the two walked down to the lake. "How guid a fisherman are ye, Mac?"

"We'll see," answered Mac.

Harry had never fished, and he had a strong conviction that Mac was as inexpert as himself. The lake was broad and blue, its shores richly wooded. The landscape was restful and lovely. Off in the distance an old man was busily cutting peat from the bog. On the hills a band of sheep were grazing.

"It's a graund day," affirmed Harry.

"It is so," agreed Mac.

For hours they sat in the middle of the lake, gazing idly across the blue water, puffing contentedly at their pipes.

"Aweel," sighed Harry, "it may not be sport, but it's peacefu'."

Mac sighed. "It's weel I mind the time I first went fishing. Mon Harry, the fish I caught *that* day!"

Harry was impressed, instantly interested. So, Mac was a fisherman after all and had never said a word about it!

"Aye," went on Mac, with the blissful softness of retrospection in his eyes. "For twa summers not a fishermon i' the country but had been trying to land one single trout. Ould he was, this trout, ye ken, ould and tough and wily the rascal. Fishermon came frae all over to try to land him, but he aye got awa'. So I waded oot i' th' water and all of a sudden I felt a tug at ma line. Declare to God, Harry, it was a pull that near yanked the rod oot of ma hand. And there was this trout. The creature was i' a fighting mood, I'm telling ye."

"Was anyone watchin'?" asked Harry in a voice not untouched by awe.

"Aye. Aye. There was a whole crowd watching me. They all got excited when they saw what trout it was I had on the end o' ma line. It was the very trout no one had been able to land. Nobody thought I'd be able to bring him in. And what a tussle he gave me! Three hours of it, Harry. Mind, *three hours!* But he wouldna' gie up—and neither would I."

"You're a firm mon when your mind's set tae a thing, Mac."

"I am so."

"But ye got him at last?"

"I did. And you'll never guess the weight of the creature."

"No," answered his companion.

"Weel, he weighed thirty-one pounds to the ounce."

"Thirty-one pounds?"

"He did so."

"*Did* he?"

"I wouldna' tell a lee."

"Thirty-one pounds is a big fish, Mac."

"It is: and it takes a strong mon to bring in a fish like that, I'm telling ye."

"Aye," agreed Harry. He gave Mac a sharp, speculative glance, but Mac's face was bland and impassive. There was a long pause during which Lauder very thoughtfully filled his pipe. "I mind th' first fish I ever caught," he remarked casually, at last.

"You? You caught a fish?"

"I did so."

"Big?"

"He was twa thousand six hundred fourteen and a hauf pounds."

"Twa thousand six hundred fourteen and a hauf pounds! What kind of a fish is that?"

"Just a bit whale," answered Harry.

CHAPTER EIGHT

There were fields beyond Scotland, fields alluring and rich. There was London with its famous music halls. An act which was in demand there could play three or even four of these halls in a single night, traveling from one hall to another at top speed, without even removing make-up. Headline Variety artistes were amassing untold wealth.

"I suppose," said Harry, whose thick Scotch accent was undergoing a gradual change as the area of his activities widened, "I suppose a mon ought to be content wi' what I have. Certainly, a few years ago if I could have looked ahead to what I have the noo, I'd say I wouldna' ask for any more."

Mac was silent a long time. "It's been graund, Harry," he said at last, "it's been graund us working together and playing together."

"It's—*been* graund, Mac?"

"Aye. Aye. We maun face the fact, Harry, that we're none of us a real success until we've been accepted i' London and played the big London Ha's. I ken if ye go to London it wull mean the end of our partnership."

"Why?"

"Why? Because ye ken as weel as I do, mon, if ye catch on i' London, even the siller we've been making here wull seem like only a wee drappie i' comparison. But you've no only me an' yoursel' to think of, there's Nance and John."

"Aye. To them I owe the best, to them I want to gie the best. Ah, Mac, he's a fine, healthy lad is oor John. I want him to go to Cambridge; and when he grows up I want him and me to be, not faither and son, but comrades."

"I ken, Harry. I ken how a' your dreams are centered around that precious laddie o' yours."

"He must never go through the boyhood that I endured," declared Harry firmly. "He must go to the best schools, and that, Mac, wull take a lot of money; it means a lot to a mon to have a good education, to have a happy boyhood to look back upon. I ken that when John grows up, I canna' save him frae th' hard knocks. I ken that for all I can do, there'll be times when he's baffled, when he's scared, when the hope is drained out o' him, but there's one thing I can do, and it's little enough—and that is to gie ma boy every possible advantage; but for me to have a try at London—they say London's a different kind of audience."

"You're wasting your time i' the north country, Harry."

"You think so, Mac?"

"Aye."

"But London's used to the best i' the world, the greatest. Am I ready for London yet?"

"You'll never know till you try."

"True. True."

"You've a way that takes wi' an audience, mon Lauder. You've a way o' singing that's different. I dinna ken what it is. I've seen your act hundreds o' times, and I've never gotten tired of it. I've watched how you've improved since we've been together. You never stop working, Harry. All the time you're off the stage, you're working."

It was true. Throughout the fifty years of his theatrical career, even in his sixties, Harry Lauder never stopped trying to improve his songs, his costumes, his stories. The vogue for Lauder was something of a phenomenon in footlight history. Seemingly it was as perennial, as unwaning, as the sun itself. It covered an unprecedented period, and it was still at its zenith when he finally retired. This simple, honest, modest little Scotsman was one of the greatest drawing cards the theatre ever knew. Even his enemies were forced to admit it. Those recognized as authorities in the world of entertainment could never wholly explain it. While recognizing the value of publicity, he never had a paid press agent in his life.

He was writing most of his material himself now, and even when he bought a song, he kept changing it over and over, until scarcely a word or note of the original structure remained. From the time of its inception until it was presented to the public, every song went through a period both of growth and of pruning which lasted for months. During that time it was seldom out of his mind. He would sing it to himself everywhere—as he walked along the street, as he bathed, shaved, dressed, in trains, in restaurants; and each time he sang it he was trying a new trick with his voice, a new emphasis, a longer drawn out "oh" or a shorter "oh." Was there too much expression here, too little there? To stand still when he sang a certain line or to move; to smile or not to smile; a turn of the eyes on this word, a lift of the brows on that, the very height at which his stick would be raised, every nuance was of tremendous importance. He never gave a careless, slipshod performance in his life.

The strange thing about it all was that despite these studied moves and intonations, his performance maintained a seeming spontaneity, a perennial freshness and vitality.

The action of the actor, his winks, gestures, walk, are called "business." Lauder was his own relentless critic. "That's a guid piece o' business," he would tell himself approvingly about a certain move of his head; or "that's a bad piece o' business"; or "I maun think up some better business for richt after ma entrance."

There was nothing involved or "highbrow" about his songs. They were kept deliberately simple. A mere reading of the words of these songs which all the world knew and loved, arouses a sense of wonder that such triviality, such inconsequential doggerel, could have produced such enthusiasm. Lauder audiences were all-inclusive. Rich and poor, cultured and ignorant, Chinaman, American, Englishman, Australian, Negro, Jew, all classes and races responded with equal wholeheartedness to the singular Lauder appeal. Here was a homely little man with an uncultivated voice and a collection of clean, simple, singable songs. Yet for over thirty years he was admittedly the greatest drawing card, and he received the highest salary, of anyone in the theatrical world. There was *Stop Yer Ticklin', Jock, I'm th' Saftest o' th' Family, She's Ma Daisy, Wee Hoose 'mang th' Heather, It's Nice to get up i' th' Mornin', I love a Lassie, Roamin' i' th' Gloamin', When I Meet MacKay, Wee Doech an' Doruis, When I was Twenty-one, When I Get back to bonny Scotland*—all of these songs were not at this time in his repertoire, but they were the songs which he sang for over thirty years in every part of the globe—and the world sang them with him. Should he omit one of them, shouting demands would arise from all parts of the house.

"Nance," he asked one day, "what would you think of ma going to London?"

"And why shouldn't you?" she answered.

"They say I've no understandin' o' what th' London audiences are like. They say London audiences are cold and critical. They say London's had a flood o' Scots comics lately, and that she's tired of them. They say Scots comics dinna catch on i' London."

She gave him one of her fond, bright smiles. "Folks like ye *here*, mon Harry, an' folks are folks everywhere. Months and months it's dreamin' o' London you've been. Hae your try at London, ma dear. I ken ye willna' fail. I ken it weel."

"I saw Dan Leno's act at the Empire. They call him the Idol o' London. He's good, Nance; I'm no sayin' he's no good."

"Is he a Scots comic, too?"

"No. He has a cockney act. But if they'll pay Dan Leno a hundred pounds i' Glasga' for singin' London songs, why wouldn't they pay Harry Lauder at least a fifth o' that for singin' Scots songs i' London? I swear ma act's as good as his!"

"And better!" she declared. "Dinna fash yoursel'. When your chance comes for London, Harry, take it."

"Chance," he repeated moodily, "chance. When ma chance comes—if I wait for that, I'm likely to be playin' i' Scotland for th' rest o' ma life. Chance doesna' come, Nance. A mon has to go out an' find it. Opportunity—I mind th' time we left Axbroath for Hamilton—we didna' wait for opportunity, we went lookin' for it. And now—" his voice took on the sharpness of sudden decision, "now the opportunity's i' London an' Harry Lauder's off to find it!"

"When?"

"I'll take th' first train oot i' th' mornin'! I wull so. I'll start packin' ma costumes an' ma props richt awa'. I'll say nothin' to anybody aboot it. If I—if I fail, nobody'll be any th' wiser."

"It costs muckle siller, I've heard, to live i' London, Harry, an' ye may not get work at once—"

They were in the kitchen, and walking over to the wooden bed in the far corner, she reached under the mattress. From its hiding place she took out a heavy stocking and started counting the money it contained.

"I'd better take twenty pounds of gold sovereigns," he told her, "an' I'll buy a third-class *one-way ticket.*"

Next morning, weighted down with two Gladstone bags, Lauder left Glasgow. It was March, 1900. Great Britain was fighting a war with the Transvaal Republic, and the aged Queen Victoria, perpetually in mourning, was worrying about the escapades of her boy, Edward. Two months previously, John Ruskin had died. Paris was preparing for a great exposition which would officially open in April. Harry Lauder was thirty, and off to conquer England with a few songs, a few props, and twenty pounds in golden sovereigns.

He did not wear his kilts. Instead he was dressed in what he believed to be the latest London fashion. His spats were yellow, his shoes a bright tan. He wore plaid trousers, a frock coat, a high white collar, a green and black cravat. He looked prosperous enough, he felt, to impress any London manager. Over his arm was the coat with the astrakhan collar.

It was evening when he arrived, and went in search of a cheap hotel, but even the cheap hotels in London cost more than he had been accustomed to paying in Scotland. He settled at last in a hotel in Euston Road—three and sixpence for bed and breakfast! Oh, well, he would economize by walking to the agencies.

The first thing next morning he began what actors call "the rounds." He decided to try Cadle's Agency first. He was not entirely unknown there, since this agency had often booked him in the English provinces.

"Well, glad to see you, Mr. Lauder," began the head of the firm cordially. "Come in. Sit down. Here for a little holiday, what?"

"I'm here lookin' for work. I thought ye might be able to fix me up at one o' th' big West End ha's."

"You don't mean here in London?"

"And why not?"

The man smiled, a pitying, kindly smile. "You Scots comics! You think all you have to do is come up to London. No, Mr. Lauder, no. I'm sorry. You haven't a chance. Not a chance in the world. London's been overrun with Scots comics lately, anyhow. It's tired to death of Scotch comedy. There have been failure after failure. Frankly, I *couldn't* book your act in a London hall. Take my advice. Save what money you have by going back to Scotland on the first train. I say this in all kindness, go back where you came from and leave well enough alone."

As he walked out of the building, Harry's short body was held very erect, and the blue eyes had taken on a certain grim defiance. There were other agents in London, weren't there? London was full of agents. There must be hundreds of them. Well, he would see them all. One man's opinion was not going to discourage *him*. He *would* not be discouraged. He would not stop until all possible channels had been exhausted. He thought what it would mean to Nance and the boy if he made good in London. It would mean that John could go to Cambridge. It would mean that they could take a house here, and Nance could have a servant or two to do the heavy work. It meant that in time they would be independent for life. It meant that he could give his mother a few luxuries in her old age. But perhaps his friends had been right, after all. Perhaps it had been foolish to come. Oh, they must give him a chance, they must! Why, he would even sing for nothing just to get that chance, or he might even *pay* some manager for letting him sing. Anything—anything, just to have his try at London!

"So, you're Harry Lauder," smiled the second agent, "yes, we've heard of you. Are you looking for some bookings in the provinces?"

"Provinces? Deil a bit, mon. I'm looking for a shop here i' London."

Again that gently derisive smile. "No, that's impossible. All you Scots comics try to break into London the minute you've had a touch of success elsewhere. But there's not a chance in the world. Go back where you came from, old chap. Take my advice. We're fed up with Scots comics here in London. Audiences won't stand for any more of them."

"But I'm *no* just anither Scots comic! Only gie me a chance an' I'll prove it!"

"I know. I know. That's what they all say. Sorry, old man, but if you want the truth, you belong in Scotland. Make up your mind to stay there. There's where you're known and liked and understood. You've as much chance of being taken on in London as I have of sprouting wings."

There were *more* agencies, Harry reminded himself doggedly. But one after the other they told him the same thing. It was late when he returned to his room in Euston Road, too weary to think of dinner, too discouraged even to write to Nance. Tomorrow was another day. Why not go directly to the managers of the halls? But what was the use, after all? These agents must know. Getting him work was as much to their advantage as to his own, since they would have ten per cent of his earnings. They had no grudge against him. If work were possible here in London, they would be only too glad to try and book him. Why remain then? It was costing money, money which Nance had saved by dint of strict self-sacrifice. Why should he think he knew more than the agents, anyhow?

But he could not, would not give up.

Next morning, feeling fresh, rested, hopeful, he started "the rounds" again. But one after another the managers laughed at him. Again at nightfall, having trudged miles through the London streets, he returned to Euston Road. Well, there was still tomorrow. There remained a few managers and agents whom he had not yet interviewed.

Early next afternoon, while still determinedly going the rounds, he heard a friendly voice cry out: "Harry Lauder! What in the world are you doing away from Glasgow?"

He was glad to see Walter Monroe. Monroe had been an agent, and Harry knew that he must have a large acquaintance among the London theatrical world.

"Wattie! Mon, this is graund! Here's a bar. Come in, I'll buy ye a drink."

Over the drinks, Harry explained his presence in London.

Monroe sighed. "Well, Harry, I'm afraid you're doomed to disappointment. I know more about this London situation than you do. You haven't a chance, that's obvious as a wart. I'll be glad to take you around to several offices, but I'm warning you beforehand that it won't do a bit of good."

Monroe's words were prophetic. The two friends went in and out of agents' offices until late in the afternoon.

"You see, Mr. Lauder," they explained, "you may be known in Edinburgh and Glasgow and Liverpool, but you're absolutely unknown in London."

"But how am I gaen to *get* known if no one wull gie me a chance to *show* masel'?"

There seemed no answer to that question. They were polite enough, but they had no use for Harry Lauder. It was too late to go to any more offices now, and Harry invited Monroe to have dinner with him at a restaurant in the Strand. Sitting there gloomily, Harry thought of Nance, and how he would have to go home and tell her that London would have none of him.

"We've seen them all?" he asked jadedly.

"Yes, I've done the best I can for you, Harry. I've introduced you to all the men I know except Tinsley. He was out, you remember. Tinsley's a fine chap and a jolly good friend of mine. He—well, by jove! Speak of the devil! There he is, just leaving the restaurant. Tom! Old fellow! Tom!"

Tinsley stopped and shook hands with Monroe. Tom Tinsley, Harry knew, was the manager of Gatti's in the Westminster Bridge Road. Though a small theatre, it was by no means unimportant. Gatti's was known for the originality of its bills.

"Sit down, Tom. Shake hands with Harry Lauder."

Extremely cordial, Tinsley shook hands and seated himself at the table. With a lordly air, Harry ordered drinks and brought forth one of his gold sovereigns. He'd show this London manager that, though he was only a Scots comic from the provinces, he was not exactly a failure.

"Lauder," Monroe explained, "is a comedian, very well known in Scotland. In fact, I was surprised to see him today because he's practically booked solid all the time."

Tinsley was genial. "Ah, came to see the sights of the big town, eh?"

"Weel, no. I'm lookin' for a shop here."

The geniality ebbed. "What did you say your name was?"

"Lauder. Harry Lauder. I'm a comedian. I—"

"That's enough. You don't need to go any further. London's a foreign country as far as you're concerned."

"But—"

"Now, my dear boy, I hope you won't be angry with me, but it's just no good you're trying to get on in London.

I remember I put on a Scotch act last year. It was a dismal flop."

"But if you'd just—"

"My doors are fairly besieged day after day with ambitious young talent from the provinces who think they can crash into London. But it's especially hopeless for a Scotch comedian. The quicker you get that through your head the better it will be for you. Sorry, old man, I'd like to help you, but—"

"But you haven't heard me. You dinna know what I can do. Just gie me a trial, Mr. Tinsley, just let me sing for you, personally, just a wee bit song!"

"No, it's no use, my boy. I know my audience better than you do. You'd only be wasting your time."

"But Harry's not like other Scotch comedians, Tom," put in Monroe. "I've seen him. He has a distinctive way of putting a song over. Now, it wouldn't take much of your time, would it, just to hear him, just to give him a little private try-out? You're trying out talent every week, you know. I'll take it as a personal favor if you'll—"

"Well, all right, since you put it that way, Walter. All right. But it won't do a bit of good and it'll only be a waste of both our time. Where are you living, Louder?"

"It's not Louder," answered Harry, "it's Lauder. As if it were spelled L-A-W-D-E-R—Lawder." He gave Tinsley the address. When the manager had jotted it down on an envelope, he rose.

"Well, I'll let you know when it's convenient for me to give you that try-out. Good-by."

When Tinsley had gone, Monroe shook his head. "You'll probably never hear from him. That's the old dodge—'I'll take your address and let you know.' It doesn't mean anything."

"I ken that," answered Harry glumly.

"I've done all I can for you, my lad."

"Thank you, Wattie, and dinna think I'm no grateful."

They rose and walked out of the restaurant. "It's no use, Harry," said Monroe as the two shook hands in parting, "you're not wanted in London and that's all there is to it."

"It looks as if you're richt, Wattie."

"I know I'm right. You might as well face it."

"Aye," admitted Harry. "Weel, guidnicht, Wattie."

"Good-by. Good luck."

Again next morning, Harry was out "doing the agencies." Toward evening he turned homeward again, his feet sore and burning. He had walked twelve miles. London agencies were crowded with actors, actors young and old, smartly dressed and shabby. The offices all looked alike. Every inch of wall space was covered with autographed photographs of acrobatic acts, soubrettes, jugglers. There were wooden benches along the walls, where the artistes sat while they waited for an interview. Usually there was a railing behind which stood the agent's assistant. "No," he kept saying like an automaton, "nothing today, nothing today. Sorry, nothing doing today."

Now and then an act would try to tell him how good they were. "We simply knocked them off their seats in Carlisle" or, "We took four calls in Stirlingshire."

"Yes. Yes, I know, but there's nothing doing today—"

"But I—we've been resting now for three weeks—"

"Yes, I know. But there's nothing doing today. Nothing today. . . ."

Not an office in London that Harry Lauder had not visited, and always with the identical result. He had seen them all, been admitted into the inner offices, talked with the agents themselves.

"Yes, Mr. Lauder, I've heard of you, but London's overcrowded with acts. A hundred acts to fill every opening. It's difficult enough to keep acts working that've had London showings. Unless an act's a topnotcher, it's better off in the provinces. No, sorry. Can't do anything for you, Mr. Lauder. Good day."

A sense of utter futility engulfed him as he walked toward his small, dingy back room. There was nothing to do now but return to Scotland. Every flicker of hope was extinguished.

Thank heaven no one in Glasgow but Nance knew that he had come to London; no one would know of his failure. Lord, how weary he was, inexpressibly weary. Even climbing those three flights of stairs seemed a task far in excess of his strength. Tomorrow—well, tomorrow he would take the first train back to Glasgow. Time, money, energy, all wasted.

"There's a telegram in your room," called the landlady as he passed her in the hall.

A telegram!

Tiredness forgotten, he climbed the stairs two at a time. Was it Nance? Was something wrong at home? Nance? John? No, it could not be from Nance. He had not yet written to her. She had no idea of his address. Even Monroe did not know where he was living. No one knew. No one of the hundreds of agents and managers he had seen had even bothered to inquire where he could be reached. No one knew except—Tinsley. Tinsley! But the telegram could not be from Tinsley. Why, only last night Tinsley had said—it was some mistake, of course. Yes, he must not let himself hope. It was some mistake. The telegram was for some other Lauder.

He had reached the room now, and his hands were trembling so that he could scarcely insert the key in the lock.

The message lay on the dresser.

Once again a telegram was to change the course of Harry Lauder's life.

CHAPTER NINE

"One of my acts suddenly ill. Can you fill place at ten o'clock tonight?
                                                                    TINSLEY."

Ten o'clock. It was after six now. Lauder caught up the bag which held his costumes and dashed down the stairs again. An hour later he was in Tinsley's office.

"Glad to see you, Lauder. Beastly luck. One of my acts suddenly got ill. I thought of you. Would you mind filling in? Just one song'll do. I warn you, my audiences are hard. Anybody will tell you that about the audience at Gatti's. They're hard and they're sophisticated. If they don't like you, they'll let you know it quick enough. Now, you understand, don't you, that this is just for one night? Just filling in for an emergency until I can get someone else?"

"Aye. I ken that an' I'm gratefu' for th' chance, Mr. Tinsley."

"You may not be when this night is over. Well, there won't be time to rehearse with the orchestra, but the leader's back there somewhere and you can give him your music. The stage manager'll fix you up with a dressing room." Tinsley became busy with some papers on his desk.

Lauder went in search of the orchestra leader, and gave him his book of music. "I'll open wi' Number One—*Tobermory*. If I get an encore—"

"Tinsley says you'll only sing one song."

"Aye, but if I—if I—*get* an encore, it'll be Number Four, *Th' Lass o' Killecrankie*. Gie me the introduction forte."

"All right," muttered the leader, and turned away.

In the dressing room, which boasted only of a chair, a shelf and a mirror, Harry hung up his costumes, laid his make-up neatly on the shelf before the large oblong mirror, stacked his walking sticks against the wall. Then he went out into the street in search of a cheap restaurant; but after he had ordered, he found that he was unable to eat. It was suddenly difficult to swallow. He sat there, nervously toying with the fork. How could Tinsley be so sure that the people would want only one song? Well, a person must hope for the best—and hoping, he would have a change of costume all ready in the wings. If he failed to make good tonight, he would go straight back to Glasgow on the first train next morning. He would forget London forever.

Back in the dressing room long before the time for his act, he put on his make-up with more than usual care. If they liked him, he was made. Well, he would give them the best he had, and a man could do no more. He thought of Nance and her reassuring statements that folks were folks everywhere. He would not let himself be afraid. He would not fail. But even while he kept saying this, his hands were shaking. The small room seemed suddenly airless.

At last he was dressed and ready, and there was well over a half hour to wait. He paced back and forth. The room had a bare floor and its walls were almost completely covered with the signatures of former acts which had occupied it. At last Lauder sat down again and stared bleakly, unseeingly at the names.

Every passing moment brought greater apprehension. It was agony, this waiting. At long last came the callboy, knocking at his door.

"Hey, you're on."

"Aye," said Harry, and his eyes had a dazed look. He picked up his change of costume, his crooked walking stick, went down the stairs and out to the stage. In the darkness, close to the first entrance, while the preceding act was finishing, he arranged his second costume on two chairs.

The stage manager, conscious of his authority, asked, "What's all that for?"

Harry's voice sounded curiously faint. There was a wild moment when he thought he was losing it. "In case I—get an encore."

"No encores!" ordered the stage manager gruffly. "You're only to sing one song, understand?"

Harry saw the man through a strange, flickering blur. "Aye," he answered.

The preceding act was taking its bows now, amid faint, half-hearted applause which ceased after the second bow.

Finally, there was the music for Lauder's act.

He always impersonated some quaint, comic, lovable Scots type. The music was fortissimo and jaunty, about two choruses being played before he made his entrance. The entrance itself was jovial and spirited. He had a peculiar, very distinct walk, a ridiculous swagger which in itself was laugh-provoking. His step was firm and quick, accompanied by a staccato beat with his heels and a thumping of his heavy, twisted blackthorn stick in time to the music. He entered laughing. First he did that characteristic little walk clear around the stage, swinging his kilt as he went. His very legs were funny; they were short, stocky, and something in the way he moved, gave the impression that his legs were both bowlegged and knock-kneed.

When he had circled the stage, he planted himself in the middle of it close to the footlights—and grinned. There was something about that grin of Harry's which compelled even the most hardened onlooker to grin right back at him. Everyone in the audience felt that that grin was personal, man-to-man, spontaneous—directed expressly to *him*. Then Harry began to sing, tempering the Scotch accent somewhat, since he realized how important it was that he be understood. This was part of the secret of his success—the spectators were never in doubt as to what he meant.

The first chorus over, he would begin a few stories. He had a regular line of patter, apropos of the song, which was extremely original. Later, people would quote him, but the stories only sounded silly when other people said them. He told these stories simply, apparently without the least striving for effect, with no attempt at what the performers would call "mugging" or "hokum." He was just a homely little Scotsman having a very good time, telling a story he just happened to remember, and which he was sure that his good friends—Mr. and Mrs. Audience—would enjoy. He had an uncanny faculty for feeling the pulse of his audience, and he would cater to that, always stopping just before they had had enough of him.

The first song over, he made his exit, changed his make-up, and returned. He might come back as a schoolboy with a slate, singing *I'm th' Saftest o' th' Family*, or he might return as a very old man singing *When I was Twenty-one*. When he grew famous and people everywhere had come to love him and to know his songs, the audience would sing with him, joining in the choruses as naturally and unself-consciously as if everyone were comfortably at home, all a lot of cronies. Even when the act was over, they would never let him go, and from all parts of the house men's and women's voices would call for the songs which he might have omitted that night.

An act in vaudeville had to be restricted to a certain number of minutes. These minutes were as carefully counted as they now are over the radio. The stage manager, who stood in the first entrance, always had a piece of paper upon which was written the number of minutes which each act might be expected to run. He watched his time-sheet closely, and if the show were "running late," he would eliminate some of the "bows" by flashing the light signal to the orchestra leader to begin the music for the following act.

Lauder always upset the schedule. Even after the name of the next act had been slid into the slot on each side of the stage, and even after its music had begun, the people would go on calling for him. In the vernacular of vaudeville, Lauder always "stopped the show." Vaudeville performers knew that the act which they were to follow could help or hinder the success of their own. Some acts were "hard to follow," while others were "easy to follow"; but as Lauder grew famous, the audiences everywhere were so expectant of having a good time and were in such good humor, that all the acts on the bill were received with kindness and enthusiasm. The spirit of good-will permeated the entire theatre, even before he made his entrance.

All this, however, was yet to come. London had not yet fallen in love with Lauder. London had never seen him, never heard of him. London was frankly prejudiced against Scots comics, and when the card went up on each side of the stage announcing "Harry Lauder, Scotland's Pride," the people lounged back in their seats and the entire house was pervaded by an air of "Well-we'll-have-to-sit-through-this-it-will-soon-be-over."

Usually his mere entrance brought a laugh and a hand. But now there was not even a slight snicker. Nothing. Complete silence.

In an instant Lauder knew the prejudice which he would have to overcome. Out of that profound silence, he heard the voice of the audience, "Make me laugh—if you *can!*" it challenged. The trepidation he had felt in the wings had completely evaporated now. He began to sing. Still utter silence, as if he were singing to a lot of stone images. A faint chuckle when he reached the chorus heartened him. It gathered momentum as he progressed. By the time he had finished the song the house was in an uproar of mirth, and he made his exit to an outburst of applause. He returned for one bow, two; but instead of subsiding, the applause increased.

"Hey, you! Scotty!" yelled the stage manager excitedly. "What's your name, anyhow?" Then without waiting for an answer, he cried, "Get back out there and give 'um something else!"

While the orchestra struck up *The Lass of Killecrankie*, Harry began changing his clothes in the wings. This number went over even better than *Tobermory*. The audience was eager to laugh now, and when the song was ended they called for more. He gave them more, but still they were unsatisfied.

"Take a bow!" yelled the stage manager. "I can't give you any more time. You're stopping the show! Just take a bow!"

But a bow did not suffice. They refused to let the show continue.

"For God's sake," yelled the stage manager, "make a speech!"

"A speech?" asked Harry.

"Yes. A speech. Say something—anything! Anything!"

Harry Lauder walked down to the footlights. "I'm awfu' gratefu' for your kindness," he assured them feelingly. "This is ma first appearance i' London, but ye ken it willna' be ma last. Ma name is Harry Lauder. Remember th' name—*Harry Lauder*. And whenever ye see that name on a London ha', come an' see me!"

"You betcher life we will, 'arry!" yelled a voice from the gallery.

As he left the stage, Tinsley was waiting for him in the wings, his face flushed, his hand outstretched. "By gad, man, you've done it! Let me shake your hand! You've made a hit, Lauder! You're made. I'll book you for the rest of the week at three pounds ten shillings!"

"Done!" laughed Harry.

"Before this week's over every agent, every manager in London will be down to see your act!"

"Ye think I'll do, then?"

"Do? I tell you, you're made! You're one of the biggest hits I've ever had. Every manager in town'll be clamoring to sign you up after this!"

Tinsley was right. Before the week had ended, managers and agents were swarming into the little dressing room.

"I've decided to hold you over for another three weeks, Harry," declared Tinsley one night.

"Sorry, I canna'. I'm already booked solid for over twa years."

"What? What? That's a fine way to treat me, that is! Well, I'm glad for your sake, of course. I suppose it won't be long now before you're playing three halls a night."

Again Tinsley's prediction proved correct. Before the year had ended, Harry was playing three and even four London halls in a single night, and his salary had mounted to seven pounds at each hall. The press began to take notice of him. Reporters wrote long articles about him, interviewed him, snapped his picture wherever he went. They snapped him in the garden of his new house in a middle class London suburb named Tooting. They snapped his bulldog, Jock; his son, his wife, and finally, his new car.

Tom, Nance, Isabella, John, it would have been difficult to say which of these took the greatest pride in him. The boy was old enough now to come to the theatre and sit on a trunk watching him make up. Walking together through the London streets, John heard cabbies, policemen, pedestrians, calling out "'Ello, 'Arry!" and Harry would grin, wave his hand, and cry, "Hello! Hello!"

"You know rather a lot of people, don't you, Dad?"

"No, son, but thank God they know me. And it's these people that're going to send you to Cambridge when th' time comes."

He bought one of the first motor cars, and riding in it, Nance and Isabella would ask themselves, could all this possibly last? Could all this attention possibly last?

"Ca' canny, Nance," Isabella would say. "D'ye think ye should hae bought sae big a hoose, lass?"

"Harry wanted a hame," Nance answered. "Harry says that a mon or a woman wi'oot a hame is like a tree wi'oot roots."

"True. There's a steady head on th' lad. It isna' likely tae be turned by a' this praise he's gettin'."

Christmas; that first Christmas in London. It was a Christmas the Lauders celebrated heartily, for every manager in London was now begging Harry to sign contracts.

Isabella's gray-blue eyes had a look of childlike wonderment. It was all too much like one of her own fairy tales. She fully expected to wake up any morning and discover that the whole thing had vanished, and that her boy Harry was back in the wee cottage in Weavers Land and on his way to work in the mines.

"Th' guid Lord hae blessed me i' ma ould age," she often thought to herself nowadays.

Her girls had married honest, hardworking men and were now settled securely in their own homes. Her sons—brawny and industrious—were working steadily and doing well. Harry was always ready to help any of them who needed it, but they rarely needed it. They were content with their lot—all except Alec, who was not getting along as well on the stage as he thought he should.

Even though his brother had made such a success, Alec Lauder was too much of an individualist to copy Harry. Although Harry willingly gave Alec permission to sing his songs, Alec never did so unless the audience insisted. Alec was also a Scots comedian, but he had his own act, his own melodies.

Isabella had grown stout now, her once abundant hair was thin, and she wore it parted in the middle and drawn into a prim little knot at the back. Her face, which had never known rouge nor powder, was without wrinkles. Its contour had broadened and the muscles were sagging, but the dimples flashed as merrily as ever when she laughed, and her eyes were keen. Her dresses were now of heavy black silk, simply made, a full skirt gathered at the waist, a tight plain bodice ornamented only with little white lace collars which she crotcheted herself.

"Nance," she would say, "I mind th' time he sang for a watch!"

Nance was looking very smart these days. Still slender, still graceful, her gowns were the latest London fashion, and her dark curls were coiffed in the chic London manner. To Harry, she had grown even more beautiful than she had been as a girl. She laughed now, and patted her mother-in-law's plump hand affectionately.

"I mind the time he said he'd make a lady of me and buy me a carriage and a hoose wi' hot water. Little did we think then that it would a' come true, and that someday we'd hae a son and we'd be planning to send him to Cambridge."

"How has Harry done a' this, Nance, just for th' singin' o' a few songs? Hoots, he's gettin' rich oot o' singin'?"

"No," answered Nance, "it's no the songs he's getting rich oot of. It's the laughter."

Laughter. It went with Lauder everywhere. It followed him in a great, rippling, never-ceasing gale. To a comedian laughter is the most important thing in the world. If he "gets his laughs" he is happy. If he fails to get his laughs, he is worried. Laughs meant success. People paid money to see Harry Lauder just to get a chance to laugh. He lived in laughter. His life pivoted on laughter. Time after time Tom or Nance would walk into his dressing room long after the performance to find him still sitting there in his make-up staring dejectedly at the floor.

"What's the matter, Harry?"

He would sigh, a deep and tragic sigh. "I lost a few laughs tonight," he answered mournfully.

With the passing of years the London world was changing, but Lauder's vogue increased. The old Queen had died, and her unruly son, Edward, was managing very well indeed. The Boers had been vanquished and the land was at peace again. A few daring women were putting on bloomers and riding bicycles through the park. Older people were saying they didn't know *what* the world was coming to, and John Lauder was growing up and wanting to be a lawyer. Some of the happiest hours of his life were those in which he could boast of having beaten his father at billiards. The boy was in his early teens now, and though he had no desire to go on the stage, he showed a remarkable aptitude for music.

Nance's fond dreams for her bairn were every one to be realized. Often she looked back to their first home in Weavers Land where she and Harry had been happy on ten shillings a week. They were still happy. Luxuries, servants, cars, big hotels, prestige, none of these had changed Nance and Harry. Nance was still an expert at saving the money Harry made.

They both realized that someday the time would come when Harry would not be earning these incredible sums. Who knew? He might fall suddenly ill. The public taste might change overnight. Too, the time would come when they would both be wanting a long rest. They must save to make themselves independent.

"*Ca' canny!*" had been Isabella's advice—and they followed it still, although she was no longer there to give it to them.

She had died in 1905, and Harry learned what it meant to go on the stage and laugh—when a loved one lay dead. He had seen other troupers do it. He had seen them standing in the wings with tears streaming down their faces, and then at the familiar sound of their own entrance music, he had watched the bowed head raise, the sagging shoulders straighten, the tear-wet face break into a brilliant smile; and when the act was over they took their bows, laughing, dancing, flinging kisses. Fellow players sympathized, but no one thought strange that the act went on as usual; no one thought it heroic; it was simply part of the game.

Harry's songs at this time included *Saftest o' th' Family, She's Ma Daisy, Tobennory, Fou th' Noo, Stop Yer Ticklin', Jock,* and *The Lass of Killecrankie.*

One night as he was leaving the theatre the stage doorman handed him a letter. It was written in a lady's hand and on scented pink stationery. Today this sort of thing is politely called "fan mail." Earlier in the century it was more frankly labeled "mash notes."

The old man winked. "So, you love the lassies, Harry?" he asked.

"I love *a* lassie," Harry answered, "and I'm gaen hame tae her th' noo."

As he walked away from the stage door the words echoed and re-echoed in his brain. "I love a lassie—I love a lassie—I love a lassie."

It was a song and he knew it—a song twitching to be written. Gradually other words followed:

> "I love a lassie,
> A bonny Hieland lassie,
> She's as pure as th' heather in th' dell. . . ."

It was being more and more suggested to him that he go to America, but Lauder was having all he could do to fill engagements in Britain. To him America was a fabulous place, a place of wealth and aggressiveness. He knew that salaries in America were even larger than those in London. He had heard of Broadway, of New York's great theatres—the Knickerbocker, the New York, The Folies Bergere, Keith and Proctor's Fifth Avenue, the Winter Garden, the Hippodrome, the Casino.

He had heard of a vaudevillian named Gertrude Hoffman who got three thousand a week, and a buxom woman named Eva Tanguay who wore white tights and got two thousand five hundred a week, and of a female impersonator named Julian Eltinge who got a thousand five hundred a week, and of Lillian Russell who got a thousand a week. The names of great American vaudeville entertainers were spoken with respect among the Variety artistes in London—Irene Franklin, McIntyre and Heath, Pat Rooney, Houdini, The Four Cohans. And Broadway was hearing about one Harry Lauder.

It was in 1907 that Lauder received an offer from America. The sum was staggering. It was to be only a five weeks' engagement in New York City. He considered it thoughtfully. If he failed in New York he would in all probability lose his great prestige in London. He knew the London audiences; he knew what they wanted; he knew exactly where to expect every titter, every laugh. Britain was home to him, but America was strange, unknown. Seemingly, the more England had of him the more she wanted, but would that be true if America proved unappreciative? Failures in show business are dangerous, even fatal. Besides, how would Nance feel about it? If he made good in America, it would mean that future bookings would compel him to travel from one end of that vast country to the other—Canada, the south, the west, the east. How would Nance feel about leaving her home for months at a time like that?

He was playing outside of London when the cable arrived, and Nance was at home in Tooting. He sent her a wire:

"Have offer to leave for America. If I accept will you go with me?

Love,
HARRY."

Her reply puzzled him. He read it, and looked up at Tom.

"Tom," he asked, "what do you ken aboot Ruth?"

"Ruth, Harry? What Ruth?"

"Ruth i' the Bible."

"Oh, *that* Ruth. Why, tae tell th' truth, Harry, offhand I canna' recall much aboot Ruth. I believe she married somebody named Boaz, but I dinna recall the story."

"Have we got a Bible, mon?"

"A Bible? Aye, I think so. It's doon i' your trunk somewhere. What do ye want it for, Harry?"

"I want to read it."

As Tom began to rummage in the trunk for the Bible, Harry read the telegram again.

"Ruth. Chapter One. Verse Sixteen.

Love,
NANCE."

"Here's the Bible, Harry. Are ye going tae read it *a'*?"

"No, just the Book o' Ruth, Verse sixteen, Chapter one."

"Here it is."

Harry took the Book and looked down at the page.

"And Ruth said," he read, " 'Intreat me not to leave thee, or to return from following after thee: For whither thou goest, I will go; and where thou lodgest, I will lodge. Thy people shall be my people, and thy God, my God.'"

CHAPTER TEN

However, when the time came to leave for America, Nance was ill, not seriously, but she needed rest and quiet, and as the trip would be a short one, Harry decided that it was best for her to remain in England; added to this, her brother Tom was ill with rheumatic fever. But the contract had been signed and must, therefore, be fulfilled; consequently, Harry and John sailed from Liverpool in mid-October.

He had a large repertoire of songs and it was a little difficult to decide which would prove most pleasing to the American audience. There must, of course, be *I Love a Lassie*. For weeks Harry labored over the words, unable to evolve anything which satisfied him, at last he took the idea to Gerald Grafton, a song writer, and between the two of them the verse and chorus were finally achieved. The melody was entirely Harry's. It came blithely singing itself into his head one day, and he never changed a note of it. This song, was to endure for over thirty years, proved a greater hit any Harry had had heretofore. England was enthusiastic about it—but America?

America was vastly different from England. Everything there would be different. For instance, in America would be daily matinees and one evening performance would play only one theatre a night instead of dashing to three or four. (How adept Tom had become at driving the small car at top speed from one hall to another, dodging in and out of traffic!)

To the theatrical manager show business is large gamble. In England, as far as Lauder was concerned, the sense of risk was eliminated. He was a sure-fire attraction. Should business fall off, an English manager knew Lauder's name outside his theatre could be depended to fill the house to capacity. But to the American put was entirely unknown. A member of the Klaw and Erlanger firm had "caught" his act in London and cabled that Lauder was a "bet." On the strength of this, Klaw and Erlanger were gambling on Lauder. As far as they were concerned he was an unknown quantity, a dark horse.

Although his salary for five weeks was assured, this trip was even a greater risk for Lauder than for the mai who were exploiting him. Shrewd in business matters, I was not insensible to the risk entailed. To a star, failures are costly, often fatal. His position in England was solid its seeming solidarity would crumble if America failed to appreciate him. He knew full well what it would mean if he failed to make good in New York. Inside of a week the news would flash throughout England that Lauder had "flopped" on Broadway, and he would return to London, his aura of success a little less shiny. In England there was always a crowd about the stage door, waiting for hours to see him enter or leave, a jolly, noisy crowd, calling out hearty salutations and good wishes. This, he had heard, was not the custom in America. The more he thought about it, the more formidable America became, and the more he regretted signing the contract.

"Why don't you try your luck in America, Harry?" For a long time now, people had been suggesting this, but he had taken no notice of it. America had always interested him. American history had enthralled him. He knew all about Lincoln and Washington, and often thought that someday he would visit America as a tourist.

And now, here was America looming ahead, closer and closer with each passing moment. Could he, Lauder kept asking himself, compete against the great American entertainers? The trip across the Atlantic took two weeks in those days, and every hour Harry's gloom and restlessness increased.

"What's the matter, Dad?" asked John when they were two nights from Sandy Hook.

"Weel, son, I'll tell ye. This five weeks' engagement is only a kind o' try-out. I might not make guid. There's no knowin'. I'm thinkin' I should hae left weel enough alone an' stayed i' London. Th' greatest artistes i' th' world are i' America."

"Don't worry about that, Dad. You'll go over all right."

"Ye think so, lad?"

"Sure. I know it. I met lots of Americans when I made my six weeks' trip to Canada last year. They'll like you, all right, and you'll like them. And anyhow, if they don't, the ships are still running back to England."

"You're only sixteen, lad, but you've a wise head on your shoulders; still—I can't help wishin' I hadna' come."

"No, no, Dad. You were right to come. You won't be sorry. You wait and see."

John's confidence was inspiring. After that talk, Harry felt better, almost like his old self again. After all, why count on the bad when the good was quite as likely?

But next day in the salon he chanced upon an old New York newspaper. Idly he picked it up and glanced through it. He had not read far when he came upon an article signed "Alan Dale." Here all his forebodings were verified. Here in black and white was the proof of what lay in store for him.

For years Dale was a power on Broadway. Actors dreaded him, feared him, winced and writhed under his criticism. His articles were brilliant, widely read, and often merciless. Harry had never heard of Dale, but Dale had heard of Harry. It seemed that Mr. Dale considered the English people slightly feeble-minded because of their enthusiasm for Lauder. According to Dale, Lauder was nothing more than a buffoon. He poked brutal fun at Lauder's voice, his legs, his nose, even the way he breathed. According to Dale, Lauder had nothing America wanted. Lauder should have stayed at home. His forthcoming debut in America was certain to be a fiasco.

Harry had a quick temper, and he was never more angry in his life than he was now. His face flushed, his eyes glittering, he went in search of John. To his surprise, John read the notice—and laughed.

"I see nothin' to laugh at!" stormed Harry. "So, that's America, is it? Condemnin' me wi'oot even hearin' me! It's like this Dale reached oot an' hit me when I wasna' lookin'. I'd like to take a poke at *him—and* I wull if I ever meet him! I wull so."

All the rest of the day excerpts from Dale's article kept flashing through his mind, nagging at him, taunting him, stinging like wasps. Lauder never saved press notices and rarely read them, and now Dale became to him a symbol of the entire American press. Moment by moment his resentment mounted. Just let him meet this Dale, that was all. Tomorrow morning they would arrive in New York. Harry wanted just one thing now, and that was to "take a poke" at Dale.

As the boat approached the harbor and the great metropolis loomed ahead, his mood increased. A gray-blue haze hung like chiffon over the city, pierced through by the tall buildings rising aloofly, coldly, sharply. That would be typical of America, Lauder surmised—sharpness, aloofness, coldness.

When the boat docked a crowd of newspaper men swarmed aboard, surrounding him suddenly, snapping questions at him with the rapidity of machine guns. He had never experienced anything quite like this, and he did not know how to cope with it. Later he was to become accustomed to the technique of the American press, but now it confused him. He believed they were all replicas of Dale, and the thought came that perhaps Dale was among them.

"Which one of ye is Dale?" he roared. "Let him come forward an' fight like a mon, that's a'!"

They laughed good-naturedly. "Dale? Who's Dale? Never heard of him!"

He knew they were making fun of him, and he was in no mood for that sort of thing.

"Hey," said one of them at last, "are you a comedian or a tragedian? What's the idea? You better lay off this fighting stuff, brother, that won't get you anywhere with us, you know!"

On the outskirts of the crowd members of the Klaw and Erlanger staff, who had been sent to meet him, were looking distrait. The report they took back to the office was anything but flattering.

"The boss sure pulled a boner this time. If that guy's a comedian, I'll eat my hat. In the first place, he wants to fight everybody. He stands up there and antagonizes the press! In the second place he had an old coat on and he looked like an immigrant. In the third place, the boob's hardly more than four feet tall."

"Yeah. He may be the cat's whiskers in England, but he certainly *ain't Broadway!*"

But there were Scotsmen in New York who knew how to welcome a compatriot. Hundreds of them, accompanied by pipers in their colorful Highland dress, were waiting on the pier and the place rang with their hooches and their calls, even topping the sound of the bagpipes which "blew the wanderer ashore" in the good old Scots tradition. Outside the pier a motor car waited, tartan-draped. The mad speed at which it tore through the crowded traffic made Harry grip the sides of it in sheer panic. When at last he and his son arrived at the Hotel Knickerbocker and the door of their room was closed, he sank breathlessly into a chair. How, he wondered, would he ever live through the next five weeks? So, this was New York—teeming, bustling, noisy. Oh, if he could only turn right around and go back home again!

He had arrived on Friday. On Monday he was to open with a matinee at the New York Theatre on Times Square. On Saturday Harry, in his kilt, and John, smartly dressed and handsome, walked along Broadway, across Forty-second Street, and down Fifth Avenue as far as the Waldorf-Astoria on Thirty-fourth Street. The height of the buildings, the tense, quick pace at which New Yorkers walked, the rumble of the elevated trains, the clanging of the streetcars, all this gave him the feeling that he was being smothered, that the buildings were going to fall on top of him. It seemed suddenly difficult to breathe. On Sunday he was desperately homesick and miserable.

"When I get back to bonny Scotland—" he began, and stopped.

"Why, that's a song! There's a *song* i' that! An' someday I'll be singin' it to ither hamesick folks. There maun be millions o' people a' over th' world as hungry for their ain native land as I am richt noo. It's to them I'll be singin' ma new song!"

Abruptly, his homesickness was forgotten. He was concerned only with the song which that moment had been catapulted into his brain. So engrossed was he in the thought of the new song that he forgot the passing of time, forgot the street noises, forgot the strangeness of the new world.

He was still thinking about the song when he and John entered the star dressing room on Monday. As they were unpacking his costumes, laying out his make-up, stacking his walking sticks against the wall, there was a knock on the door and Harry opened it to find a dark, pleasant-looking young man smiling at him as if they had been friends all their lives.

"Hello," said the newcomer, "I'm Will Morris. I'm in charge of the bookings for the Klaw and Erlanger office. How are you?"

"Oh, I'm fine," answered Harry, and went on with his unpacking. "Never felt better i' ma life. Come in. Come in."

From accounts received at the office, Morris had expected to meet someone disagreeable, belligerent, temperamental. He was an expert at dealing with stars who were "hard to handle," and had come prepared to pacify, but here was only an amiable, simple little man with the friendliest grin in the world. He liked Lauder at once and Lauder liked him. For well over twenty-five years these two were to be associated with each other and contracts in writing were never necessary between them.

Later, people were to say that Morris "made" Lauder, while others as steadfastly maintained that "Lauder made Morris." Severing his connection with the Klaw and Erlanger office, Morris later became Lauder's American manager.

"The house is sold out," announced Morris, "standing room only. I bet every Caledonian in town has bought a seat to see you. I suppose you'll find the American audiences a lot different from the English audiences, though. Of course, the critics'll be out there, too, and I warn you, Mr. Lauder, these New York critics can be pretty rough."

"I ken *that*," replied Harry feelingly.

"Well, I just wanted to make sure everything was all right. Good luck to you—the best in the world."

"Thanks." As Morris turned to leave, Harry asked, "What does an American audience do if it doesna' like ye? Does it boo? Does it throw things?"

"No, not any more. Nowadays, if an American audience doesn't like you, it just—*freezes*. It exudes ice. And when it's froze, believe me, it stays *froze!* You might as well play to a lot of corpses. On the other hand, if it likes you—well, good luck again."

"Hmm," muttered Lauder when the door closed. "Weel, th' best I can gie them is th' *most* I can gie them. I mind th' time your mither told me that audiences 're just folks, an' that folks are folks everywhere. Your mither's usually richt, laddie. I've trusted her judgment for a long time. I've been thinkin' so much aboot th' new song, I've had no chance to contemplate failure. It's odd—on Friday I thought that failure was a possibility. On Saturday I decided it was inevitable—but today, laddie, today it's—unthinkable!"

John seated himself on the old hamper.

"Dad," he announced knowingly, "*you'll paralyze them!*"

CHAPTER ELEVEN

New York audiences cold? Aloof? Lauder felt their warmth, their responsiveness before he had been on the stage two minutes. Their enthusiasm was a vitalizing thing, and Lauder was giving them one of the best performances of his entire career. It is a stimulating and inspiring sensation, this sense of being one with an audience. His act usually ran from sixty to seventy minutes, but it was two hours before they let him go.

Sitting out front, Morris kept saying to himself, "This fellow's not good—he's *great!* He's one of the greatest comedians America's ever seen!"

Lauder's act over, he left the theatre hurriedly, but he knew everybody and everybody knew him. Consequently, he was stopped many times before he reached the street.

"This man's marvelous!" people exclaimed. "This man's a *bet!*"

To which Morris laughingly replied, "You're wrong. This man's a *sure thing!*"

He reached the stage entrance, just as Lauder and his son were leaving. "I want to have a talk with you," he said. "There's a quiet little restaurant near here where we can talk in peace."

When they were seated at the table, Morris spoke earnestly. "Lauder," he leaned forward, his fine dark eyes glowing, "you're not only a great comedian, you're the best comedian I've ever seen. You're coming back to America. No vaudeville house in the country will be big enough to hold the crowds you'll draw. You'll travel. You'll go everywhere. You'll pack 'um in. You won't travel in your own private car, I'm going to get you the President's private car! You won't make thousands, you'll make millions."

Harry laughed. "Weel, if you do only *half* of that, it'll be guid enough." He signaled the waiter. "Do ye ken what a Scots contract is?" he asked.

"No, sir."

Harry turned to Morris. "Gie me your thumb."

Wonderingly, Morris reached out his hand. Lauder linked his own thumb tight with Morris', lifting both their hands in mid-air for the waiter to witness.

"*This,*" he announced to the waiter, "is a Scots contract. He's ma manager!"

The Scots contract was the only one the two men ever had.

Next morning while Lauder still slept, John rushed out, bought every newspaper and read them all.

"Harry Lauder Triumphs!"

"Lauder, the Merry Scot, captivates New York."

"Dad! Dad!" cried the boy. "Dad! Wake up! Wake up!"

"Wh— what is it, laddie?"

"Notices. The press notices. Let me read them to you. Listen. Here's the *New York Telegram*— 'Lauder comes, sings, conquers. Merry Caledonian wins big audience at New York Theatre!'"

"New York," said Lauder, when his son had finished reading the notices, "I love you!"

Eyes bright with excitement, John sat on the edge of his bed. "I knew you'd do it. I knew you'd do it!"

"I think you're surer o' me, lad, than I am o' ma sel'."

"I just knew you'd do it," answered John.

Harry always maintained that these first five weeks in America passed like a "dwam." The winds were high and brisk. There was something invigorating and electric in the very air of New York. Every theatre was open. To Harry, everything and everybody seemed marvelously, intensely alive. Reporters waylaid him in the hotel lobby. Invitations poured in upon him from everywhere. There was a stream of brilliant receptions, banquets, luncheon and even breakfast engagements. Crowds waited outside the hotel for a glimpse of him. Only now and then could he find an hour when he could wander through the streets alone with his son. Why did everybody hurry so? How could people live in this endless turmoil?

"It's wonderful, isn't it. Dad?"

"Aye, laddie, it's wonderful. It is so. It's so wonderful it near takes ma breath awa', but I wouldna' *live* i' this town for a million dollars. Do they never get tired o' th' bustlin' an' th' scramblin'? What're they a' hurryin' *to*? An' what are they a' hurryin' *for*? Ah, but she's graund an' bonny, is America. I wish we could stay longer."

But British bookings did not permit this, although now every city in America was clamoring for him. It seemed now incredible that he had been reluctant to come, and he was strongly tempted to throw over all British engagements and accede to the almost frantic pleas to remain. The wealth to be made in the United States was beyond anything he had ever imagined. Yes, he would come back.

Never had Lauder been happier than he was on the *Carmania* as she sailed for England. An enormous crowd had gathered at the pier to wish him Godspeed, and he had stood waving at them as long as he could see the glint of a single handkerchief.

The trip home was an endless delight. Not only was it two weeks of much-needed rest, but most precious of all it was two weeks of uninterrupted companionship with his son.

Growing interest in Lauder had prompted him to write a book, *Harry Lauder at Home and on Tour.* He had enjoyed the writing of it, and he discussed with John other books that he meant to write—when he found the time. They had so much in common, these two, so much to talk about. His work had permitted him little opportunity for companionship with the boy, but this had not affected their singular closeness. Pacing the deck of the ship together those early December days, Harry would sing over to John the new song, *When I Get Back to bonny Scotland,* which now took definite form and rhythm. Perhaps because its melody was developed largely while strolling the *Carmania's* deck, it had taken on a marching, rollicking air. John played it over and over on the ship's piano, as vitally interested in its progress as was Harry himself.

Life, thought Lauder, had given him everything, even more than he had asked or imagined. Most of all, it had given him Nance and John. He was thirty-seven. His health was robust, his vitality seemingly inexhaustible. Never had he earned so much as he had during these brief five weeks, and this affluence was only a sample of the vast wealth that lay ahead of him.

Other performers, even those who at one time had been as famous as himself, found themselves penniless in their old age and sometimes benefit performances were given for them. This must never, he decided firmly, be the case with Harry Lauder. He had known poverty, its ugliness, its bitterness, and he had inherited his mother's horror of ever accepting one penny of charity.

Lauder's "closeness" became something of a legend. "Bawbees" is the Scotch word for half-penny; roughly the word means "money," and it was common knowledge that Lauder was "verra fond o' th' bawbees." At first these stories irked Harry and he began by fiercely resenting them. But he was beginning to realize that the stories of his stinginess were news, and it was he who now began to tell them upon himself at every opportunity. Too, being a first-rate showman, he would often put on a little act for the benefit of the newspaper men.

There was a particular landing when Lauder was encircled by newspaper men and by a crowd of strangers. Since each song required a complete change of make-up, he was compelled to carry with him a vast amount of baggage. A porter, grunting and perspiring, piled trunk upon trunk, bag upon bag, and finally stood there, mopping his brow, gazing expectantly at Lauder. Lauder grinned and walked over to him while the press looked on, scenting a story.

"Weel," smiled Harry, "thank you and—take this for your trouble."

The porter stretched out his hand—and Lauder dropped a dime into it. It made a laughable story. It was "good copy." No one knew that before the porter had touched one of those bags, Lauder had sought him out, privately told him to exaggerate the grunting and the brow-mopping—and in utmost secrecy had given the man a twenty-dollar tip!

Nevertheless, the "bawbees" had an important place in Harry's life. When he died he meant to leave John and Nance well provided for. Besides, in the uncertainty of the theatrical world, who knew when the tide of public approbation might turn? How often had he watched it turn, seemingly for no reason, and sometimes almost overnight? The thing to do was to save and to keep saving so that he and his could be independent. Let them call him "close" and "mean," he owed them nothing—and, please God, he never would.

Fortunately, Nance was not the sort who craved luxuries. Neither he nor John had ever worn any socks or gloves but those which Nance had knitted. She was never happier than when she sent the servants away, tied on a big apron, scrubbed the kitchen, cooked parritch, mixed up a great batch of scones and oatcakes. She was four years younger than Harry, his exact height, and she still had about her that singular quality of freshness and spotlessness which had characterized her as a girl. Seemingly, her eyes were bluer and brighter than they had ever been.

Though their lives had been spent almost entirely in cities, the three Lauders felt a kinship with the country, with broad open fields, with the moors and the hills. They dreamed of one day having a farm somewhere on the banks of the Clyde, a place of wide acres and great old trees, of their own sheep grazing in the valley, and vegetables popping up out of their own earth. It would not be long now, they realized, before that estate would be a reality.

Harry still found it amazing how much money there was to be made in show business, not alone in the theatres, but with his records. Phonographs were the rage, small wooden boxes, like tiny coffins, from which sprouted a great, lily-shaped horn. In lonely hillside cabins, in palaces, on farms and houseboats, people everywhere were winding up phonographs, slipping a little wax tube on a metal cylinder, and listening to the voices of Harry Lauder, Ethel Levey, Eddie Leonard, Fritzi Scheff, or even Caruso and Melba.

Yes, the country estate would soon be an actual, tangible thing, a place of infinite repose, a place away from the noise and the dust and the lights, where Harry would live like a genuine Scots laird; a place where he and his could go walking for miles over the heather on their own land, and all about them would be the green, quiet hills. And one day John's children would be there, and every Christmas they would all cluster about the great fireplace and Harry would tell them stories.

"An' *that*" he maintained, "wull be ma best audience."

On his return Lauder found himself in greater demand than ever with the London audiences. Though he had no press agent, scarcely a day passed without an article about him in the newspapers. His every move was of interest.

"Harry Lauder makes triumphant return."

"Harry Lauder seen last Sunday at Brighton."

"Lauder buys son an American car."

"Lauder's son runs car into ditch."

Scarcely had he disembarked in England before cables began arriving beseeching him to return to America. He was eager now to make the trip. It was not only the money which drew him back and back year after year, it was America itself. Never did it lose its charm for him, never did he cease to delight in the singular vitality of this strident, energetic new world.

The second American tour in 1908 was to last only fourteen weeks. Bookings, at a salary of five thousand dollars a week, called for a week in Boston, Chicago, Pittsburgh, Philadelphia, and ten weeks in New York City.

He arrived on the *Lusitania* and the Cunard pier was black with the hundreds of people waiting for a glimpse of him. This time these consisted not only of his own countrymen, but of a multitude of his fellow vaudevillians, who had banded together forming a powerful beneficent organization called "The White Rats."

Critics now were even more enthusiastic than previously over "The Inimitable Lauder." Everywhere one went, these days, one heard sophisticated New Yorkers singing:

"She's ma Daisy, ma bonny Daisy . . ."

or:

"I'm th' safest o' th' family,
I'm th' simple Johnnie Raw . . ."

Constant adulation, coupled with the vast amounts of money which kept rolling in in exhaustless golden waves, left Harry speechless.

How long ago it seemed now since he and Mac had sat on opposite sides of beds in cheap Scottish hotels calling themselves rich when spread out between them on the counterpane was a hundred pounds, out of which must be paid railroad expenses, salaries, advertising.

Back in England in 1909 Lauder played his first command performance.

It was September. Edward the Seventh was visiting Rufford Abbey as the guest of Lord and Lady Saville. When Her Ladyship asked His Majesty what entertainment he would prefer, Edward answered promptly, "Harry Lauder!"

"John," asked Harry some days later, his blue eyes twinkling with merriment, "how would ye like to make a trip to Rufford Abbey to see th' King?"

"Fine!" answered the boy with a broad smile.

"We'll start tomorrow, then."

"You mean it? You're really serious, Dad? It's a command performance?"

"Aye. An' I'll want ye to accompany me."

"Me?"

"You're ma favorite accompanist, lad."

"Righto, Dad. I'll do my best."

"Done!" said Harry, and laughingly, they shook hands.

Arriving at the Abbey, he presented a list of his songs to Her Ladyship. "If His Majesty wull just indicate th' songs he prefers to hear—?"

"Yes, Mr. Lauder. Quite. I'll submit this list to His Majesty and let you know his decision."

An hour later she was back. "His Majesty says that you are just to start at the beginning and he'll tell you when you're to stop."

This proved to be one of the smallest audiences to which Lauder had ever played. It consisted of not more than fifty people. Seats had been placed in rows about a small platform. In the center of the first row sat Edward, gray-bearded, bulky, handsome. Small though it was, this audience proved no different from other audiences, for they joined heartily in the choruses, the voice of the King topping them all.

"I love a lassie," sang the King of England, "a bonny Hieland lassie. . . ."

Then came *Tobermory* and *Stop Yer Ticklin', Jock.* After each song Harry's eyes met those of his King anticipating an uplifted hand as a signal to stop the program, but the King kept on beaming, singing, applauding. The twelfth song on Harry's list was *When I Get Back to bonny Scotland*, and for this His Majesty's applause was as vigorous as it had been in the beginning. Finally the little Scotsman walked to the front of the stage and addressed his Sovereign.

"I'm sorry," he announced simply, "I didna' bring any more of ma music!"

The King laughed and applauded. Some minutes later he sent word to Harry's dressing room that he wanted to meet him. Hale, jovial, democratic, Edward, now sixty-eight years old, had the knack of putting everyone at his ease, and so the man who had been bom in a "but and ben" and the man who had been born in Buckingham Palace, talked and laughed together like old friends. It was the proudest moment of Lauder's life, not when the King told him that he had enjoyed his performance, but when he congratulated Lauder on his son and said how much he had enjoyed John's playing.

Nine months later Edward was dead after an illness of three days.

Long live George the Fifth.

Edward had been crowned the year after Harry had come to London. His nine years on the throne had been a time of peace and prosperity for England. What was in store for the new King, the short man with the brown beard and the grave, kindly eyes?

One heard a great deal, these days, of the efficiency of Germany, of the scientific research that was going on there. Germany's power in trade and manufacture was striding ahead rapidly. She was commercially energetic, rich and shrewd. But what of that? England was rich, too, and so was America. Harry had a swift recollection of Theodore Roosevelt, who had invited him to visit the White House last year.

His second term was nearing its close, and Roosevelt told Harry of his plan to visit England after he had finished with the African hunting trip to which he had been looking forward.

"I'm going to places where they say I can't go," declared Teddy, "but you know, Lauder, the word I hate most in the English language is *can't!*"

Harry's first impression of this man was one of aggressiveness, keen eyes, huge shoulders—and teeth. They were friends from the start. Not even King Edward, Harry thought, had a greater sense of humor than Roosevelt, and no one in the world could laugh more heartily.

The estate the Lauders had dreamed of was now theirs. Surrounded by twelve acres, it was in Dunoon, a popular watering place, near Glasgow.

Here, though they had servants, Nance arose early, cooked the breakfast, often did the washing, wiped up the flagstones of the kitchen floor, dusted and swept, went to market in her pony cart, and brought all her purchases home herself. In the afternoons and the evenings she went about in the village visiting the old people and cuddling her neighbor's children.

By 1911, Lauder's tours in America were lasting as long as six months. He was now the highest-priced man on the stage. His salary was one thousand dollars a night, all expenses paid. Nance was a little plumper, her cheeks a bit more rounded, but she was still as incapable of putting on airs as she had been when she was just Jamie Vallance's daughter, Annie. John was at Cambridge now, continuing his music, studying law, and she was as proud of her son as she was of her husband.

Never had the American stage been more brilliant. The country was honeycombed with road shows which spent a night or a week in every hamlet and city. The Stage Hand Union had not yet made the cost of production prohibitive, and both vaudeville and dramatic theatres were springing up like proverbial mushrooms.

In New York the Ziegfeld Follies was presenting Bessie McCoy, Fannie Brice, Leon Errol, The Dolly Sisters and Bert Williams.

Legitimate theatres blazed from their marquees such illustrious names as Richard Bennett, Margaret Anglin, Ruth Chatterton, Billie Burke, Marguerite Clark, Blanche Ring, Edmund Breese, David Warfield.

Vaudeville theatres were "packing 'um in" with Gallagher and Shean, Vesta Victoria, Valeska Surratt, Emma Carus, Blossom Seeley and Belle Baker.

Never had America been more amusement-conscious. In ballrooms people were dancing the *Turkey Trot* and the *Texas Tommy*. Caruso was reigning in glory at the Metropolitan. The streets were becoming more and more crowded with Oldsmobiles, Fords, Cadillacs, Marmons. Everyone was reading Edith Wharton. Every debutante had to learn to manage a train before she appeared in an evening gown; button shoes were ultra-smart; white fox was worn on everything; billboards flung out the greeting, "Good morning! Have you used Pears' Soap?" and Harry Lauder was playing golf with President Taft.

They made an ill-assorted twosome, Taft very tall and fat, Harry very short. It seemed to Harry that Taft smiled all the time. Looking back upon that day he could not remember a moment during their game when Taft was not smiling, even when Harry beat him by two holes.

People were becoming interested in a new kind of entertainment, called moving pictures. Those "in the know" agreed that of course it could not last. It was just a craze. The public was sure to tire of it. But each vaudeville performance ended with one of these new moving pictures, and strangely, people remained to see them. The new media brought new names—John Bunny, Henry B. Walthall, Alice Joyce, Mary Pickford, Bronco Billie Anderson.

Lauder was forty-one, his handclasp as firm, his laugh as hearty as ever, his zest for singing unabated, and songs still had a way of tumbling out of the nowhere into his brain. He had little time to spend at Laudervale in Dunoon, but the tranquil hours there were among the happiest of his life. Strolling alone one evening along the banks of the

Clyde, puffing at his pipe, it came to him how good and beautiful the world was. Behind him was the very house of which he and Nance had dreamed, with its stately rooms and huge old fireplaces. About him were his own acres, stretching off into the distance. Ahead of him walked a young couple, arms about each other.

Frankly romantic and sentimental, Harry smiled. "There they go, bless them! It's the ould, ould story—a lad roamin' i' th' gloamin' wi' his lassie."

Suddenly he stopped. Roamin' i' th' gloamin'—why, it was a song! He started walking again, puffing at his pipe, his blue eyes alight with the holy joy of creation.

> "Roamin' i' th' gloamin' by th' bonny banks o' Clyde,
> Roamin' i' th' gloamin' wi' ma lassie by ma side. . . ."

But it was two years before the song was presented to the public. During that time Lauder rehearsed it every day, sung it often after he got into bed at night, laid awake thinking about it. The costume underwent innumerable changes before it suited him, but finally *Roamin' i' th' Gloamin'* took first place among the Lauder songs.

1912—and Germany growing richer, more vain, more arrogant.

For years now teachers had been instructing German youth with the idea that Germany was greater than any country on earth. Germans were superior both physically and intellectually to all other peoples. Germany, they said, was destined to lead the world. Other nations? Hopelessly inefficient and decadent. The Germans were a race of conquerors.

The rest of the world smiled tolerantly at this. It was a world at peace, a world engrossed in spending, working, dancing, dining. For all her wealth, her growing navy, her pompous and assertive claims, Germany seemed only a little absurd.

Germany's Emperor, Victoria's grandson, went swaggering all over Europe—Rome, London, Constantinople, Vienna, Palestine—a man with stiffly up-twirling mustachios, a crippled arm, and a penchant for splendid uniforms with long, flowing white capes. Pictures of him were printed everywhere, wearing a helmet, perched upon which was a silver eagle with greedily outspread wings. His navy was increasing, his army was growing. God, he proclaimed, was his "divine Ally," and from one end of Germany to the other rang the feverish, adoring cry, "*Hoch der Kaiser.*"

Britain's king was a quiet, unassuming little man with no liking for flowing capes and helmets, and no taste for the spectacular. Edward's son, George, with his Queen, Mary, often came to the Palace Theatre when Lauder played there.

One night George Ashton, a concert agent, came backstage saying that Their Majesties wanted to have a talk with Harry. Still in costume, Harry entered the royal box.

Delightfully informal, Their Majesties congratulated him warmly upon his performance, and the King questioned him about America. When Harry had answered George's questions, Mary asked, "How do you get your ideas for your songs, Mr. Lauder?" And when Harry had told her how a song would project itself unbidden into his head, seemingly out of a void, George wanted to know how long he practiced a song before he presented it.

It was a pleasant, friendly chat, and Harry left the royal box, returning to the stage by a door which led from the box itself. Just outside the door he stopped for a time talking to George Ashton, and finally Ashton moved away.

"Weel, guidnicht, George, an' guid luck!" Harry called after him.

As he was speaking, the door of the royal box opened, and King George stood before him.

"Good night and good luck to *you*, Harry!" called the King cheerily.

That was the type of king England had—and loved.

CHAPTER TWELVE

D o ye never get tired o' singin', Harry?" asked Nance a little wistfully.

"Never, Nance, never. I love it as much as I ever did. I love th' stage. I love th' applause. I love it all."

"Your heart's still i' your singin'."

"Aye. As much—more—than it ever was. Of course, I'm no sayin' there are not times when I'd like to sit doon an' take a wee bit rest."

Yes, there were times when he longed just to sit quietly at home, longed for more opportunities for companionship with his son. But once on the stage all that was forgotten. By 1913 Lauder had been all over Great Britain countless times. He had traveled from one end of America to the other, and now he was booked for Australia.

When the Lauders left Dunoon in 1913 they knew it would be a long time before they saw the place again.

Lauder was booked solid for years ahead. Laudervale in Dunoon—

how seldom he saw it. And Glen Branter, the new Highland estate he had bought in Argyllshire on the shores of Loch Eck—a week-end or two was all the time he had been able to spend at either place. There was never a vacation for Lauder. Sometimes nowadays he would plead to be released from engagements even for a single week, but contracts signed were contracts to be filled. Time was passing swiftly, too swiftly. How little he had seen of John!

The boy had everything in the world he wanted. He was almost finishing at Cambridge now, and he could only travel with them as far as Glasgow. They were going to Australia by way of America, and the plan was that as soon as John had finished at Cambridge, he was to start on a trip around the world, meeting them in Sydney. Harry was glad that he could give such a trip to his son. He gazed at the boy now with a deep sense of pride—slender, immaculate, looking more like Nance every day. From John, Harry's eyes wandered about him appreciatively. The small steamer that was carrying them to Glasgow was just pulling away from the little pier at Dunoon. The Clyde was serene and bonny. The snow-topped hills loomed with majestic tranquillity in the distance. How lovely, how *peaceful* the world was. As usual, a huge crowd of neighbors had gathered to bid him good-by. On the pier were the pipers, and above the sound of the bagpipes came the cries, "Good luck, Harry! Come back soon!"

At Liverpool where they sailed for New York, the crowd was even greater, but it was not so great as the crowd that awaited him in New York itself.

"Hi-ya, Harry!"

"There he is! That little guy in the kilts! That's him! That's Lauder!"

"Hello there, Harry! Welcome back!"

In America, as in Britain, people were talking of the advantages of peace. It seemed odd to Harry that people should have so much to say about peace when there was no war, and no one believed that there was likely to be any war. It was a dance-mad, amusement-mad world. Ethel Barrymore, Maude Adams, Helen Ware, Frances Wilson, Wilton Lackaye, Mary Nash, Elsie Ferguson, Otis Skinner, Ina Claire, Viola Allen, Julia Sanderson, Guy Bates Post, Nance O'Niell—these were a few of the great names that illumined the magic street called Broadway in 1913.

In Germany amusement was comparatively unimportant. Credulous young Germans were being gorged with the idea that one day they were to rule the world. Preachers shouted it from pulpits, teachers thundered it in the schools. One day this great Germany would dominate the world. Inculcated in the German mind was Count Moltke's belief that "War is an element in the order of the world ordained by God."

Other countries were beginning to view all this now with suspicion, even apprehension. Britain, vaguely alarmed, had said, "Let us stop building ships, each of us, for one year."

The Kaiser refused to consider the proposal. Bluntly he declared that his navy must increase until it was superior even to that of Britain.

Britain, however, had other things to worry about. There was this question of Irish Home Rule which was being debated so hotly in Parliament. Ireland, arming herself with guns from Germany, was talking boldly about Civil War.

Lauder's American tour ended in San Francisco. Despite the fact that he had traveled in his own special coach and had his own cook, the tour had been long and hard. It was now February, 1914. Year after year for seven years, he had been coming to America, playing small as well as large towns, and never had America been so spontaneous in its appreciation, never had it been more friendly. Lauder stories were legion.

One night during Harry's performance, someone in the gallery continued to create a disturbance. Annoyed, Lauder nevertheless kept on singing. At last a Glengarry cap came hurtling through the air to land at his feet. He smiled to himself, realizing now that whoever was creating the disturbance was one of his own countrymen. Looking up into the gallery he could see an usher walking down the aisle, bent upon ejecting the fellow.

Suddenly a frantic voice screamed, "Harry! Harry! Dinna let them put me *oot!* I kent ye i' Glasga'!"

To which Harry, stopping in the midst of his song, yelled back, "Dinna *let* them put ye oot! Remember, you're a Scotsman! *Hang on!*"

The audience roared and applauded.

This tour of 1913 had netted more enormous profits than any of the tours preceding it. In Gordon's Flax Mills, in the Lanarkshire coal pits, he had not imagined there was so much money in the world. Why should he go on working, anyhow? But new contracts were arriving all the time, and he would hold the pen poised while he looked up inquiringly at Nance.

"Ye maun please yoursef, Harry," she said.

Much as Harry loved America, the incessant travel had been exhausting, but now he realized that every turn of the car wheels was bringing him closer and closer to the reunion with his beloved son. Throughout that long journeying the thought kept recurring that it was unjust to himself to be separated from John like this. He tried to talk himself out of it. "But think o' a' th' long years that's ahead for both of ye," he would argue silently. "John's young, and you're still young. It's th' best time of a' that's comin'. It is so."

As usual, there was a good-natured, waving, laughing crowd at the San Francisco pier. As the boat pulled out the enthusiastic cries of hundreds of friends reached him, "Come back to us, Harry! Good luck, Harry! Come back to us *soon*, Harry!"

"Aye," he called, in his clear, hearty voice. "Aye, I'll be back!"

Nance saw his small eyes misty with tears. "You'd think you'd be used to that by now, mon Harry," she told him gently.

"No, Nance. It aye moves me, makes me feel humble. Th' world is such a *friendly* place, Nance, such a friendly, jolly place!"

They made a stop of one day at Honolulu, then the boat proceeded to Pago Pago. Each day in their stateroom, Nance and Harry studied a map of the world. From time to time their eyes met. "John'll be *here* by now," they'd assure each other, or, "now he'll be i' *this* place." And still smiling, Harry would close his eyes. Nance knew what he was doing. He was thanking God that He had been so good to him, so good as to let him be able to give his boy so much.

"John, oor John a barrister, Harry," Nance would say. "An' it won't be long before we'll be seein' him i' his wig an' gown—och, that important and handsome he'll look! Why, it seems only yesterday that he was a wee laddie."

"We maun arrange, somehow, to spend mair time wi' him, Nance. It's no richt for parents to be separated as we have been frae oor only child. Certainly there's nothin' i' th' world that means as much to us as John—and these days it keeps worryin' me that I've seen so little o' him."

Never had they been more impatient for a voyage to end. At last the great ship was actually putting in at Sydney harbor. About them were ships from every corner of the world. The sunlit sea glistened ahead of them like a pathway strewn with rhinestones. There was a fresh, invigorating wind.

Nance, Harry, Tom stood at the rail, and as their own boat drew nearer they could make out an amazing activity on shore. Flags were waving in the spring breeze. Bands played. The dock was black with people. Bells began ringing; sirens; foghorns from near-by ships added to the din. Beyond the dock, along the waterside, the crowds were lined up, waving, shouting.

"What is it?" asked Harry. "Can it be that th' King is comin', or th' Prince? I hadna' heard aboot it. It maun be that they're expectin' th' King."

Nance's little hand crept into his; her eyes were bright with excitement; her face was flushed and glowing.

"It's for you, mon Harry. It's a' for you!"

"Me? Me? Not a' *this*? Oh, no, Nance, no!"

"Aye," murmured Tom. "Listen. Ye can hear th' voices now!"

"Flags wavin'? For me? No, I'm no worthy o' this."

"Listen!"

Hundreds of voices now reached him from the shore.

"Harry! Harry!"

"Welcome to Australia, Harry!"

"Welcome, Harry! Welcome!"

He had known no greater ovation in his career. As the car drove through the streets toward the hotel, the crowds were lined up all along the curb. Night after night for an entire month the Theatre Royal was packed to capacity. Harry Lauder was forty-four now, in the full glory of his artistry. Though not corpulent, his body had grown heavier, and because of nearsightedness, he wore glasses on the street. But his singular mastery over an audience had increased with the passing of time. Other actors, famous ten years earlier, had already been labeled passé, and many had even been forgotten, but there was a perennial buoyancy about Lauder's performance, something ageless in his songs.

After New Zealand there were more bookings back in Australia—but best of all, there was John, looking fit and handsome. It had been a whole year since they had seen the boy.

In Australia there was a sense of removedness from the rest of the world. The papers had declared that Britain was on the verge of civil war, that there had been riots and bloodshed in the streets of Dublin, but none of this was alarming or even important now that John was here.

He had been training as a subaltern in the Argyll and Sutherland Highlanders, and Harry thought the training had done him good. Scarcely were the greetings over before the young man asked, "Dad, what's the news? Looks bad, doesn't it?"

"News, son? Oh, ye mean aboot this threat o' war? Nobody here seems worried aboot it. Everyone's sure it'll blow over."

John shook his head. "No, Dad. It looks serious. I think people don't realize how prosperous Germany is, and how strong."

"But even if there's war, son, why should England get mixed up i' it? If Germany wants to fight Russia—"

"If there's war, Dad, England's in it, let's not fool ourselves."

"And—i' that case, son, you'll be recalled?"

"Oh, yes, certainly. At once."

"Weel, we maun hope an' pray for th' best. Th' world's been a bit uneasy for a long time—since 1911, wasn't it, that Italy annexed Tripoli an' had her war wi' Turkey? Greece is ambitious. Th' Balkans 're restive, fightin' an' arguin' amang themselves, but then th' Balkans 're aye doin' that."

"What about America, Dad?"

"America?"

"Yes. Is she preparing for war?"

"War? No. No civilized country is preparin' for war."

"Germany's preparing and has been for years. If the Germans attack Russia, France will support Russia instantly. In that case, Germany will dispense with France first, and then go on to Russia. They'll invade France through Belgium."

"Oh, John," begged Nance, "do stop talkin' aboot war as if it were a certainty. Why, you've only just arrived, son.

Tell us aboot your trip. Tell us aboot yoursel'. Tell us—"

"Mum, dear, you're like everyone else. Nobody wants to think about war or talk about it. It seems incredible."

They were silent, thoughtful. Their minds went back to that day in June when the heir to the Austrian throne had been assassinated. That had started things. Austria had declared that Serbia was the cause of the murders, and in late July was sending an ultimatum to Serbia. War between the two countries had been declared. But, argued the Australians, it was only a local war, a war among the always fighting Balkans, nothing to worry about. By the 30th of July, Russia was mobilized. On the 31st, John had arrived in Australia. On August 1 st, Germany had declared war on Russia.

"Germany *wants* war," John asserted, gravely. "She's prepared for it. She has planned for it. It won't stop there, either."

News came that Germany had invaded Belgium and was marching on France. Still, Australia seemed a long, long way from war. News became momentarily more exciting.

The whole world was shocked at the horrors to which Belgium was subjected by the invading Prussian hordes. The ruthlessness, the unnecessary cruelty of it, the shooting of innocent Belgians, the looting of Belgian homes—it was ferocious, terrible, incomprehensible that such things could happen in this modern, civilized world. The "Huns" became symbols of terror, of unmitigated greed. On August 2nd the entire world stood aghast, horrified, at the savagery which had taken place in the little Belgian town of Visé. Why, asked a stunned and stricken world, must the Germans set the entire village ablaze? Why must they kill hundreds of noncombatants for the alleged shooting of a single German officer? One can respect and even admire a scrupulous and clever enemy, but such things as this were the work of suddenly unleashed fiends.

One saw now, fully exposed, the long years of sinister planning that had gone on beneath the supposed culture of a hitherto respected nation. Abruptly, the German Kaiser became something more than a strutting braggadocio with a withered arm. The world saw him now as a soulless monster, the manifestation of all that was diabolical and hideous. All this havoc could not go on unrestrained and unchallenged. Something had to be done to stop it.

On August 5th, five days after his arrival, a cable came for John while he and his parents were at luncheon in the hotel. He read it quietly. Then he passed it to his father. Harry knew what it was, for only yesterday, August 4th—which was Harry's birthday—England, roused by the devastation into which Europe had been so abruptly projected, had declared war on Germany.

The cable was brief. "Mobilize. Return," was all it said.

John's voice was calm, strangely calm. "Well, Dad?" he asked.

"This is th' time for action. Your country needs you, son."

"Right! I'm off."

"Off?" asked Nance, her body tense, her face ash-white. "Off? Off where?"

"To the ticket office!"

They sat there mutely, gazing after him as he hurried away.

CHAPTER THIRTEEN

The show must go on.

There were bookings in America, beginning at San Francisco and ending in New York. America, safely entrenched behind the mighty bulwark of the Atlantic, was firm in her determination to remain strictly neutral. She was at peace and she told the world bluntly that she intended to remain at peace. It was not, she steadfastly maintained, her fight. Britain, France, Russia, Japan, Belgium at war with Germany and Austria? Well, they must fight it out among themselves. It was all too bad, of course, but America wanted no hand in it.

But the world seemed no longer secure.

For a time, in Britain, people were completely dazed, muddled. The thing had happened too suddenly. They had had a long peace and could not conceive of war, could not contemplate what war would mean to each individual British soul. Workers, planning August vacations, went right ahead and took them. The slogan was, "Business as usual."

But Germany was moving swiftly, as for years she had planned to do. She felt herself invincible. Her methods, her equipment were modern and efficient. France, completely unprepared as was Britain, began the war with outmoded weapons. Neither country had anything to compete with the devastatingly thorough high explosive shells of Germany and the powerful new machine guns turned out in volume by the Krupp works.

England had a small army of but seventy thousand men, which was driven back with great loss at Mons on August 22nd. The Prussians now were more boastful than ever, certain of easy victory; but the French and English, recovering quickly, drove them back in the Battle of the Marne in September.

It was not until the spring of 1915 that Lauder returned to a vastly changed England. People were beginning to realize what war meant. There was no conscription, but the women had found an effective way of forcing men to enlist. They were quietly handing out white feathers to every able-bodied man in civvies.

John had not as yet been sent "over there." He was in the Midlands with his regiment, where Harry and Nance rushed to see him. He had been made a First Lieutenant, and he looked, they thought, more handsome than ever in his uniform with his natty Sam Browne belt and his swagger stick.

"If I could only go wi' you, son!" cried Harry. "If I could only go wi' ye an' fight!"

They talked of the fighting at Ypres, where the British line had held so valiantly. They talked of Australia which, when Harry left it, was momentarily expecting invasion due to German-held bases not far distant. Everyone in Australia kept asking where the great German navy was. Who knew but what it might be on its way to Australia? Australians had been dashing into recruiting offices. They talked of America. America had been confident and serene. Lauder told his son how he had made speeches in America, and how good-naturedly America had scoffed at him.

"Prepare, you Americans!" he had cried. "You won't be able to stay out of it!"

"Stick to your singing, Harry! We don't intend to *let* ourselves be drawn into it. There's not a chance in the world of *us* being drawn into this mess!"

But America was a little less neutral when she learned that the Germans had used poison gas. This was not the work of men, it was the device of devils. Throughout America the pro-Ally sentiment was steadily increasing.

"Weel, tell me now, what d'ye need, son?"

"Men, Dad, men!" the boy answered promptly. "Enlistment is voluntary and the response has been wonderful, but we'll need more men. It's going to be a long, hard war."

Lauder had not anticipated this answer, but now he said quietly, "A' richt, son. You've told me how I can do ma bit."

How was he going to get men to enlist? How? Speeches? Yes, of course. He would go everywhere making speeches. But he must do more than this. They had called him stingy, but now he was ready to give every dollar he possessed to the great cause of freedom and democracy.

He hit upon the costly idea of organizing his own band of pipers for which he alone furnished costumes, salaries and traveling expenses. To Harry's mind nothing on earth was as attractive as music. His plan was that these men would station themselves on a busy corner and play their rollicking airs until they had gathered a crowd. Then, still playing, they would move away. The crowd would follow—to the nearest recruiting office. This simple procedure proved amazingly effective.

Harry's heart now was not only in his singing, but in his speaking. In addition to his theatrical appearances, he spoke everywhere, vehemently urging young men to get into the fight. He went to hospitals and sang. He sang in camps. He was indefatigable.

The only happy times he knew during that trying year were the times when John could get leave and they could spend a week-end at Glen Branter on the shores of Loch Eck. Here, Harry was superintending a new house he was building, not for himself this time but for John and John's bride-to-be, Miss Mildred Thomson. His parents were happy that the boy was going to get married and that the young people would live close to them. John was eager to get into the scrap and he had no doubt but that he would emerge from it unscathed.

Glowing and splendid were the plans he had for the time when "the show" would be over.

When Harry left for America on the next tour, he realized that it would be one of the hardest tours that he and Nance had ever made. For six months they would scarcely lodge in a single hotel. Their home would be their special train.

It was 1915 and they both knew that they might never see their son again, for he was certain to be sent "over there" during their absence. It was necessary to make this tour, however, for Lauder was coming to America primarily to do propaganda work for his country. In May, 1915, Italy had become one of the Allies. He was going to tell America how and why the Allies were fighting. He was going to make America realize how splendid had been the French at Arras, and how intrepid were the Russians at Galicia. He was going to tell of the miles and miles of trenches stretching all the way from the North Sea to Switzerland, where millions of human beings were living and suffering and dying. He was going to tell of the stupendous problem of feeding these men and supplying them with ammunition. "They shall not pass!" affirmed the French. "Ils ne passeront pas!"

He meant to speak of the Zeppelins that came roaring over the east of England, and the airplane raids over Paris. America must realize these things.

As he talked to Woodrow Wilson during tea at the White House, Harry knew that Wilson's chief thought was not war, but peace. It was not the first time Lauder had been a guest at the White House, but it was his first meeting with Wilson. Wilson, at fifty-six, was an idealist. At first Harry thought him stern and cold. The long, scholarly face of Wilson was grave as they shook hands. Wilson was always impeccably groomed, and this fact particularly impressed Lauder at their first meeting. Even then the President of the United States was dreaming of a League of Nations which would make future wars impossible.

"So you believe America will inevitably be drawn into the war, Mr. Lauder?"

"I do, sincerely, Mr. President."

"I will do all in my power to prevent it. There is nothing more horrible, nothing more costly than war."

"True, and no country on earth loathes war mair than does England, but this is a righteous cause. I'm goin' a' over America, Mr. President, an' I'm going to say what's i' ma heart to say."

And from one end of the country to the other he said it.

"America and Britain *must* stand shoulder to shoulder i' this crisis! A gang of cutthroats have plunged Europe into hell because they want to dominate all th' nations of the world. You canna' much longer stand aloof!"

It was early in 1916 that the Lauders returned to England, and John, now Captain Lauder, was home from France on leave, seemingly stronger, more fit than when he had left for the trenches a year ago. It was a straight, boyish, wiry body, and Harry had never been more proud of his son than he was now. War had come to seem almost a natural thing. It seemed natural to be getting letters postmarked "Somewhere in France." John's letters had come regularly. He wrote as well as he talked, but he did not want to talk of the war and the sights he had seen at the front. He wanted to talk of the days that lay ahead, while Harry, oddly enough, wanted to talk of the days that lay in the past.

"Do ye remember when ye were fifteen, laddie, how we went doon to Rufford Abbey and you played for me while I sang to th' King? And d'ye mind th' time i' Glasgow when it was rainin' an' you were only a wee bit lad. . . ."

Only a few days could they spend together at Glen Branter, for Harry had engagements to fill, and there was always an engagement to sing at a hospital where he saw bodies of youths like his own son so mangled that the memory kept him from sleeping at nights, and there were rehearsals for a revue called *Three Cheers*, in which he was to be starred in the fall.

Long before it opened, John had returned to the front, and again began the anxiety of watching for letters, the worry when a letter failed to arrive in the usual post, the waiting for the next post. Every day the newspapers published long lists of casualties. Harry bought each newspaper with dread, always uppermost in his mind the question: Would the name of John Lauder be among that list today?

London itself was quietly tense. Only lately the British had developed anti-air raid guns, but even now these were far from efficient. Despite the danger of raids, theatres were crowded. *Three Cheers* was a success. John's letters arrived promptly; cheerful, hopeful letters, still talking about all that he meant to do when "the big show" was over. Harry Lauder's heart never left his boy. He kept remembering John as he had been at their parting—lithe, debonair, eager. It had been a simple farewell, without heroics on either side. Just—

"Weel, good-by, son—good luck."

"Good-by, Dad. I'll be all right."

Sometimes Harry thought it was wrong for him to be standing up on the stage singing, dancing, joking, laughing, when his country was at war, when his only son was perhaps at that very minute facing death "somewhere in France." But his friends and acquaintances kept insisting that England needed laughter, needed songs, needed jokes now more than she had ever needed them before.

Nance's eyes had a perpetually anxious expression these days. When a letter came she read it over and over, and then she would sit holding it tenderly in her hands, staring off into space. Would there be another letter tomorrow? Might not this be the last they would ever receive from him? Often she and Harry prayed together, and they both knew that it was their prayers which sustained them during that dreadful time.

There came a day when no letter arrived. "It doesna' mean anything, Nance," declared Harry. "It—it's naught but some trouble wi' th' post, that's a'. Th' letter wull be here tomorrow."

But the next day there came a telegram, announcing only that John was wounded.

Wounded. How badly? In a hospital. What hospital? They could do nothing but wait. The show went on, and all that week no further word came. Anxiety had increased to fever pitch, and then at last came word from John himself.

It was nothing much, he assured them, nothing to worry about at all. His nose had been hurt and his wrist wounded.

"It means he'll be comin' home to Blighty!" declared Harry.

"Aye. Aye."

She gazed at the letter again. "Don't worry about me," she read. "Lots of fellows out here have been wounded five or six times and don't think anything of it."

The letters began coming with regularity again, but the sight of a telegraph messenger made them both suddenly start trembling. Each day seemed an eternity. Harry Lauder's Band was still traveling from one end of Great Britain to the other, Harry was still making speeches, and finally, John had gone back to his business of fighting. War had become an integral part of life. Yet every day it grew harder for Harry to go on the stage and crack his jokes. *Three Cheers* was one of the gayest shows in London.

Finally, a letter came from John that he was to have leave again soon after Christmas and that he and Mildred planned to be married when he arrived.

"Why, he'll likely be here for New Year's!" exclaimed Nance, and her eyes were so bright that Harry thought she looked scarcely a day older than when he had married her.

"You'd better leave at once for Scotland so as to have everything ready for th' lad when he comes hame," Harry suggested.

"Aye. I'll get everything ready. They'll have th' marriage at Dunoon—and a graund weddin' it wull be, too!" She laughed softly. "Do ye mind oor weddin', Harry, a pay-weddin'? An' you wi' your first white shirt? An' oor lovely, lovely honeymoon i' McLeod's Wax Works? An' do ye mind th' time we—och, but I canna' stand here talkin'. I maun get ready. Oor John's comin' hame!"

Harry was lonely after Nance had gone. Never in all his life had he been lonely like this. London was full of his friends and they were eager enough to entertain him, but he had the singular feeling that he had to be by himself all the time. And why, he asked himself sternly, should he feel like this? Why? He had everything in the world to be happy about. In a few days John would be home and they would all be together again. Yet the depression grew. Even while he was on the stage, he could not shake it off. He knew the old Lauder verve was lacking from his performance. He knew that several times he had even been guilty of committing the unforgivable sin of "muffing" a laugh. But it did not seem to matter. He could not seem to *make* things matter. The world seemed suddenly unfamiliar, and he felt lost in it, lost and curiously deadened.

New Year's Eve found him more depressed than ever. He *must*, somehow, shake off this feeling of deadness that engulfed him mentally and physically. Tom Vallance was the only person he could bear being with, and he spent New Year's Eve, a Sunday, with Tom and his family in their house at Clapham.

Clapham was a quiet suburb and Harry was glad to get away from the noise and bustle of London. The Vallance house was a gracious, cheerful place, but for Harry the day dragged on unmercifully. Friends dropped in, but their holiday mood failed to revive Harry's spirits.

"I havena' heard from John for two days," he explained to his brother-in-law.

"Weel, Harry, that doesna' mean anything i' these times. Maybe Nance has heard, or Mildred, an' they just have had no time to get i' touch with ye."

"True. That might be it."

Evening came, and he still could not bring himself to enter into the conversation of those about him.

"I—dinna ken what's th' matter wi' me," he kept saying apologetically. "I—just—dinna want to talk. I hope—I keep hopin' th' boy is a' richt."

"Of course he is, Harry. Of course. If anything had happened to John, they'd let you know quickly enough."

"Aye, that's true. I sent him a box o' cigars—he's likely handin' them around th' noo. I—I wonder, this time next year, wull oor lads still be i' th' trenches?"

"No. No. It can't possibly last that long. Cheer up, Harry."

Tom stood in the midst of the room, his glass raised. He was a slender, boyish figure still, with a thin, delicately chiseled nose like his sister's, and a small neat mustache. Again Harry thought how much he and Nance resembled each other.

"Here's to the New Year," cried Tom, "—and victory!"

"Aye," echoed Harry, "to th' New Year—and—peace!"

He left the house early and returned to his hotel, the Bonnington. It was a little before midnight, and there was a message for him to call

Sir Thomas Lipton. He did so at once, trying to inject something of the old ring in his voice.

"Happy New Year to ye, Tom!"

"Happy New Year, Harry. How are you and Mrs. Lauder?"

"Oh, fine—fine."

"That's good. When did you hear from the boy?"

"A few days ago. He—he's comin' hame on leave, he says."

"That's splendid, Harry. Well, good night. Happy New Year!"

Lauder went to bed, but for hours sleep was impossible. What would this coming year bring to John? What would it bring to England, to the world, to this badly battered world? Would Lloyd George who had taken Asquith's place as Prime Minister be able to speed up supplies to the front? Out there, somewhere in France, vast armies seemed to be in deadlock. And what about the tanks, these strange new contraptions that Britain had begun to use only last September, would they really prove a deciding factor? Russia was exhausted; everybody knew that. And where was John? What was John doing at this very minute?

Habit finally forced him to lapse into the old prayer his mother had taught him, the prayer which Nance had taught John.

"As I lay me doon this night tae sleep,
I pray th' Lord ma soul tae keep. . . ."

He sank into an uneasy slumber from which he was awakened by a rap on his door. He woke with a start. It was daylight, but he knew at once that the day was new. Why should they awaken him at this hour?

A porter stood there holding out a telegram. Shakily, wordlessly, Harry closed the door and tore open the envelope.

"Captain John Lauder killed in Action December 28th. Official.

WAR OFFICE."

CHAPTER FOURTEEN

He could not at first realize it. Sinking into a chair he read the telegram over and over, brain and body numb. John Lauder killed in action. It was simple, crisp, unmistakable. December 28th.

Harry knew that he had to get to Nance. Show or no show, nothing on earth could keep him from her now. The news that Lauder's son had been killed spread quickly. Early as it was, friends began crowding into his room. Telegrams were arriving. He saw people blurredly. They seemed unreal. The words they spoke were only a weird mumbo-jumbo. He sat there, hunched, stupefied, trying to realize how it would be not seeing his boy again, not planning for John's future. He stared dismally into space, finding no words with which to voice his confusion and despair.

Dead. Dead. He began to understand what that meant now. It was as if suddenly, too suddenly, everything had come to an end. He moaned, buried his head in his hands, and sobbed. After a time his sobs abated, and he sat, trying to recall the sound of his boy's voice, the way John walked, whistled, smiled; the way he looked as he sat at the piano; the way he looked as he leaned over the billiard table. It was as if he were trying to bring his son to life again in his own mind and hold him there, warm, living, vital. He saw John in his kilts. He saw him as a baby, as a child, as a young lad in an Eton jacket and his first long pants.

Then came a fearful hatred of war, an almost insane fury against the Germans, the people who had made this war, killing millions of boys like his own because of an insatiable greed, a lust for domination.

John—twenty-three his next birthday. Twenty-three, such a splendid age to be alive in.

"You wouldn't have kept him from going, Harry, even if you could," someone said.

Aye, that was true—that was true enough.

Another voice cried, "Why do these dreadful things have to happen? Is there a God?"

In the midst of the voices, Harry kept asking himself what he was doing here, what was he doing here in London, anyhow? His place was at Dunoon with Nance. She knew it by now and she was alone. A few minutes later he glanced about him seeing no one, no one save Tom standing near. Tom had made all the people leave, yet Harry had not even known that they were gone.

"I'll see to th' tickets, Harry," said Tom brokenly. "We'll leave for Glasga' th' nicht, and tomorrow we'll be i' Dunoon wi' Nance."

He nodded and sat watching Tom as he left the room.

Why? Why? Why? Why do these things have to happen? Is there a God? Alone, Harry Lauder, comedian, fell to his knees. He spoke simply:

"Lord, gie me th' strength to bear this, just strength—to go on. Gie Thy strength to Nance, too. Help Nance to bear up under it."

Tom and Harry left London on the Midnight Mail. Tom's suitcase was filled with letters, cables, telegrams. Later, he knew, Harry would read and answer them, but not now. Now he sat, hunched, staring, old, his face ashen.

Next morning they were at Dunoon, and Nance was waiting. There were no dramatics, no hysterics for Nance. She was calm and strong. Her face was white and bleak, but her voice and her hands were steady. It was she who mothered Harry, watching over him, caring for him. For a long time they knelt together, praying.

"We were proud o' John while he lived, mon Harry," Nance declared. "We're proud o' him i' death. Thousands an' thousands o' mithers an' faithers are facin' this verra same grief. Every day o' this war there'll be those thousands weepin' for lads who wullna' come hame. We maun remember, too, Harry, that oor John died for a holy cause, for th' sacred cause o' liberty. No mon on earth could ask for a better cause than that to dee for."

Gradually the conviction came to both of them that they had not really lost their boy, that there had been no annihilation for John, that he was still associated with life, with activity, with vitality and laughter, that they were bound to meet him again sometime, just as if the three of them were coming together from vast distances as they had so often done in the past. Harry Lauder felt very sure that one day he would see his boy again; and this thought brought comfort.

For three days beginning January 1st, *Three Cheers* had been closed in respect to Harry. For almost a week Harry and Nance saw no one, wanted no one but each other. The idea of ever going back to London was unthinkable. As for the stage—no, that was over. For the first time in his life, Harry Lauder's heart was not in his singing. Go before an audience again? Laugh? Tell funny stories? Waggle his kilt? No, never—never. Nothing could make him go back, nothing on earth.

"The public are calling for you, Harry," the manager insisted. "They want you. I can't fill your place; you know that!"

Friends came, asking when he was going back to work. The manager begged. It was no use. It amazed Lauder that they should all expect him to go back on the stage again. Didn't they *know* it was impossible?

"I canna'. I canna'," he told Nance wretchedly.

"No, Harry," she agreed. "They shouldna' be askin' it of ye."

There was enough for the two of them to live on if they were careful. It was not so great a fortune as it had been, for of the millions Harry had made, most of it had been given to the war effort. He was not a rich man any more, but that did not matter.

"Well, Harry," asked the manager over the long distance wire, "I suppose you've reconsidered, old man? Business has fallen off since I've been trying to run the show without you."

"I said I was no comin' back an' I mean it."

"What? Not at all? Not ever?"

"No. I'm through."

"But think what this means! Good Lord, I'll have to close! Think of the people it'll throw out of work. Hundreds of them—chorus girls, stage hands, wardrobe women—"

Friends came. "No, Harry, you mustn't. Why, you're only forty-six. The world needs you, Harry. Never has it needed laughter like it needs it now."

"No. No. I tell you, I'm finished."

Letters and cables all carried the same message: "Harry, don't leave us now!" The cry came from people of whom he had never heard. "There's enough sorrow in the world, Harry. You can make us laugh. Come back to us. You can make us forget the Hun for a little while. There's so little happiness in the world these days. We *need* laughter, Harry. Don't leave us now!"

"We canna' just think of oorselves, mon Harry," Nance said. "These people are richt. Ye maun think o' the ithers, Harry. Think o' th' people i' th' show, thrown oot o' work when work's so scarce. Three hundred people i' th' cast, Harry. I've been thinkin' o' them. Hardly a one o' them but what has someone dependin' on their earnin's—a child, a parent. An' most o' them need th' siller so!"

"But Nance—"

"You'll be bringin' sufferin' upon them, mon Harry. Have ye th' richt to do that?"

"I ken, Nance. I ken. I've thought of it. Only—I—I canna' bring masel' to go back. I just—couldna' go through wi' it. I'm sure I couldna' go *through* wi' it, Nance."

"I think ye should go back," she insisted quietly.

"It's your duty to your fellow-actors, Harry," maintained Tom.

"And Harry," went on Nance, "think o' th' thousands o' mithers an' faithers a' over Britain and France an' Canada that have had telegrams like we had. Do ye think they can stop doin' *their* work?"

"But ma work is different, Nance. I tell you, I canna'! I would if I could, only I ken I'd never get through wi' th' show. I'd break doon an' make a fool o' masel', Nance. I—"

He paused as a servant came in with a letter. She handed it to Harry and went out again quietly. Harry read it aloud.

Mr. Harry Lauder,
Dunoon, Scotland.
Dear Sir:

You do not know me, but I was one of John's brother officers. I have no time to write at length, but I thought you would like to know what his last words to his men were. I was close by him and I heard them very distinctly. They were just two words— "carry on" . . .

"Carry on!" echoed Nance.

Tom spoke decisively. "Harry, as far as your goin' back is concerned, it's no a question o' how ye feel, it's a question o' your duty. There're hundreds o' people i' th' cast that're dependin' on ye. Do ye think John was speakin' to his men alone? No! He is speakin'—straight t' *you!* John would want ye to carry on. Those were his last words. To whom? To *you*, Harry—*carry on!*"

"You're richt, Tom. Thank you. I—we'll leave for London at once."

CHAPTER FIFTEEN

Carry on. Carry on.

As they brought him Londonward the wheels of the train kept saying it. Always before this, Harry Lauder had felt perfect assurance of his power over an audience, but now he was not sure of anything. With every passing moment as the train approached nearer and nearer to London, his nervousness, his fear increased. Tom, sitting silently and sympathetically beside him, had wired the management of his return, and already the news had spread from one end of the city to the other—Harry Lauder was coming back.

As for Harry, his fear of facing the audience was so great that when the train arrived in London, he had to be assisted from it, and as if he were blind, Tom led him through the crowded station and into a taxi. Harry thought of the glaring spotlights, of the chorus girls in their gay, semi-nude costumes, of the rollicking tunes which composed the score of *Three Cheers*. No, never again could he possibly be a part of all that. It was suddenly alien, mocking, grotesque.

When the time approached for them to go to the theatre, he knew quite surely that he would have to tell Tom to phone the manager and say he could not make it. But when Tom said, "It's time we were starting, Harry," he rose like an obedient child.

Arriving at the theatre, a group of actors awaited him inside the stage door. In silence they moved toward him, but Tom shook his head and muttered, "No, no, dinna talk to him th' noo."

But they had seen him. They had seen the shaky body, the bleak, tortured eyes, the drawn, white face. They looked at each other tensely. "He's on the verge of collapse," they said. "He'll never be able to go on."

Harry walked into his dressing room and seated himself before the brilliantly lighted mirror. Then he turned his head slowly and looked about as if he had never seen a dressing room before. There was blankness in his eyes—until they rested on the old hamper. Watching him, Tom flinched and cursed himself for not remembering to have that hamper removed. It was old and battered. Harry must have bought the thing back in 1901. It was John's favorite seat. Time after time John had sat there on that hamper, watching his father make up.

In what he knew to be a futile effort to divert Harry's attention, Tom said, in a voice curiously hoarse, "Th' hoose is sold out, Harry."

Harry did not answer. It was doubtful if he heard, but he turned from gazing at the hamper, and habit made him reach out for the right cosmetics and dab them over his bloodless face. The grease paint first, put on in little splotches and then blended into the skin. He tried to remember what he said, what he did on his first entrance, and found that he could not recall a single line, a single bit of business. Now and then a knock came gently on the door, and Tom, opening it only a crack, said, "No. No. Leave him alone. He's better alone."

As he got into his tunic, Harry was trembling so that Tom had to help him with the buttons. His hands, icy one minute, were damp with perspiration the next. At last he sat there in his funny costume, staring fixedly at the wall.

"Fifteen minutes!" came the voice of the callboy. "Fifteen minutes, Mr. Lauder, please."

Harry made no move.

After what to Tom seemed an eternity, that vigorous young voice came again.

"Overture. Overture. Overture, Mr. Lauder."

"It's—overture, Harry," said Tom.

Harry seemed not to have heard him.

"First act. Places, everybody! On stage! First act. Curtain! Curtain!"

"Tom!" cried Harry distractedly, "I canna' do it! It's impossible. I canna' do it. Tell them! Tell them. Say—say I'm—I'm sorry—"

"Nonsense, Harry."

"No. No. You'll see. I'll make a fool o' masel'. They'll have to ring doon th' curtain!"

"No. No, dinna fash yoursel'. Wait till ye get out there, Harry. Ye wullna' feel so, then."

"It was silly o' me to try to do this, Tom. I kent it a' th' time. I canna' sing when ma heart's no i' it. I canna' sing when ma heart's—breakin'."

"Nonsense, Harry. Come, it's most time for your cue. Time for your cue, Harry."

Lauder rose, and with Tom beside him, walked out into the wings. Members of the company made a little silent aisle for him as he moved toward the entrance. Already the orchestra was beginning the gay introduction to his first song. The actors stared at him, making no attempt to speak, their eyes filled with tears. They saw how he trembled. They saw the strange, panicky look in his eyes.

"They're a' your friends out there, Harry, remember that," whispered Tom.

"Tom! I canna'. *I canna' do it!*" He made an abrupt volte-face and started back toward the dressing room.

Tom caught him firmly by the arm. "D'ye mind John's message to ye, Harry?"

"Eh?"

"*Carry on!*"

"Aye," he answered, dully. "Aye."

The orchestra played the introduction again. Harry Lauder squared his shoulders, and ran smilingly toward the footlights.

From the audience for a moment there was complete silence, profound, strange. Then suddenly came a very thunder of applause, shouts, cheers. He could look out at them—were they crying? Aye, women and even men were frankly sobbing, sobbing as they cheered.

They thought the funny little man up there on the stage was only waiting for the noise to die down before he began his song, but Harry Lauder did not know what the words of that song were. He was not even thinking about it. Wildly, chokingly, he was praying.

"Help me, God. Be good to me again, God. Help me through this show. Help me to carry on. Gie me th' strength I'm needin.'"

The cheering had subsided now, and Lauder found himself singing. His voice was as firm and true as ever. All the brightness, the laughable walk, the contagious little chuckles, the subtle pieces of business—not one of these was omitted. It seemed to him as he cavorted that the people out front were far, far away, curiously remote, that the music reached him only vaguely as if from a vast distance.

The act progressed, and he kept saying his lines on cues, going through the business, cracking his jokes. The laughs came, curiously enough, in the same old places.

With the descending of the curtain, shouts rang spontaneously from every part of the crowded auditorium.

"Bravo! Bravo, Harry!"

Helping him change for the next act, Tom murmured, "It was a graund performance ye gave th' nicht, Harry, as good as ever. It was so."

But it was not over, thought Harry, and the end of it seemed to stretch out into infinity. Seemingly, this performance would never be over. It would go on and on and on.

He kept going on with it—that, to Harry, was the amazing part of the whole thing, that he kept standing on his feet, speaking lines, dancing around the stage, and finally—finally—they were approaching the grand finale.

This was a brilliant and spectacular ensemble. The entire three hundred members of the company, augmented by a genuine Scots guard, lined up about and behind a little man in green tunic and gaudy tartan while he sang the song that all London knew, *The Laddies That*

Fought and Won. Two lines toward the end of the chorus, Harry himself had written in during rehearsals:

"When we all gather round the old fireside,
And the fond mother kisses her son. . . ."

He sang the verse and chorus jauntily enough until he reached those two lines. He could not sing them now. He choked, stopped, tears streaming down over his grease paint. Simultaneously, as if by a prearranged agreement, the orchestra, the chorus, the Scots guard swelled out in unison. Almost at once Harry was himself again, carrying on in the age-old tradition of the theatre, and ending the performance with *God Save the King.*

When at length the curtain came down and the audience stood in the aisles cheering, Harry took no curtain calls. He lay on the stage in a faint.

"Weel, Harry, ye did it," said Tom as they were driving back to the hotel.

"Aye. I did it, Tom."

"An' ye can do it again. Ye can finish oot th' run."

"Aye."

Yes, he could go on night after night singing about the fond mother kissing her son. He would not, he knew, break up like that again. He could sing those lines and sing them with gusto, for there *would* be sons coming home—someday; not his own, but other laddies. For some there *would* be those genial gatherings around the fireplaces.

Nance joined him before the week was over. "There's work we maun do i' th' hospitals, mon Harry, both of us, an' you'll go on makin' your speeches for th' war charities. It wull help us forget oor ain grief if we help ithers bear theirs."

Nance was right. There was much for them both to do in London. The enemy had ceased using Zeppelins now, and was using airplanes to bomb the city. Never a moonlight night but what the enemy craft came and there were the shrill screeching of the police alarms, the roar of the antiaircraft guns, the hiss of shrapnel, the exploding bombs— and then inevitably the shriek of the ambulances and the fire engines.

On the seas, submarines were taking voracious toll of English ships, and food was increasingly scarce. The fury of the powerful German submarines increased every day. England was blockaded.

Since the sinking of the *Lusitania* in 1915, American sentiment no longer sought to mask itself under the word "neutrality." It was a world gone mad. Turkey at swords-points with Egypt. Dardanelles being bombarded. Bulgaria joining with Germany, the Serbs were retreating through the Albanian Mountains, the English army was surrounded and beaten in Mesopotamia, the war was everywhere—France, Russia, Turkey, England, Asia. More and more the Allies were learning the value of the airplane. No one had ever heard of aerial fighting before. Winston Churchill in the British Admiralty had battled valiantly for the use of tanks, while people said he was insane. The British armies were being slaughtered, and it was those tanks which later did much to weaken German morale, for the Germans saw these monstrous contraptions with a consternation which was close to panic. Russia was fast reaching exhaustion. Rumania, having entered the war on the side of the Allies, was crushed. The Germans were in possession of Serbia, Belgium, Rumania, much of France and Russia. Seemingly there was no stopping the Hun.

In and out of hospitals and camps went the little Scotsman in kilts, still making people laugh in spite of it all, still making them sing with him in the midst of destruction and death.

"I've made up ma mind to enlist," declared Lauder, "but they'll have to promise they'll no gie me a saft job here at hame. It's at the front I want to be. Oh, if they'd only let me go into the trenches and avenge my boy!"

Of course, agreed the authorities, he could enlist, and there would be no difficulty whatever about securing a commission.

"But I want to go out an' fight!" he insisted. "I want to fight th' ones who killed oor John!"

They smiled. "No, Mr. Lauder, you're a bit too old for the trenches."

"Too ould? I'm only forty-seven. I'm as fit as I ever was i' ma life."

"As a matter of fact, you can do more good where you are. We don't need you in the trenches, but we do need your laughter."

"Then in God's name, if ye wullna' let me *fight* i' th' trenches, I can *sing* i' them! I can sing to th' laddies that're i' th' trenches. Let me do that much!"

"No, that's impossible. It's just never been done. You can visit the bases in Belgium, if you like, or in France, but the trenches? Sorry, old man."

"I can cheer up th' laddies i' th' trenches, I tell ye! I can encourage them. It's th' lads i' th' trenches who need laughter more than th' hame front!"

"We-ell, we'll see what can be done about it, Harry. We'll see."

He knew intimately many men in important governmental positions. He went to them all. They shook their heads and agreed it was not a bad idea, but—well, it had just never been *done*. Weeks passed, and he heard no more concerning it.

With the closing of *Three Cheers*, he returned to Scotland for a few days' rest, but rest was impossible.

"It's no time for a mon to be restin," he declared. "Oh, if they'd only let me go right i' th' trenches an' sing for th' laddies!"

Dunoon, Glen Branter, both he and Nance found it impossible to remain in either place. They were too full of memories. Here were John's guns, his horse, his clothes, the billiard cue he most liked to use, his fishing tackle, his music, and here too was the fine, modem house all ready, all furnished—the house where he was to have brought his lovely bride.

Restive, miserable, the Lauders returned to London. Letters came to Harry from the front, letters from men he did not know, some of whom had seen his performances, while others had only heard his records. "Come on, Harry, come on over," pleaded the letters. "Give us a song and a laugh."

Finally, almost as he had given up hope, came the official permission to do so.

"Nance," he cried when the permission came, "I'm going to France, too! I'm going to sing where th' fightin's thickest. I'm going to sing for the Argyll and Sutherland Regiments—oor John's ain regiments. And for th' Camerons an' th' Gordons an' the ither Scottish troops. What shall I take them? What can I gie th' laddies i' th' front lines?" "Songs," she answered, "songs an' cigarettes."

"You're richt, Nance. I'll buy thousands o' cigarettes. I—" he put his hands on her narrow shoulders and looked deeply into her eyes. "Nance, you'll no be worryin' aboot me, wull ye?"

"No, I—I'll try not to worry, Harry. I'll keep verra, verra busy i' th' hospitals an' a'. I'll try not to worry."

"Because—I'll be a' richt, Nance, I'll be a' richt."

She had a clear, swift recollection of another Lauder who had gone off to the trenches with that same blithe assurance, "I'll be all right." But she must not let Harry know what she was thinking, for now he was more like his old self than he had ever been since that dreadful New Year's Day.

"I'm sure you'll be a' richt, mon Harry," she answered steadily.

CHAPTER SIXTEEN

Lauder managed to get a piano so small that it could be transported in an ordinary motor car. In addition to the piano, which Nance called "cute," he bought five hundred dollars' worth of cigarettes and set sail from Folkestone in June, 1917.

It was a time when the Allied prospects for victory had reached their lowest ebb. Russia was in utter chaos. For over a year her Allies had worried lest she contract a separate peace with their enemy, and in March the food riots in Petrograd had developed into a revolution. One great source of hope had arisen among the Allies—America had joined them in April. But—was it too late? asked the people of France and Britain. Was it not too late?

Folkestone was a beehive of activity. Ships were loading and unloading. Airplanes were roaring overhead. Soldiers were everywhere.

At Boulogne, where Harry landed, an even more feverish activity prevailed. Hospital ships were being loaded for their trips to England. Men on leave were returning home. Ambulances were speeding back and forth from the docks. Planes gleamed in the sunlit sky. The little piano looked curiously out of place among the guns and the ambulances.

A young officer approached Harry, saluted, then reached out a friendly, welcoming hand. "Godfrey's my name, sir, Captain Godfrey. It seems I'm—er—to be your manager during this tour."

"Weel, Captain, I'm under your orders. An' so far, ma managers have a' been ma good friends. Where an' when do I open?"

"The Casino here in Boulogne is being used now as a base hospital. Perhaps you would like to give your first concert there? And then, of course, there's the Y. M. C. A. hut."

"Th' nicht?"

"Yes, tonight. We'll have to leave quite early in the morning."

"Of course, Captain. We'll put on twa shows th' nicht, one i' th' Casino, the ither i' th' hut."

"Good. Is there anything you need?"

"Weel, I brought a piano an' I could do wi' an accompanist. I didna' bring one wi' me because they told me there were no lack o' musicians i' His Majesty's forces."

"An accompanist? Quite. The simplest thing in the world. I'll find you one inside the hour."

Godfrey was as good as his word. He found a young Yorkshireman named Johnson who, though convalescent, was not yet ready to return to active fighting. Johnson proved cheery, obliging and capable.

Harry's heart was in his singing now as it had never been before; never had he given better performances than he gave that night, and never had he played to more enthusiastic audiences. At the Casino many of the men were brought in on cots and wheelchairs. Harry loved every one of these battered, tortured men. They had fought, he knew, for his own freedom, for his divinely ordained privilege to live his life in safety and peace.

The Y. M. C. A. hut was densely packed with laughing, khaki-clad men, all standing about in a great circle, with Harry, Johnson, and the piano in the center. Lustily they sang his songs with him, and boisterous were their shouts for more. The show over at last, Harry went straight to bed, for Captain Godfrey had told him that they must be up at six o'clock the next morning and on their way to Vimy Ridge.

Long before it was time to start, Harry was ready. The two high powered motor cars in which the party traveled moved at breakneck speed over the crowded roads. All traffic, official cars, trucks, ambulances, racing to and from the docks at Boulogne, set the same perilous pace. Overhead a festive sky was almost hidden by airplanes. The sun was high and clear, the country was a lush, fresh green, the air was gentle. In the fields aged peasants labored stoically. Old men, old women of France took up the farm work which the youth had dropped. France was in desperate need of food, and only the very old and the very young were left to raise it. They worked quietly and steadily, their wrinkled faces impassive. "C'est la guerre," they said, with a weary shrug.

Coming now to a turn in the road, the Lauder party was passing some marching troops. The troops turned out to the side of the highway, and despite the speed of the car, a hundred voices along the line rang out, "Hello, Harry!"

"Lord, if it eyn't 'arry 'imself! Lor' bless ye, 'arry!"

They could hear now a faint rumble, minute by minute growing more distinct. No one mentioned it. It sounded like distant thunder, but they knew that it was not thunder.

At another turn in the road they came upon a slow-moving second company of soldiers. Captain Godfrey explained that these men had just left the trenches and were on their way to hospitals and rest billets. Clothes and faces mud-splashed, they moved tiredly, carrying their packs as if every step required a gigantic effort. These men, Godfrey went on, were ill, but not ill enough to ride in the much-needed ambulances.

"Driver!" called Harry. "Stop here!"

When the car had stopped, Lauder hurried out of it and addressed a gaunt young Lieutenant who seemed to be in charge.

"Would your men like to hear a few songs, Lieutenant?"

The young man glanced inquiringly at Captain Godfrey. Godfrey nodded.

"Why, that—that's very good of you, I'm sure. Fall out!"

The men squatted on the side of the road, shoulders sagging, eyes blinking in the sun. While Harry distributed some of the cigarettes he had brought, the tiny piano was lifted from the running board. Suddenly from the midst of the crowd a thin, piping cockney voice cried: "Lor' love us! Don't cher know 'oo this bloke is? If it eyn't 'arry Lauder! 'Ello, 'arry!"

The men were alert now, their tiredness forgotten.

"Go it, 'arry! *I love a Lassie*, 'arry!"

"*Wee Hoose 'mang th' 'eather*, 'arry!"

"*Roamin' i' th' Gloamin'*, 'arry!"

In the field, doing his laughable little walk, wagging his kilt, Harry gave them the songs they wanted. Beneath the grime, faces were animated now as the men joined in the choruses. Every one of them loved some lassie, every one of them dreamed of the wee house that was home, and every one of them liked to believe that someday he would be roamin' i' th' gloamin' away from the roar of the big Berthas, away from the cooties and the mud.

Glancing at his wristwatch, Godfrey told Harry that he was sorry but they would have to be moving on. By noon it was evident that they were nearing the front, for the Captain calmly announced that it was time to don their steel helmets. No longer was the noise of the firing like thunder. It was sharper, an incessant, singular throb which occasionally was interrupted by an ear-splitting detonation. The aspect of the fields had changed. The ground was strewn with wreckage, torn and mangled with shells. Sometimes on either side of the car great clouds of dirt bilged up into the air. The earth was pock-marked with craters.

"Well," smiled Captain Godfrey, pointing ahead, "there it is, gentlemen. There's Vimy Ridge."

"*Yon?*" asked Harry.

So that was the famous Vimy Ridge. Why, compared to the rugged majesty of his own Scottish Highlands, Vimy Ridge was not even a hill! All the world knew about Vimy Ridge. Up that shell-racked slope in the very face of devastating German fire, the Canadians had charged and planted the flag of Britain one April day in 1917. Every inch of that ground had been covered with the dead bodies of Canadians. The Germans had fought stubbornly to maintain their position. The Kaiser's advisers had assured him that Vimy Ridge could not be taken. Well, thought Harry grimly, the Germans knew better now.

The Huns were still shelling it. Something that looked like myriad balls of white cotton, which gave off a white smoke, filled the air. It was shrapnel from the guns of the enemy. The sun was hidden by the thickness of the planes.

Shrapnel bursting everywhere about them, the men left the cars.

There was a mile to walk before they came to the ridge itself, and shell holes made walking difficult. On the ridge, well concealed, a Canadian battery was firing at the Huns. The artillerymen were calm, businesslike, their faces inscrutable. Behind their enormous guns these men worked with the precision of machines; not a moment, not a movement, was wasted.

Lauder was in the thick of battle now. Below him he could see the flat, war-devastated country. About him was a constant droning, like a million bees. He was here, where he had wanted to be for so long, actually watching the guns belch flame. He had fully expected to be afraid, but he was not. He was only excited at being so near the Huns, the detestable, insatiable Huns, bent upon the destruction of his country, possessed with the idea of dominating the world.

The men gave a shout as the little comedian, his helmet slightly askew, stepped among them. It was hot now, exceedingly hot, and hotter than ever here in the battery. Most of the men were stripped to the waist. Bodies and faces were streaked with sweat and grime.

"Hello, Harry!" someone called. "Lord, but it's grand to see that mug of yours!"

"Hello, Harry!" cried another. "Remember me? I met you once in Toronto."

"Hello," exclaimed Harry heartily. "How would ye like a wee bit song?"

"Fine! They told us you were coming, Harry. We got a theatre all ready for you."

"We'll have lunch first," decided Godfrey. "Although you'll find it not quite the fare you're used to, I fancy."

Close by the battery was a little stream. Not so long ago that stream had run red with blood. Even now there had been no time to bury all the dead that had covered the ground after that fiery assault on Vimy Ridge, and here and there were skeletons. Some of the skeletons were Germans. It was easy to distinguish them by the huge boots which were still on the feet, for the German shoes were heavy, their thick soles studded with nails.

When they so confidently began this war, the Germans had not expected to encounter any strong British resistance. They had known that Britain was completely unprepared, and this fact, coupled with the civil war in Ireland and possible mutiny in India, would bring Britain to her knees early in the conflict and force her to sue for peace on any terms which the German High Command chose to inflict; but Britain had met the challenge and was still meeting it, doggedly, desperately. She made blunders, stupid, costly, but she recovered from them with a quickness and resiliency that astonished not only her Allies but her opponents.

"You didn't take the men seriously, did you," asked Captain Godfrey, when lunch was over, "when they said they had a theatre all ready for you?"

"No, of course, I dinna' take them seriously, mon. That was only a wee joke. A theatre on Vimy Ridge!"

"No, I assure you, it wasn't a joke. We *have* a theatre for you. Come and see it."

The theatre was large and deep—a huge cavity in the ground.

"Weel," smiled Harry, as he scrambled into the middle of it while hundreds of khaki-clad figures grouped themselves about the rim and peered down at him, "it's a bit different from any theatre I've ever played i', but I never felt mair like singin' i' ma life."

"*Roamin' i' th' Gloamin'*, Harry!" shouted a dozen voices from above him.

"A' richt, lads, and when I come to th' chorus, ye maun sing it wi' me. Ye ken th' words?"

"Sure!"

Above the roaring and the coughing of the great guns they sang:

"Roamin' i' th' gloamin',
By th' bonny banks o' Clyde . . ."

The guns were so loud now that it seemed to Harry that the entire von Hindenburg line was practically upon him, but his audience remained calmly smoking, smiling, applauding—and Harry kept on singing.

When the concert was over, the men crowded about him, shaking hands.

"So long, Harry. Good luck and—thanks."

"Thanks, Harry. Thanks a million for the songs."

"You'll no be thankin' *me* for what I'm doin' for *you*, laddies. It's me that must be thankin' *you* for what you're doin' for *me*." He grinned. "To say nothin' o' th' fine big theatre ye went to a' th' bother o' diggin' oot for me."

They laughed. "*We* didn't do it. Fritz saved us a lot of trouble, Fritz did. It was sweet of him, wasn't it, to make this hole just yesterday, just in time for you to sing in it?"

Back in the car again, his great load of cigarettes considerably lessened, Lauder asked Captain Godfrey where they were going now.

"To a rest billet. You'll sing to a bunch of men just in from the trenches."

The cars had gone only a little over a mile, when they saw moving toward them a regiment of Somerset men on their way to Ypres. Harry gave the signal to stop and instantly Johnson and the driver were lifting the piano from the car without being told to do so. Again in the roadway Harry sang, again the men sang with him, and a half-hour later the piano was back in its place, the cars were roaring down the road, the Somerset men cheering as they went. Scarcely had they gone five miles when they came upon a crew of two hundred repairmen working on the road. Again the car stopped, the piano was lifted into the field, and in less than two minutes Harry was singing. It was growing late now, and when the concert was ended Captain Godfrey suggested that they had better not stop again else they would fail to reach Aubigny on schedule.

At Aubigny was a rest camp and an old château. Scots troops were waiting here, men who, because of their kilts, the Germans called "Ladies from Hell." Leaning back in the car, Harry's body commenced complaining, insistently telling him how tired it was. Harry began talking back to it sternly.

"Tired! We'll hae none o' *that* th' noo!"

His body reminded him that it had been a long, hard day, and that it was no longer as young as it once was.

"There's an audience o' seven thousand Scots soldiers waitin', most o' them have been fightin' since Mons. Maybe *they're* a bit tired, too, but if they can keep fightin' for you, Harry, you can keep singin' for them. An' we'll hae no mair o' this nonsense!"

On the grounds of the château the piano was set up and the concert began. When it was over there were old friends to greet—stagehands, fellow vaudevillians, schoolmates from Arbroath, miners with whom he had worked in Hamilton.

It was dark when the Lauder party left, black-dark, for the road was unlit and there were no headlights on the cars. This, however, caused no slackening of the speed at which they traveled. The halt finally came at Tramecourt where the party was to spend the night. Here, though the guns sounded close enough, they were not actually in the zone of fire. Immediately dinner was over, they went to bed and not even the noise of the guns could disturb their rest.

So far the enemy had left the stately château of Tramecourt untouched. Rare old furniture was everywhere, priceless pictures still lined the walls. Here was not only comfort, but luxury. From this place the party was to start out every morning, each day's itinerary having been carefully planned in advance. It meant that they must rise at daybreak and be off at once after breakfast.

Day after day along the roads whenever they came within sight of marching troops, the chauffeurs would automatically jam on the brakes and Johnson would become very busy helping to lift the piano. Men fresh from the trenches or going to the trenches went all the better for a song and a funny story. In rest billets they crowded about in a circle as Lauder sang, their number often augmented by smiling French peasants who, though they could not comprehend the words of the songs, could enjoy the lilt of the music. Never less than a hundred miles did the Lauder party travel in a single day.

At last they left Tramecourt for Arras. In this locality every town had been demolished by German bombs, not a house was left standing. Summer was well on its way and the going was hot, but men forgot the heat to cry out:

"Here's Harry!"

"Got a song for us, Harry?"

In what had once been the market squares of small towns, Harry sang, often merely standing up in the car if the party happened to be behind schedule. Immediately outside Arras a company of soldiers started cheering even before the car had come to a stop.

"Hey, Harry! Got a song for us?"

"Aye! What do ye want?"

"*Wee Hoose'mang th' Heather!*"

There was a swift and painful moment just before he began to sing when he wondered how many of these brawny, eager-eyed men would return to their own houses. God, the fearful, senseless toll of war!

The red of the poppies, the blue of the cornflowers stood out in sharp contrast to the ruined buildings and the guns.

Overhead was the whirring of airplanes and the frantic whizz of the shells, while a hundred men swayed to the rhythm of a song they all knew and loved.

> "There's a wee hoose 'mang th' heather.
> There's a wee hoose ow'er th' sea . . ."

CHAPTER SEVENTEEN

Harry Lauder had seen much of the devastation of war, but never could he have imagined anything so mutely tragic as was Arras. It was a bright day in late June, and the sun poured out its gladsome rays upon what once had been a town, stately, serene and beautiful. No house, no wall, remained. Nothing but bricks and debris. Streets were piled high with dust and stones. Only the main road had been cleared and over this great trucks were constantly passing, laden with food and ammunition. Outside of the town had been, not long ago, a battlefield. Now there was only a maze of barbed wire, eloquent testimony to the ingenuity of the human mind.

As the car entered Arras, Tommies seemed to spring up by magic from among the ruins, the dust, the stones. They kept coming until there were over five thousand of them, demanding a song. They sang, unmindful of the clouds of dust that rose in the wake of the swiftly-moving trucks, unmindful of the shells that went whizzing through the air at regular intervals.

Harry had scarcely finished singing when he saw a hardy young Scot in khaki kilts determinedly pushing his way toward him.

"Harry," announced the lad, "they've sent me tae get ye."

"Sent ye? Who?"

"A' of them. I'm tae ask ye if you'll come oot an' sing tae them."

"Where are they, lad? Who are 'they'?"

"They're at a railroad cut atween here an' Lens. We're Hieland regiments, several companies o' us, an' we're holdin' th' cut."

"Of course I'll come."

"Th' noo, Harry?"

"Th' noo, lad. That is, if Captain Godfrey, ma manager, is agreeable."

Godfrey nodded. "It's a risk," he said. "The enemy is very close, you know. He has just been driven out of Lens. I don't promise that we'll ever even arrive at the cut, but if you gentlemen want to take the risk—"

"This lad risked a lot to come wi' th' message, didn't he?"

"He certainly did."

"Then—let's start at once," said Harry.

They arrived at the cut without difficulty, and the men cheered, yelled, waved at the sight of them. Everywhere one looked were shell holes and dugouts. It was a scene grotesque, ugly, stark. In the midst of his boisterously cheering countrymen, Harry looked about him. God, how terrible it was! Inconceivably terrible, like a picture painted in hell. Could the world ever forget what the Germans had done to it? Could the world ever forgive?

"Go ahead, Harry, sing!"

He smiled, told them a funny story and began his song. He had just reached the chorus when not far away a shell exploded. Harry ceased singing, feeling a little sick and dizzy, but none of the soldiers seemed alarmed at the closeness of the shell or the fury of its roar when it exploded. Resolutely, once the noise had died down, he began his song again.

This time he had sung only a few lines when another shell struck the railroad bridge not two hundred yards distant.

"We've been spotted!" yelled an officer.

There was a steady rain of shells now, and through this the men scampered toward the dugouts. Here for a half-hour they waited, laughing, smoking, some squatting on the floor, some sitting on tables, some leaning nonchalantly against the walls while outside the frantic bombing continued.

It was horrible, thought Harry. Suppose a shell should hit this dugout? Suppose the lot of them should suddenly be buried under tons of earth? The men about him were not concerned with such questions. One of them had taken a soiled deck of cards from his pocket, and at the far end of the dugout a game was in progress. After what seemed an eternity, someone said: "Looks as if they've gotten a bit discouraged. Let's go on with the conceit. What do you say, Harry?"

"Done," he answered, and they all trooped into the sun again.

The entertainment lasted an hour, but it was not again interrupted. Lauder knew that getting away was not going to be easy. The bridge had been utterly demolished, and the railroad embankment, along which they must travel, was still being relentlessly shelled. As he and his party moved forward the deluge of shell increased. Seemingly at any second one of those on-coming shells must hit the car and catapult them all into oblivion. Only when they reached the road did Harry draw a full breath.

At last they arrived at headquarters where a platform had been built, upon which Johnson and his piano were already ensconced, while in the wide field beyond the audience was waiting.

The concert over, Godfrey said they must leave at once for Tramecourt. As they were making their way through the debris that was once Arras, the enemy began shelling the place again, but the car traveled safely through the bombardment, and reached the place where the Eleventh Argyll and Sutherland Highlanders waited. This had been John's regiment. Standing there before them it seemed to Harry for a fleeting moment that he saw his son among them, smiling at him. The illusion lasted only a second and he knew that he had imagined it, but his charm had never been more vibrant than it was during that performance, he had never sung so well, never felt more free and vigorous.

It was dark when they finally arrived at Tramecourt and the feeling of buoyancy which he had known earlier had completely evaporated. Lauder was more tired than he had ever been in his life. It was a nagging, aching tiredness and he thought longingly of bed, but the beautiful grounds around the château were athrob with animation. All he could discern in the darkness were small moving lights, like fireflies, seemingly millions of them. Directly in front of the château itself was a single lighted spot. The light was so white as to be blinding, and it covered a wide area. All else was pitch dark. He could not even distinguish the tall old poplars amidst which the château sat enthroned like a tranquil, aged queen.

Out of the darkness a voice cried: "Is that 'arry?"

"Aye," he answered, completely mystified.

"We're all 'ere, 'arry, waitin' for yer. Been waitin' hours, 'arry."

"What—what is a' this?" asked Harry. "I canna' see a thing."

"It's about four hundred men," explained Godfrey. "They were working ten miles away on a road job and they heard you were at Tramecourt. They've put in a hard day's work, but they walked the ten miles hoping you'd give them a song. They've waited a long time. When they saw that it was getting dark they said they didn't care how late it was, they'd wait until you came. So while they waited they rigged up that spotlight from some headlights. What do you say, Harry? I expect you'd like your dinner first, eh?"

"No, I'll sing first. Tell Johnson to have th' piano brought up."

So Harry sang for an audience he never saw. The spotlight was too blinding to see beyond it, but now he knew that what he at first thought were fireflies were lighted cigarettes. It was odd, hearing the laughter and the applause, yet singing into total darkness. As he sang an army of bats, attracted by the lights, flew blindly back and forth past his face, all about him. Involuntarily, he kept dodging them, but he continued singing. The men refused to let him stop. They, too, had put in a long day, and when the show was over they had a ten-mile walk ahead of them; despite this, it was well after midnight before the concert ended.

Next day the party left for Albert. The one building which remained even partially standing in Albert was a church, before which was a large statue of the Virgin and Child. High above the surrounding desolation, as if forever aloof from time and strife and hate, it seemingly maintained its position only by a miracle. Above passing armies, friend and foe, it swayed and tottered. Apparently at any moment it must surely fall.

"No," Godfrey declared, "it has been like that for a long time. When a storm comes, it sways almost horizontal with the wind, but it is always there intact in the morning. To the peasants around here it's an inspiring symbol. It—"

He broke off, for a company of Australians were almost abreast of the car, and one of them shouted, "Look, it's Harry! It's Harry Lauder!"

For the first time Harry did not want to stop, for the way led to Ovilliers—to John's grave. That grave had become to him a Mecca, the finale to a kind of holy pilgrimage.

"Give us a song, Harry?"

"How about a few songs, Harry?"

"Aye, lads, aye. I'll gie ye a song. Of course, I wull. But first, did ye ever hear aboot th' Scotsman who. . . ."

To those who were with him it seemed odd—a comedian stopping to sing rollicking songs, stopping to tell jokes to a company of Australians whom he had never seen—while he was on his way to the grave of his only son.

But when it was over and the car had started again, they saw him slump back in his seat, saw the desolation and hunger in the blue eyes. No one spoke as the car sped along Bapaune Road. A trim young soldier, little more than a boy, had joined them as guide. When the cars stopped, the youth stepped into the road and said, "It's this way, Mr. Lauder."

Stretching out before them was a veritable sea of white crosses, among which Harry and his guide moved slowly, soundlessly. So neat, so orderly, those mounds, so white the crosses, thousands of them, covering an area so vast that one could not see where they ended. Finally on a little hill the young soldier stopped and merely pointed, then he turned back to the car.

Harry fell prone upon the soft earth, beneath which lay the body of his boy. Above him the sun, warm and kindly. About him silence and death. The comedian lay upon the grave, sobbing unrestrainedly.

At long last he rose, walked back among the crosses, and silently entered the car. No one spoke.

Lauder did not feel like singing that day, but he sang, nevertheless, and went on singing day after day over the highroads of a battered but unbeaten France. As the time for his return to England drew near he began formulating a plan.

For a long time he had been thinking, not of the men who had died in France, but of the men who would return, those of them who would be almost helpless, adrift, unable to fill their old jobs. He could not help all of them but he could help his own countrymen, the Scots. They would have their pensions, of course, but they must have more than this—some little business which would make them independent and self-respecting. They did not want charity, and Harry was determined that his plan should not be regarded as such. The idea was that each man who returned to Scotland physically unable to resume his means of livelihood, which the war had interrupted, should be given enough money to let him have a fresh start in the world which he had fought so valiantly to save. How was Lauder to get so much? It would require at least five million dollars.

More and more as the plan evolved, took form in his mind, became something practical and concrete, it possessed him to the exclusion of all other interests. He would never stop until he raised the sum he needed. He would go anywhere, everywhere, do anything to raise it. He must not and would not stop until his purpose had been accomplished. He knew that he would not be able to devote his entire thought and energies to the achievement, for there was other work to be done. He would work until he dropped for Britain and for her Allies. He had had a first-hand glimpse of war. He knew its grimness, its bitterness. The most he could do seemed comparatively small—raising money, lecturing, singing in camps and hospitals. It seemed so little. Besides doing all this, and fulfilling theatrical contracts, he meant to write a book which he intended to call, "A Minstrel in France."

He had been back in England only a few months when he was approached by a representative of his government and asked to go to America. America knew him, respected him, loved him. Would he go to America and tell the American people what he had seen at the front?

"I'll go anywhere," he answered, "I'll do anything; but I'll speak to them i' ma ain way."

While these plans were progressing, a cable arrived from America which discussed the details of his next tour. He cabled back his acceptance on condition that he would be free to speak in the allied cause at any time or in any place. When it was known in the States that Lauder was to come this time not solely in his capacity as entertainer, the American Y. M. C. A. invited him to speak to the American youth.

Already "The Harry Lauder Million Pound Fund for Maimed Men, Scottish Soldiers and Sailors" had been well organized. Night after night he had lain awake worrying about the boys who would come back, some with eyesight gone, some without an arm or perhaps a leg. He had seen so many of them in the hospitals. They, too, he knew, must be worrying about what the future would hold for them. How often had he seen old soldiers selling pencils on street corners? Well, now it was a certainty that Scottish men who had fought in this World War would not be subject to such indignity. If a man needed a hundred or even two hundred pounds to launch himself in business, he would have it. It would be, not lent, but given.

Newspapers had been glad to give such a plan publicity. Five million dollars, a million pounds sterling, was the goal. He went to Glasgow, London, Edinburgh, Manchester, and addressed enthusiastic meetings. The Honorary President of the fund was the former Prime Minister, The Earl of Roseberry. Its treasurer was Lord Balfour. Already much money had been raised, and the Scots in America would contribute more. Little envelopes with plaid borders would be distributed among the audience; in these contributions would be sent to a New York bank. Nance would stand in the lobbies after each performance, selling stamps which were like the Red Cross seals. Everyone was eager to help. Money was showered upon him as he stood singing. Stagehands voluntarily donated their week's wages.

He had, he felt, so much to tell America, so much to tell that he had seen with his own eyes. The little cemetery at Mont St. Quentin, for instance, where the Germans had dug up the dead. He was going to beg America to hold fast to her faith. He was going to repeat in America what hundreds of British soldiers had said to him: "We fight in a righteous cause and a holy war."

The Atlantic in those days was not the safest place to be, but the thought of helping America with her Liberty Loan Drives, raising money for his own fund, speaking in behalf of England, dwarfed the risk almost to triviality. Throughout the nights the *Mauretania* ran without a single light, but she reached port safely.

America at war was a vastly different America than that which Harry had previously known. America, young and strong and spirited, meant business. Everywhere—on buses, in theatres—women were knitting. Armories were holding Saturday night dances for the soldiers and sailors. White sugar was almost never seen, even in the smartest restaurants. There were heatless days and meatless days. Food prices were soaring, and "food slackers," those who failed to comply with regulations, were watched and punished. The only places permitted heat on Mondays were the theatres, and not a theatre in the city but was crowded to capacity on Mondays. Enormous sums were raised each night in the theatres. There was no escape from these appeals. Famous people sold Liberty Bonds on every busy street comer. In Healy's, Jack's, Rector's, Mouquin's, every smart restaurant, the Minute Men went about from table to table. France had sent over the Chasseurs, the famous Blue Devils, who also added their efforts as bond salesmen.

Profits to be made in war work were unlimited. Silk shirts, selling at twelve dollars a piece, were so universally worn by the men on the home front that it was called the "Silk Shirt Era." Women were taking the places of men on elevators and as streetcar conductors. Effigies of the Kaiser and the Crown Prince, called derisively the "Clown Prince," were hanged on Fifth Avenue.

The only songs which caught the popular taste were war songs— *My Buddy, Roses of Picardy, Over There, Smiles, Tipperary.* Taxes were steadily rising. War-saving stamps were so much in demand that the government had difficulty in getting enough of them off the presses. Overnight, industry had swerved to war production. This was, America declared, "a war to end war." She told the world she knew what she was fighting for, not for aggrandizement, but "to make the world safe for Democracy."

The Sunday night following his arrival, Lauder spoke at the Hippodrome. This first speech brought such amazing results that invitations followed to speak in other large cities. In addition to these propaganda speeches, never a day passed but that he went out on the street corners selling bonds. There was one noontime, speaking in front of the Sub-Treasury, when he raised half a million dollars in only a few minutes. To him, it was astonishing. Never before had he been so profoundly aware of the untold resources and the generosity of America. The Allies *could* not lose, he knew it now.

The response to appeals for his own fund was equally gratifying. He had completed his book, "A Minstrel in France," copies of which were auctioned off in behalf of the fund. A single copy went for five thousand dollars at the Metropolitan Opera House.

There were towns in America, however, where a strong pro-German feeling still lingered tenaciously. Often Lauder was insulted and even threatened, but nothing could stop him. To lecture, to help with the loan drives, to give his performances, to raise money for his fund, to give concerts in encampments and hospitals, this was what he was here for.

One day Nance brought him a copy of the *New York Outlook*. "Here's a poem," she said, "aboot you. It's beautiful. It's by someone we dinna ken, someone named Amelia J. Burr. It's called *The Fiery Cross*. Listen, Harry, listen:

He stood behind the footlights and he set the crowd a-laughing
With the same old crooning chuckle that we loved in other
    years,
And only those who knew could guess the grief behind the
    daffing,
But for those who did, the laughter had a secret salt of tears.
Then at the last he came out in his grass-green coat and bonnet
With his gaudy tartans coloured like a garden in the sun,
The same quaint little figure—but a different face was on it
When he sang about the laddies that had fought so well and
    won.

A face lined hard with furrows where the plough of pain had
　　driven,
Blue eyes that now were shadow-set through many a sleepless
　　night,
The face of one who more than life ungrudgingly had given,
Who called on us to do as well—and ah! we owed his right.
We saw in him the Fiery Cross of Scotland, charged and gory
And our spirit burned within us to the challenge that he gave,
For the player was a prophet as he spoke his people's glory,
'We're a wee land, and a puir land, but by God above, we're
　　brave.'

"You see, mon Harry, there are people who understand what you're
tryin' to do."

"What I'm tryin' to do, Nance? Think what these American lads are
going to do. Ah, but they're splendid, these young Americans, splendid! They remind me o' oor ain Scots regiments. Lookin' at these boys,
big, clean, handsome lads, makes me realize as I never did before,
what a graund an' vital nation this America is."

It was the winter of 1917. There had been food riots in Berlin. The
Russian army was in a state of mutiny, the Soviets had overthrown
the Kerensky government, and Russia, impotent, desperate, was now
no longer a part of the war. Still uppermost in the minds of the German High Command and the German people was the subjugation of
Britain. Food rations in Britain had been so drastically reduced that
famine seemed inevitable. The Italian front had been utterly crushed.
But America was fresh, confident, seemingly inexhaustible.

Again in the White House, President and Mrs. Wilson, Mr. and
Mrs. Lauder were having tea. Wilson thanked Lauder for all that he
had done, but the President's voice was tired, his long, scholarly face
was unsmiling, thinner, amazingly older, than when Harry had last
seen him.

"No mair ardent American ever lived than Woodrow Wilson,
Nance," declared Harry as the car drove them away from the White
House that day. "Aye, he's a great mon, is Wilson. I wonder if th' people
appreciate him? I wonder if they realize just how great he is."

"He is that, and a tired, worried mon, too. Ah, dear, little did we think, mon Harry, when you were diggin' awa' i' th' darkness o' th' pits that one day we'd be havin' tea wi' th' President o' the United States, and he'd be thankin' ye for helpin' America. We've come a long, long way, Harry.

Do ye mind th' first time ye played here i' America, how nervous ye were, and how ye wanted to turn richt around an' go back to Scotland?"

"Aye," mused her husband as if he had not heard her, "a great mon is Woodrow Wilson, but Nance, do ye ken his mither had Scots blood i' her? Aye, she was th' daughter of a Scots meenister."

"You'd know he was a schoolmaster just to look at him, and dear, dear, isn't he *henspeckle?* Losh, I wonder if those dreams o' his wull ever come true? Wull there ever be a war to end war, I wonder? Wull this war *really* make th' world safe for Democracy?"

"I dinna ken, Nance. It *could.* It's no an impossible dwam that men should hae a safe world to live i'. That's th' kind of a world Wilson is contemplatin'. He's a stem mon, is Wilson, but I love him. An' what a difference there is atween him an' Teddy! Nothin' o' th' schoolmaster aboot Teddy." He closed his eyes wearily, for in half an hour he was due to make another speech.

Although he always achieved the effect of speaking extemporaneously, these speeches of Lauder's were no more spontaneous than were his performances. Every word, every pause had been worked out well in advance. Almost constantly, however, he was forced to make last-minute changes in order to combat some sly new trend in German propaganda, for Germany was determined to break up the unity among the Allies.

New Year's Day he and Nance spent on the train. Middle-aged, lonely, they sat in their stateroom trying not to remember that New Year's Day a year ago.

"Do ye mind that Christmas i' Hamilton, Nance, when I thought I had failed and th' world didna' want Harry Lauder? And how you encouraged me. You've always encouraged me, a' th' days we've been together. I'm thinkin' th' right wife can make a mon or mar a mon. I couldna' hae done it, Nance, wi'oot you."

"Of course ye could, Harry."

"An' do ye mind th' Christmas Eves i' the ould country, an' a' of us loungin' aboot th' roarin' fire an' tellin' ghaist stories? What stories ma mither could tell! Make th' shivers run a' doon your spine. Weel, here it is. New Year's Day 1918. Are there tears i' your een, Nance?"

"Aye, I'm a bit hamesick, Harry," she admitted. "On holidays I long for hame most of a'. Ah, to just bide a wee quietly at hame!"

He, too, was homesick. Memories of his beloved Scotland arose within him, memories of things which he had noticed without knowing that he noticed, the simple, everyday things. How spectral and lonely are the rushes when you would be looking at them through the still, slow dawn. And the cheery sound of birdsong just before candle time. And the smell of the grass after a rain. And the drear sound of the rain on the turf. And an owl's ghostly cry of a moonless night. The stones in the fields. The cows grazing on the moors. The noise of the carts along the country roads. The old women making lace in the doorways of the little houses that are flush with the streets, those small limewashed houses straggling along winding, unpaved roads. Sheep that watch you as you pass, their eyes as sad and reproachful as the eyes of the doomed. The larches at Dunoon.

"Someday, Nance," he proclaimed, "we'll retire."

She gave him a glance that was wise and skeptical.

"I mean it. We'll retire—someday. But we're young yet, Nance. I'm only forty-eight and you're only forty-four." He sighed. "1918. What wull it bring to th' world? Can there be peace i' 1918? Wull there *ever* be peace i' th' world again?"

"Forget th' war for a minute, Harry."

"I canna'. It's a fine lot o' men America's sendin' to France—and why should there be strikes amang those who stay at hame? How can there be strikes when those braw laddies are goin' awa' to fight an' die—an' ither men who stay behind strike for a few cents mair pay! Strikes—i' wartime! It's inconceivable. Strikes—when there's so much of everything i' America. In Britain th' noo they've no milk for their tea i' order that th' bairns may have it."

They were silent a long time. It was a weary business, this business of constant traveling. He looked across at his wife. Her body remained persistently girlish. Were there tiny wrinkles around her eyes? Harry Lauder never saw them. Was there a strand or two of gray in the soft, dark hair?

He patted her small hand lovingly. "After Canada, there's hame, Nance—Dunoon, Glen Branter, an' I'll do a bit o' fishin' i' th' loch."

But Glen Branter with its large, modern house, its moors, its mountains, its loch and its larches, only depressed them. They could not, after all, remain here. There was only one thing they must do, and then they would shut up the place forever.

On the main road from Dunoon to Strachur was a knoll. The view from this knoll had been a favorite of John's, and his parents decided to put up a monument to him here. It would stand proudly in the middle of an enclosed space, an iron fence around it. Within the fence, on each side of the monument, remained room for a single grave. One day they would both be buried here, Nance on the right side, Harry on the left.

The monument complete, they left Glen Branter for London. There were contracts to fill in London and another American tour to follow.

Things were going badly in France until July when the entire picture suddenly changed. It was in July at the Battle of Château-Thierry that the Americans proved their fighting ability. The British began to meet with success in Belgium. At Amiens the German line collapsed. By October, Germany was in retreat. In November, the Kaiser fled to Holland, and on November 11th the Armistice was signed.

Peace. Peace at long last, and a world safe again, safe for Democracy. Thirty-five million people had died because one country had set out to subjugate the world, but, declared those who were left, a thing like that could not possibly happen again. It had been a lesson dearly bought, but it had been a lesson learned. Now there were lights in London, and now there would be an end to the air raids, the blockade, the casualty lists.

It was a little difficult at first to get used to peace, just as at first it had been difficult to grow used to war, for all production had been geared to war; but it was to be a new kind of world, a better world for everybody. Mr. Lloyd George declared that he was going to make England "a land fit for heroes."

Harry Lauder, who had made enormous sums and had been called stingy, was now almost bankrupt because he had given unstintedly of his income to the cause of freedom. It was shortly after the war that the British government offered to buy Glen Branter for purposes of reforestation. He was glad to sell it. He and Nance had imagined that they wanted to rest, but now they found that they could not.

Glen Branter, with its quiet, its larches, its flowering shrubs, its rolling hills—they had loved it, and John had loved it. Had he lived, nothing could have made them part with the place. But now Laudervale, the house in Dunoon, was enough for them. They were strangely restless. Work and travel. Travel and work. This seemed imperative.

The first steamer leaving for America after the Armistice was the *Mauretania*. The Lauders and the Vallances were on it, along with five thousand homeward bound American troops. No longer did the great ship sail in darkness, no longer was there fear of torpedoes.

The American tour of 1918 ended in San Francisco, and again there were contracts in Australia. On Lauder's arrival, Sydney turned out with a welcome as great as the one she had given him five years ago. It was the 1st of March, 1919. The boat had docked that morning, and at noon the Lauders and the Vallances were having luncheon in the Hotel Australia, with them were two old friends, John Tait and T. C. Carroll.

A page brought Tom a cablegram. Harry, Tait and Carroll continued their conversation until Tom rose, walked gravely around the table and stood at Harry's side, his hand outstretched. Harry gazed up at him questioningly. Was this another of Tom's jokes?

"Congratulations," said Tom. "Congratulations—*Sir Harry!*"

Harry blinked. Nance gasped. Tom turned to his sister. "Nance," he announced, "you're now—Lady Lauder!"

Knighted. Sir Harry and Lady Lauder.

"The telegram," cried Tait, "what does it say, Tom?"

"It says that His Majesty the King has been graciously pleased to confer upon Harry a Knighthood of the British Empire!"

Nance's eyes filled with tears. Yes, they had come a long way from the coal pits of Hamilton.

CHAPTER EIGHTEEN

For weeks afterward the Lauders were deluged by a steady inpouring of congratulatory cables.

"I'll cable back ma thanks to every one o' them," exclaimed Harry, his face flushed with excitement.

"Hoots, mon," said Tom with a humorous and characteristic lift of his narrow brows, "do ye ken how much it'll cost?"

Harry's blue eyes grew sober. "Weel, maybe I could speak ma gratitude wi' mair eloquence i' letters," he decided prudently.

For two weeks his every spare moment was spent in letter writing. Already it was becoming natural to hear Nance addressed as Lady Lauder; but everywhere Harry went the same old friendly, informal salutations greeted him.

"Hello, Harry!"

"God bless you, Harry!"

A friend strolling along the street with him one day asked, "I say, Harry, do you know all these persons?"

"Never saw them before," he answered cheerily.

"But—they address you in a most familiar fashion, old chap."

"And why not? I never saw them before, but they've seen me, thanks be! And as for familiarity—they helped me buy th' shoon an' th' claes I'm wearin'. They paid for th' parritch I had for breakfast, and th' bit o' beef I'll be eatin' for ma dinner. If it weren't for them, and th' likes o' them, I'd still be diggin' coal i' th' pit i' Scotland."

He knew, did Lauder, that an actor must love his audience before an audience can love an actor. He knew that every audience demanded much, but most of all it demanded sincerity. He had spent many splendid years in the theatre, but he had been knighted for his patriotic services during the war rather than for his mastery as an entertainer. He was proud of the title, grateful for it. Sir Harry Lauder. Harry Lauder—a knight! He could see himself a barefooted, ragged urchin mixing swill for Wattie Sandiland's pigs; he saw himself a young boy, begrimed and strong, descending among the rats in the pit night after night. He saw himself tramping from agency to agency begging for a chance to sing. Knighthood. What did it symbolize, after all, but service, service to Crown and country? In the ancient medieval days, knighthood was associated with chivalry. And what was chivalry but being steadfast to one's God, one's sovereign, one's lady, living up to one's highest concepts of honor and courtesy?

"Why," he exclaimed one day out of a deep silence, "this bonny world is fu' of them!"

Nance looked up from her sewing inquiringly. "Fu' of what? Are ye daft, mon Harry?"

"Fu' of knights! A mon can be a knight wi'oot havin' a 'sir' attached to his name!"

She nodded, and her thin face lit up with a bright, mischievous smile. "Ye dinna look any different bein' a knight than ye looked bein' a mister—an' your tie's aye squint an' your kilt needs pressin'!"

"Does it?" he asked with the astonishment of a credulous child.

"It does. Losh, i' the ould days it would have taken a' ma time polishin' your armor. I dinna ken *how* I would have done it, for th' noo I'm kept verra, verra busy straightenin' your ties!"

They laughed together, and he kissed her.

"Harry," she asked dreamily, "do ye mind th' time we were roamin' i' th' gloamin' along Lanark Road, an' you promised you'd make a *lady* out o' me?"

"Aye, Nance, an' those were th' graund days, too."

She sighed and leaned contentedly against him. "They were so," she agreed softly.

"Well, Harry," invariably asked his friends, "no doubt you'll retire now?"

"Retire? Retire? A young lad like me—retire?"

"But why not? You have fame, wealth, honors. What else is there left to work for?"

"There's th' joy o' th' work, itsel'," he answered.

From 1919 to 1923, he saw about him a swiftly changing world. For a time immediately after the war, it had seemed confused. Prices were soaring, yet everywhere one heard of unemployment. The demand for luxuries was increasing. It was a day of rash and unprecedented speculation. Particularly pronounced was the change in the entertainment world. One by one the palatial theatres heretofore dedicated to vaudeville and drama were being turned into moving-picture houses. But the vogue for Harry Lauder was as great as, and even greater than, ever. No one who saw him saw him but once. They came again and again. They heard the same songs, watched him go through the identical "business," yet the Lauder performance remained the vanquisher of boredom, as timeless as the sun.

The enormous fortune which had dwindled during the war was now as substantial as it had been back in 1913. When he walked along the street everyone was sure to recognize the clean-shaven little man with the bald head, the long nose, the wide mouth, the strong chin, the kilts, the pipe and the walking stick. Though from time to time new songs were added to his repertoire, the public continued to demand the old ones. In his mid-fifties, despite increasing weight, he was as zestful and as agile as he had been during his first London season. Though the risqué was becoming a touchstone of cleverness, Lauder's act was kept deliberately wholesome. He had no need and no inclination to descend into the off-color in order to get his laughs. His audience would laugh at him now before he spoke a word. All he had to do was come on the stage, give that characteristic little chuckle, a wag of his kilt—and the laugh came.

His philosophy was simple.

"Harry," asked one of his friends during a rare quiet evening at Laudervale, "what would you say was the greatest thing in a man's life?"

Behind their glasses, the blue eyes looked over at Nance, knitting serenely in a far corner. "Love," answered Harry feelingly, "love is th' greatest thing i' a mon's life."

In 1925 he gave another command performance, this time for King George and Queen Mary at Balmoral Castle. Their eldest son, Edward, was one of Harry's most treasured friends. His friendship with the Prince of Wales had assumed a delightfully informal tone.

The Prince, whom all England adored, visited Harry often in his dressing room and brought him back walking sticks from his many voyages. Still dapper and immaculate, the heir to England's throne looked tired, these days. Like all of Britain, Harry loved him, expected great things of him, and wanted to see him suitably married.

"Your brother, th' Duke o' York, has set ye a fine example. He has so—marryin' Lady Elizabeth Bowes-Lyon, a Scottish bride. Ye should follow your brother's example."

The Prince nodded, smiled. "I might do worse, Harry," he agreed, "I might do worse."

Harry was playing the London Hippodrome when rumor had it that at long last the Prince was surely in love. Only—who was the lady? All London was curious about this. But the Prince, suave, lithe, good-looking, maintained his usual silence on the subject. He sat in the box now, and as Harry finished singing one of his newer songs, called out brightly, "I Love a Lassie, Harry!"

Harry faced him, grinned, and called back, "Aye, we ken ye do, but what we a' want to ken is—*who is she?*"

The Prince laughed, the audience applauded.

There was always a great deal of good-natured heckling directed at

Harry, especially from his English audiences. He joked with his audience and his audience joked with him. His answers were quick, spontaneous, witty. It was a common occurrence for men to call out that they had worked with him in the mines. There was one performance in London where a spectator continued this raillery until it became objectionable, not only to Harry but to the audience.

"Harry!" shouted the man, at last, "I worked i' th' mine wi' ye!"

"Aye," answered Harry, "and if I'd had a wooden head like yours, I'd *still* be i' th' mines!"

"Bravo, Harry!" cried the audience, and laughed until it was hoarse.

No matter how often he played a town, he was always besieged with reporters begging for interviews.

A reporter once asked, "Harry, you seem to be the happiest man in the world. What's your recipe for happiness?"

The answer came readily. "Forget aboot it."

"Eh?"

"Th' quickest way to be happy, lad, is to forget a' aboot happiness, an' just work hard at th' job i' hand. An' th' thing to get busy on is th' job o' makin' *ithers* happy. That's th' secret o' real contentment. Look around ye for a job o' work that wull brighten up someone else's existence."

"And success, Harry? How about success?"

"Success," he affirmed, "is never impossible, never entirely oot o' reach, so don't you get downhearted an' think that it is. Just grin an' sit up an' reach oot a bit farther till ye do get hold of it. I've had enough hard knocks i' ma time to ken that sittin' doon under them is th' worst thing possible. That gets success no nearer, but it makes one real disheartened. It does so. Get on wi' th' next job to hand—you'll feel less sorry for yoursel' then—an' watch like a cat for anither chance to succeed. It always comes if ye work an' watch for it—or so I've found, anyway. An' dinna count on good luck any more than on bad. Nothin' worth while comes to us except by th' result o' oor ain sweated labor; if we try hard enough, we can ensure success."

"Who won the war, Harry?" he was asked at a large banquet in New York.

Harry smiled. "Weel, after long an' serious consideration on th' whole subject, I've come to the conclusion that the English an' th' French an' th' Belgians an' the Americans a' admirably assisted Scotland to win th' war!"

He was getting old and he looked it, but he had not yet even begun to feel it. Often he sat thinking back over his life and counting up the things he had for which to be grateful. Lauder had an unfailing sense of gratitude for the friends he had made. Friendship to him had always been one of the most precious things in life. It was not alone the friends that were rich and famous like Thomas Lipton, Lord Dewar, Henry Ford, Andrew Carnegie, Marshall Field, John Wanamaker, John L. Sullivan, Jim Corbett, Jim Jeffries, Bob Fitzsimmons—these were not the only friendships he treasured; he treasured the friendship of old miners who would now and then come backstage to see him, of plain men with whom he could talk so freely. Too, there was Will Morris, William Blackwood, Ted Carroll, Sir Alexander Murray, Al Smith, Donald Munro, but the best and closest friend of all was Tom Vallance. For over thirty-five years he and Tom had been inseparable. They had traveled everywhere together and now when they were both old, they were doing more traveling than ever before.

No reception in Lauder's long career was greater than the one which awaited him in Capetown, South Africa. After South Africa there had been America again, London, Ireland, Hong Kong, Shanghai, Rangoon, Benares, Calcutta, Bombay, Lahore, Delhi, Singapore, New Zealand, Manila, Tasmania, back to Australia.

"It's time we retired, mon Harry," said Nance, as they sailed to the Straits Settlements from India.

"Aye, Nance, as soon as these present contracts are finished, I'll no sign anither."

As he spoke, a fellow passenger, strolling along the deck, was saying to his companion, "When I meet MacKay. . . ."

Nance smiled. "That mon is aye talkin' aboot th' fine times he's going to have when he meets that friend o' his, MacKay—'when I meet MacKay,' that's a' th' mon can think of."

"When I meet MacKay—" echoed Harry thoughtfully.

There was a long pause. Nance closed her eyes, and was almost asleep in the deck chair when Harry's voice rang out enthusiastically.

"It's a song, Nance! We've a song there!"

"Song? What song? Where?"

"A graund song it'll be, too! 'When I Meet MacKay'!"

She smiled and shook her head. "Harry, Harry, you an' your songs! When these contracts are ended, you'll sign fresh ones. Your heart's i' your singin' as much as it ever was."

"True, Nance. I tell masel' I'll stop, but I don't. Maybe because I canna'. Somehow, it seems as if I maun keep goin'. I'm like an ould clock that's wound up an' canna' run doon."

She sighed. "It's been worse ever since—the war."

"Aye. Aye. Weel, here's a new song—'When I Meet MacKay—When I Meet MacKay'—"

Songs, he found, were not the only things he could write. *Harry Lauder at Home and on Tour* in 1907; *Minstrel in France* in 1918; *Between You and Me* written and published in 1919, these had brought him genuine enjoyment. Now there was a serious book of memoirs which he meant to write as soon as he could find the time, and which would be called *Roamin' in the Gloamin'*. He and Nance often talked about it, and Nance was even more eager than himself that the work should be undertaken.

In 1926, Lauder announced that he was making his farewell tour.

"There'll be another one next year," predicted Will Morris in Lauder's dressing room at the Century Theatre.

In 1927, they were back in Glasgow. In a few days now, they would take the little steamer for Dunoon. At Laudervale in Dunoon were innumerable mementoes of their travels. Silks from India. Ivory from Delhi. Gold ashtrays from Lahore. Bedspreads and ebony from China. The parquet floor in Harry's study was of mahogany from the Philippines. Yes, everywhere they looked was a reminder of the fact that together they had seen all that was best in the whole wide world. Hardly a spot on the globe where Harry had not fished, played golf and sung; and now he was going to write about all that. He was at last going to begin his memoirs. He had laid in a generous stock of paper, his Waterman was filled, and in July, 1927, while they were still in Glasgow, he set to work.

"Dinna forget to tell aboot that time i' Toronto when there was a smallpox scare an' we a' had to be vaccinated," Nance said, "an' dinna forget to tell them aboot th' time you bought a coal mine i' Mexico that didna' even exist!" She laughed. "Oh, Harry, mon Harry, it'll be a graund book! It wull so. I can hardly wait for it to be finished an' published. What a lot o' travelin' you'll hae to talk aboot! But I—I'm hopin', Harry, that most of oor wanderin' is over th' noo."

"Aye, Nance, when th' next farewell tour ends, that'll bring us up to 1929, an' after that we'll settle doon at Laudervale. We wull so."

"Get on wi' th' book, Harry, I'm anxious to be readin' it."

Each chapter finished, he read it to her and she would criticize it, discuss it, recall forgotten incidents. It came to him how helpless he would be without Nance. Why, she was as much a part of him as the very breath that he drew; Nance—tender, brave and compassionate. Together, during the writing of the book, they re-lived the past.

With the exception of his brother George, who had died recently at Dunoon, the Lauders were scattered. Matt was in California. Jock was in Newcastle, New South Wales. Alec, who for a few years had an act like his brother's, was now in business in Hamilton. Bella, Jean, Mary were all married. Because of his incessant traveling, Harry had seen little of them, and their place in the book would necessarily be a minor one.

"Dinna forget, Harry," Nance would say, "it was on that tour, wasn't it, that we had breakfast wi' th' Hardings at th' White House? Losh, what a handsome mon he was—and that cordial! I mind we had bacon an' eggs. An' afterwards you an' he played golf together oot at th' Congressional Golf Course. Or—no, it was during that tour that we met th' *Coolidges*. It was wintertime, because I mind I wore ma seal coat."

"What would ye think if I gie th' Presidents a whole chapter to themselves, Nance?"

"Please yoursel', Harry," she answered, and gave a long, wistful sigh. "Dear, dear, it makes me feel ould."

"What? What does?"

"Everything. Th' memories that keep comin' back of oor long years together. These flappers wi' their closely clipped hair an' their skirts up to their knees. An' you—makin' farewell tours. I dinna ken why it is, but lately I'm feelin' verra, verra ould. You're fifty-seven. I'm fifty-three. It's time we were restin.'"

"Aye. When I'm traveling I think it would be pleasant to sit quietly, to fish, to read, to write, to listen to this newfangled radio; an' then when I'm doin' a' that, it seems strange not to be smellin' th' grease paint, not to be havin' to catch trains. Well, now, let's see—let's see, where was I i' th' book? Oh, yes. I was just about to tell ma readers aboot Captain."

The book was half finished in August when Nance was taken suddenly ill. Though never robust in appearance, Nance had been seldom sick. She had been looking tired lately, but she begged him to get on with the book and not to worry about her.

In three days she was dead.

They took her back to Glen Branter and buried her beside John's monument.

CHAPTER NINETEEN

Alec, Harry's fourth brother, Alec's wife and his young daughter, Greta, came to him at once, and remained with him because they saw how deeply he needed them. It was good to have them there, young Greta, especially—sweet, gentle, understanding Greta whose eyes, so clear, so tender, kept reminding him of his mother's eyes. But despite their efforts to make him comfortable, it seemed to Harry impossible that he could go on living, eating, fishing, without Nance. There would be years, perhaps, long years—without Nance; and how to face those years? How to face each day that must follow—until he, too, reached the end of the road?

It was, he thought later, the book that saved him. There it lay—stacks of paper upon his desk. The half-finished manuscript kept telling him how eager Nance had been for him to finish it. He picked up his Waterman again and went on—went on writing, page after page, day following day. Writing, it seemed that Nance was right there in the room, watching over him, inspiring him as she had always done. Dead? Nance, dead? Not a bit of it. She had come to the end of a road, that was all. But for her, as for John, the road had not really ended, and one day, surely, as surely as the sun shone, the three of them would be together again.

And there was no deadness about it. There was only life—life, vitality, action, joy. This conviction sustained him.

It sustained him that Christmas, the first Christmas at Dunoon without Nance. The telegrams helped, too; they kept pouring in from everywhere, so that it took him and Greta hours to open them all.

When the book was finished, there was the next American tour which included six straight months of one-night stands. Only yesterday's actors know what six months of one-night stands can mean—a new hotel, a new theatre, a new town each night, catching trains at odd hours. It was the most difficult tour Lauder had ever made, yet he welcomed it, for the incessant traveling, the excitement, the new scenes, new faces, all this helped him through the days wherein he must wander alone.

"HARRY LAUDER'S SIXTH ANNUAL TOUR" was completed in 1930. Before it was finished, he signed a contract to make several motion pictures in London. The most successful of these was *Huntingtower*. But making motion pictures was not Harry's idea of enjoyment—it was the audience he loved, the friendliness and the laughter of an audience, an audience he could laugh back at, an audience he could see.

The pictures finished, there were radio contracts waiting.

In the early days of his career, stage fright had not been unknown to Lauder, but "mike fright," he discovered, was a hundred times worse.

Realizing that much of his ability to put over a song depended upon mannerisms and make-up, Lauder faced the microphone in his familiar costumes and went through his "business" just as he had on the stage; but it was strange and uncomfortable, not having the "feel" of an audience, not hearing the laughs, the applause. Had anyone been listening to him, anyone at all? Had anyone chuckled during his songs, had anyone laughed?

He realized how vast was his audience when basketsful of letters reached him, letters from hospitals, from lonely island places all over the world. The new audience was larger than any he had known in the past, yet when the contracts ended, he did not renew them.

In 1932, Lauder wrote another book, a jolly little book called *Wee Drappies*, which had an encouraging sale. It brought joy to countless people, but a deep grief touched its author that year when Tom, who had been almost an alter ego, reached the end of the road.

In 1934, Lauder decided it was time he retired. Lauder Ha' at Strathaven, twenty-five miles from Glasgow, was a comfortable and roomy place, a proud, substantial house of brick and stone, which he had bought after selling Dunoon. Alec, his last remaining brother, died that year, but there was still Greta and her mother, competent Scots housewives both, and at Lauder Ha' the three Lauders settled down to long, quiet, uneventful years.

It was a pleasant place in which to grow serenely old.

There was a tranquil back-drop of hills, green-clad, majestic; there was the garden and the larks that came to sing in it; there was the long, deepening afterglow when the restful, blue-gray mist hung like a sheer veil over the quiet fields. There were the streams, fairly bulging with fish.

Years were passing, and the trunks which held the costumes remained locked. And, oddly, it seemed quite all right that this should be so. The singing, bustling, brilliant years were all behind him. Now there was rest, now there was peace. The world was a bonny place—to fish in, to live in, to laugh in, and to "bide a wee" in until the end of the road. There was peace here at Strathaven, peace all over the world.

And then suddenly, there was no peace—not in Strathaven, not anywhere.

It was 1914 all over again.

Another strutting braggadocio ruled Germany. Instead of "Hoch der Kaiser," the idol-worshiping cry of a deluded people was "*Heil Hitler.*" Again the German youth was being taught that every other nation was decadent, ineffectual, that Germans were superior to every race on earth, divinely endowed to rule the world.

Again the world faced a Germany on the loose, her distorted mind aflame with the unholy zeal to disrupt and destroy. Again, blindly,

America was maintaining that it was not her fight. Again France and England were caught completely unprepared. Again the youth of Scotland was in uniform.

Again Harry Lauder went forth to serve.

In 1939, he was sixty-nine. The wrinkles in that strong, homely face were deep, his head was bald, but his grin was as broad, as contagious as ever.

"Come and sing to us, Harry!" called the voices from the army hospitals.

"Come and sing to us, Harry," cried the ammunition workers and the dock workers. "We're workin' hard and long, an' we could do wi' a bit laugh!"

"Come and sing to us, Harry," cried the youth in the training camps of Scotland. "Sing to us as ye sang tae oor faithers. We can do wi' a bit song, Harry."

And finally, there were the Yanks. Boatloads upon boatloads of them, swarming into camps.

Since September, 1939, Harry Lauder had not so much as thought of a fishing rod. Funds must be raised for defense—and his singing and his laughter could help. The new song would help, too—*Keep Right on to the End of the Road*. All of Scotland was singing it, these days.

> *Keep right on to the end of the road,*
> *Keep right on to the end;*
> *Though the way be long,*
> *Let your heart be strong . . .*

He gave his first concert to the fighting men on Sunday, October 23, 1939. Reared in the Scots tradition to hold the Sabbath as a day of rest, at first he hesitated about singing on Sunday. "If the laddies can fight on the Sabbath," he decided, "I can sing on the Sabbath."

Winston Churchill called him "That Grand Old Minstrel." Lauder Ha' at Strathaven—pronounced "Strai-ven" by its residents—rarely saw him nowadays. Not for him to pick the times and places where he will entertain—he went anywhere, everywhere. Blackouts, bad weather, inconvenient transportation, long distances, short ones, it does not matter. On August 4, 1943, "that Grand Old Minstrel" was 73 years old, and his voice was still so strong that even when he sang in halls seating over four thousand people, he needed no microphone.

Down into the valleys went the small, aged figure; up into the hills where the streams ran cold and clear; across the brooding moors; through the chill of the morning mists; through the rain and the sun—wherever there were men and women serving their country.

"D'ye ken the *ould* songs, lads?"

"You bet we do, Harry! Give us *Roamin' i' th' Gloamin'!*"

"How about—*When I Meet MacKay,* Harry?"

With his crooked stick, his briar pipe, his Glengarry jauntily tilted, and the waggle of the kilt as comical as ever, Lauder sang. Well, he thought sometimes, it had been a long road. It had so.

In mid-November, 1942, he went up to Glasgow to greet America's First Lady. Standing beside her as the boat carried them down the Clyde to visit the great shipyards, he thought how this woman typified all that to him was America—the ability to smile in spite of strain and fatigue, vitality, keen intelligence, quickness, humor, graciousness. All this belonged to America, and all this belonged to America's First Lady.

As the boat pulled into a dock, the place was black with cheering workers. American flags were everywhere. When Eleanor Roosevelt had finished speaking to the workmen, it was Lauder's turn. She had seen him years ago when he had played in New York, and now, listening to him, she realized that he had lost none of his irresistible magnetism. Finally, after a stirring speech, he sang to them, and led them in singing *The End of the Road.* Here, she thought, was the same apparently effortless performance, that same infectious zest, that same sure grip on the emotions of an audience, the same vigor of thirty years ago.

She had heard that he had been singing to the American troops almost every night, yet he looked extremely well, he seemed vigorous, and his voice, she admitted later, was still excellent.

Next day, at a luncheon given in her honor by the Lord Provost of Glasgow, they spoke of the war and of the bonny world to be built when it ended. She was returning to America almost at once, and

Lauder bid her Godspeed with the old Scots song, *Will ye No Come Back Again?*

Some days later, back in America, Eleanor Roosevelt consented to broadcast on November 20, 1942. She spoke feelingly of the American boys in camp, of conditions in England, of the need for fuller understanding between the two great Allies.

"People like Sir Harry Lauder," she said, "who devotes many an evening to the entertainment of our boys in the Glasgow American Red Cross Club, are adding day by day to the good feeling which must eventually exist between us."

And back in Scotland, Greta was asking: "Uncle Harry, dear, do you never get tired, rushing here and there with the troops?"

The small, blue-gray eyes twinkled back at her. "My heart's i' my singin'," he told her.

BIBLIOGRAPHY

The material presented in this book was derived from the following sources:

British Information Service, 30 Rockefeller Plaza, N. Y. City.

Between You and Me, Sir Harry Lauder, James A. McCann Co., N. Y., 1919.

Face of Scotland, Harry Batsford & Charles Fry, B. T. Bats-ford, Ltd., London, 1933.

Harry Lauder at Home and on Tour, Harry Lauder, Greening & Co., Ltd., London, 1907.

History of the Nineteenth Century Year by Year, A, Vol. III, Edwin Emerson, Jr., P. F. Collier & Son, N. Y., 1900.

In Search of Scotland, H. V. Morton, Dodd, Mead & Co., N. Y., 1930.

History of the Theatre, A, George Freedley & John A. Reeves, Crown Publishers, N. Y., 1931.

Outline of History, The, H. G. Wells, Garden City Pub. Co., Inc., Garden City, N. Y., 1920.

Minstrel in France, A, Harry Lauder, Heart's International Library Co., N. Y., 1918.

Roamin' in the Gloamir', Sir Harry Lauder, J. B. Lippincott Co., Phila. & London, 1928.

Wee Drappies, Sir Harry Lauder, Robt. M. McBride & Co., N. Y., 1932.

So You're Going to Ireland and Scotland, Clara E. Laughlin, Houghton Mifflin Co., Boston, 1932.

Robinson Locke Scrapbook, No. 311.

N. Y. Herald-Tribune, November 13, 1942.

N. Y. Times, January 17, 1943.

Correspondence with Mrs. Franklin Delano Roosevelt.

Correspondence with Miss Greta Lauder.